NAKED RUN
TO

M ... G

NAKED RUN
TO
MORNING

WILLIAM E. SNEED

iUniverse, Inc.
New York   Bloomington

NAKED RUN TO MORNING

iUniverse books may be ordered through booksellers or by contacting:

iUniverse
1663 Liberty Drive
Bloomington, IN 47403
www.iuniverse.com
1-800-Authors (1-800-288-4677)

Because of the dynamic nature of the Internet, any Web addresses or links contained in this book may have changed since publication and may no longer be valid. The views expressed in this work are solely those of the author and do not necessarily reflect the views of the publisher, and the publisher hereby disclaims any responsibility for them.

ISBN: 978-1-4401-3692-4 (sc)
ISBN: 978-1-4401-3694-8 (dj)
ISBN: 978-1-4401-3693-1 (ebook)

Printed in the United States of America

iUniverse rev. date: 4/15/2009

DEDICATION

CHARLOTTE E. SNEED

Photo taken at Hotel Dieu School of Nursing in Beaumont, Texas. School no longer exist, including building. Photo source untraceable.

This book is dedicated not only to military troops here and abroad, but to the hundreds of Merchant Mariners who deliver the goods on time anywhere. And the book is largely dedicated to my wonderful wife, Charlotte, "Tootie", a name I have called her since the first day we met back in Beaumont, Texas, in January 1968. She continues to tolerate the many moods of my writing efforts and a lot of other faults and miseries of mine over the past 40 years. She is truly an angel sent by God to help me navigate this rough life here on earth. When Judgment Day comes, the Lord will surely say to her, "Well done good and faithful servant." And I'm sure he will add: "So well, Mrs. Charlotte, that here (He will pat the seat), come up and sit by my side."

Our daughter, Alison Oney, in Ft Worth, Texas, also deserves recognition as she was a young Navy wife in Scotland, then in Jacksonville, Florida. So she easily relates to military people and separations from family.

Contents

NAKED RUN TO MORNING 1

A coming-of-age story of three boys in League City, Texas in the summer of 1956 while on a camping trip on Clear Creek. The boys have their clothes stripped off by an escaped convict, then they must make it back to their starting point without being seen. Other teenagers cause more conflict, then Billy, main character, boldly faces his greatest challenge after his pet saves his life.

SNIPS 91

A short tale of a young sailor who gets drunk because he is lonely. He gets into a fight. The Cambridge, Mass. Police Department breaks up the brawl and everyone goes to jail. A come-to-realize story, but then, does he?

RED, RIGHT, RETURNING 103

A 12 year old boy escapes from his stepfather's island near Galveston, Texas. He must cross a busy shipping lane in thick fog with his beagle, Woody, in a small row boat in shark-infested waters. (This story was written the last year of the author's Naval career. It sold for $325, but was never published)

DIXIE CUP ANNIE 121

A young sailor visits a high school friend of his in New York City, but finds that the friend has changed considerably. He cuts the visit short, very hurt and disappointed. (This story won 3rd place in an international short story contest for the military. It was later selected for publication in an anthology of short fiction by the Northeast Texas Writer's Organization: NETWO: www.netwo.org)

MERCHANT NAVY IN THE HEAD 129

A merchant mariner and a Navy man, both drunk, get into a scuffle in the ship's head. Humorous and up lifting ending.

FRUIT OF THE POISONOUS TREE................................. 135

Three days into Desert Storm from Desert Shield, two ex-Navy CPOs, now crew members of the Navy's Military Sealift Command, have intentions of just going to the base bowling alley for a few nice, relaxing beers; quiet and calm, but it doesn't turn out exactly like this. The whole Navy Base, including the Naval Air Station, and emergency vehicles from the city of Norfolk get into involved!

MILITARY PHOTOS & OTHER.. 161
New Book Prologue.. 177

Sequel to recent published novel, BLACK OIL CHIEF, USN as Chief Phillip Keith and his black friend, Chief Boatswain Mate Lucas "Boomer" Newman try to make good civilians as sheriff deputies. The prologue pulls people and conflicts that later involve Keith and his previous shipmates, Kris Palmer and Janet Lowery. (book to be published later in 2009 or afterwards)

Readers write:

"Although I had great faith in your writing abilities, you overwhelmed me! Read the whole thing in three days. The ending was perfect! And there has to be a sequel. You developed Phil so well that another book is a natural. Phil now has a life!"

Great book!!! Major Albert Perez, USAF (Ret) Lockhart, Texas

"Mr. Bill, My daughter gave me your book for Christmas. Once I started it was hard to put it down. As a Yeoman in the Navy, I never experienced the life or times of the real workers, the real sailors, but I could just imagine, reading your book how interesting and exciting your job was. I want to read your next book. Please put me on your mailing list!"

BL Dallas, Texas

"It kept me interested all the way. I am not a qualified as a critic, but I will say that your objective of promoting Christianity was well done!" Harold Wade, author of "*Cold War Fighter Pilot*. Order this book by going to: halbwade@bellsouth.net

"Read your book. It really gets hold of you and won't let go! Every once in a while, just between you and I, I got choked up a tad. Yep, darn good book. I think just maybe the Lord will be proud of you. Now that I read this book, just maybe, just maybe, I can get something done around here. Good read!"

Chuck S. Middletown, Ohio

"Chief Bill. Book read. Good read! Congratulations! Nice job!"

JL in Wisconsin, Master boiler technician, USN (Ret)

"You finally did it, Chief! Excellent military book! It would sure make a fantastic movie!"

Randy Mancuso, (ex-BT aboard USS Jouett CG 29) Brooklyn, New York

"Black Oil Chief, USN is one of the few military novels written with a Christian undertone. Believers will love it, especially the uplifting ending!"

Gayle Westmoreland, Marshall, Texas

"It is my sincere hope that this novel finds its way to many readers, and that Mr. Sneed will continue to write."

Johnny W. Gordon, South Carolina

Visit Website: **www.writerbillusn.com**

THE NAVY BLUE

Say, girl, I saw you sneer just now.
Don't I look good to you?
I'm not one of your class you say;
I wear the Navy Blue.

You think I'm not fine enough,
For such a girl as you.
Men who would not hold your hand,
Have worn the Navy Blue

How many folks in civilian life
Will take the time to think;
That sailors do other things
Besides carouse and drink?

We're only a common sailor boy
Til wars kill starts to brew;
Then, dear friends, you are the first
To cheer the Navy Blue.

When we are dead, when we are gone,
We'll not be barred from heaven's gate,
When life's last cruise is through;
For wearing the Navy Blue.

So when you meet a sailor boy,
I'd smile if I were you.
No better men are made by God,
Than the Boys in the Navy Blue.

Author Anonymous

US Navy Photo, Public Domain

NAKED RUN TO MORNING
A NOVELLA
BY
BILLY SNEED

One dark night on Clear Creek
In the summer of 1956 in League City, Texas the lives of three boys
change forever, especially for Billy Sneed.

Billy Sneed

1

NAKED RUN TO MORNING

We never told anyone. We promised. Anyway, who would have believed three young boys telling such a tale in the summer of 1956, especially in a small town like League City, Texas? Albert Perez was 15, same as me, Billy Sneed. "Nono" (Raul de los Santos) was 14. That was fifty-two years ago. We hid it all these years.

Now it's time to talk.

I can tell it now, but all the emotion and the pain is still there. It always will be. I have thought about that night thousands of times over the years. Now it's time to go back to being fifteen years old again on Clear Creek. With my simple mind, that's the *only* easy part!

If we had had any inkling of the horror that night would bring, we would have all stayed at home under our bedcovers. I would have even *touched* that slimy-looking, three-foot chicken snake that Albert carried around his neck for the past two weeks. We even got kicked out of T.A. Kilgore Grocery Store when we forgot about the snake draped across Albert's shoulders. Man, did the girls scream! Women fainted. Next thing I knew, we were pulled by the ears and tossed outside on the sidewalk. There was even a blurb in the county newspaper, the Galveston Daily News, about the "Snake Invasion at Kilgore's Store." Gee, couldn't anyone take a joke in League City?

League City, Texas. This was our small coastal town. The population was between 1,200 and 1,500, but that's probably pushing it. 'Half way 'tween,' Houston and Galveston," most town folks would say about League City's map location.

The thriving businesses, besides T.A. Kilgore Grocery Store with its hardware department and lumber yard, was the fig plant at the end of

Railroad Street, and the mop and broom factory on Iowa Street across the main drag. Back over the railroad tracks on the west side of town, Snell's Grocery Store was in an old building with worn, tongue-and-groove wood floors that squeaked when walked on. But, like Kilgore's, Snell's had a meat department in the rear of the store where everything was hand-cut, even fresh sliced baloney. Across the street was the Dairy Dream, where a big cheese burger could be had for 30 cents. It was also a hangout for teens looking for night action. Or you could go (if you were lucky enough to have a car) to Falco's Drive-in three miles away in the town of Dickinson. Also on Main Street down from Snell's was Smith's Pharmacy, its soda fountain a gathering place for old folks during the morning, and a hangout for teens after school. Smith's Pharmacy had the best cherry cokes and root beer floats. And the popular pharmacist, "Smitty" was always open to conversation, advice and humor. You had to watch this guy as he would surely pull some prank on you, and sometimes it involved two Texas Highway Patrolmen: Sgt. Gilmore and Billy Crook. Smitty was also always paying for some kid's college education. I can't count the number of young people he put through college.

SMITH'S PHARMACY
Your Friendly Druggist
Phone 8-6611
DAY OR NIGHT
League City, Texas

For further recreation, there was the Rose Theatre on Highway 3, where good westerns could be seen with Audy Murphy, Randolph Scott, or perhaps a rerun of the *East Side Kids* with Leo Gorcey and Huntz Hall. Seems this gang was known as the Bowery Boys, too. It was also the place I first viewed *Gone With The Wind*. It was normal to see the feature, a newsreel, and a cartoon all for a dime, if you were twelve years of age or younger. We were always "under" until we were caught. Back then most kids told the truth when quizzed by an adult. And if you smoked while sitting, or made loud noises you got thrown out of the theatre like we had so many times! But they always allowed us in at the next picture show, paying the adult price, of course.

The railroad tracks were considered the dividing town line. Why? Who knows. Dumb kid rumor had it that those on the west side were better folks than those on the east side. Well, I didn't know about that since we had the Kilgore clan on our side; even Lillie Longbotham, Gerald Mathis and others so…so much for adolescent gossip, huh?

While it is said that there were Japanese families in town, I never recall seeing any. But I know we had an awful lot of rice farming. While there were other industries, my fifteen-year-old mind was, as usual, operating below normal back then. Years later I reasoned that my skull was–and still is, probably–functioning about three to five years behind the rest of my class. Well, at least I'm old enough now to admit it. It is said that the human brain can only function at about 10% of its real capacity. I guess when God was giving out brains I thought he said canes. I wasn't old and I surely didn't want even one of those things! Ten-percent capacity? Amazing. Staggering, really. But my hummingbird brain was at a-2% on a scale of 1 to 3, not 10. I was always embarrassed back in the third grade when Mrs. Dorothy Tippen would call on me to do math flash cards in front of the whole class. Division? Forget it. At least no one had to tickle sides to make the class laugh! Man, I sure envied those "brainers" like Jeff Millar, Mike Davis, Gerald Mathis, Bennie Lenox, Wayne Smith, Albert Perez, Lillie Longbotham, Jane Hardin, and others. Of course, at the top of this list would be Teddy Kilgore. But I don't recall him at our school. Seems he went to some "rocket scientists" school in Houston or elsewhere. He was "Mr. Einstein" anyway. His brain functioned at a 15 plus! Hey, I remember that his father build a huge shrimp boat in his shop that faced Colorado Avenue. It was wall-to-wall, front-to-back. Too large to get out of the shop. Well, they had to burn down the building to get it out. Why didn't the shrimp boat go up in flames too? Why it was water-proof, that's why! Man, I was one intelligent cool cat, huh? Who said you had to be dumb to be…unpopular?

The closest thing to a town square was the city park by the railroad tracks, right across Main Street from Kilgore's Store. The park was lined with big oak trees on all four sides. In plain view across the street by the tracks was the old railroad depot. It was made of wood and washed a dull fainted, old yellow color that didn't even look like paint. There was a ticket window that had bars, just like in western movies at the Rose Theatre. Cool, man. There was even an ancient baggage wagon, the type that was hand-pulled. It had spaced boarded siding and large steel wheels that had skinny spokes. Real western, yessir. The city park itself only had a basketball court on the north end. The hoops were rusted, bent and had no nets. There were several big cracks and buckles in the cement court. You had to be extra careful roller skating. But it was fun to jump the gaps and fly in the air for several seconds; that is, if your skates didn't pop loose from the soles of your shoes. Then you had the frustration of trying to tighten them with a worn key, or with a pair of your dad's pliers you borrowed and hoped to return them to his tool chest before he discovered them missing.

Author, Billy Sneed at League City Park. Depot in background.

And when the siren on the big water tower by the fire station shrilled and woke everyone up in town, the volunteer firemen rushed to the station below that only sheltered two rather ancient-looking fire trucks. But they were red, had ladders, hoses, and screaming sirens. Sights and sounds kids loved. But that was uptown. We were down at the creek. Clear Creek, to be exact.

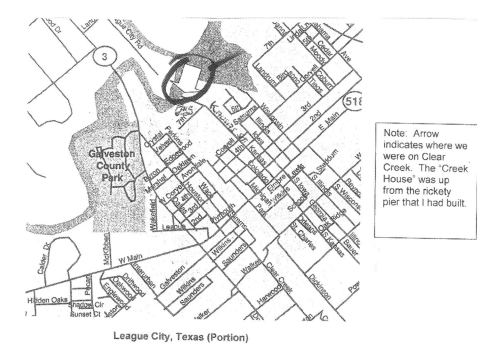

Note: Arrow indicates where we were on Clear Creek. The "Creek House" was up from the rickety pier that I had built.

League City, Texas (Portion)

League City, Texas (arrow indicating where we were at on the creek)

Then there was Clear Lake, down toward the bay that was separated by the small town of Seabrook (on the Harris County side) and Kemah (on the Galveston County side).

Clear?

Not in my lifetime! Maybe when the Vikings sailed the waters, but not in the 50s.

"I wish Albert would hurry up," I said, pacing the creek bank. "He said he'd be here 'fore dark. It'll be midnight now before we get to our campsite!" I rubbed my bare chest, feeling the sweat.

"Ah, hold your horses, Billy," Nono said. "You know how Albert's dad is with his side job from Kilgore's. He'll cut grass 'til he can't see it no more. Albert'll be here. Don't worry."

I grimaced, looking up the incline to the crushed shell road that lead to the sand and shell piles to my left.

Nono wiggled his feet in the water, sitting on the side of my boat. "You know Mr. Perez never starts a yard job if he can't finish it that same day. Shoot, they might even be on that five-acre yard, still pushing them lawnmowers. Even if every mower broke down on the job, Mr. Perez would finish it using his and Albert' teeth. Yeah!" Nono laughed that high-pitched tone of his.

I smirked, then blew a sigh, hands on my hips. "Well, he'd better get here or we're gonna shove off without him", I said, feeling rivulets of sweat running down my bare back. Like Nono, I had on blue-jeans rolled up just below my knees. Shirtless, of course. Usually it was just a bathing suit, and no shirt, for sure, on Clear Creek. I looked back at Nono. I didn't mean what I threatened. Nono knew it, but it sounded mean. We'd wait for our friend all night if we had to.

Albert & Nono in front
of Smith's Pharmacy

Earlier Photo of
Albert Perez

We were at the rickety pier I had rebuilt last winter when the tide had been unusually low, and I could see where to dig holes for the old fence posts that I used for pilings. For our parents' information, we were at what we called the "shell pile." (*refer to hand-drawn sketch of what Iowa and Kansas Streets, the Gully and the creek area looked like in 1956*) There was also a huge sand pile beside the creek. The mountains of shell and sand were located behind a wooden fence a few yards away. My shoddy pier was in a small inlet in this area. This creek front property belonged to the Kilgore family.

There was an abandoned house up the hill from where I stood. It was a desolate, lonely, and spooky joint. It was also a short walk to the cemetery on Kansas Street, also known as Old Highway 3. At night it was dark and spooky there, the owls hooting at the ghosts. However, there was a light pole up by the gate which provided a dim light down by my pier. It wasn't much, but it helped some. It also provided enough light so that the Kilgore's "**burn-down-the-shop**" shrimp boat could be seen tied at its well-constructed platform nearby.

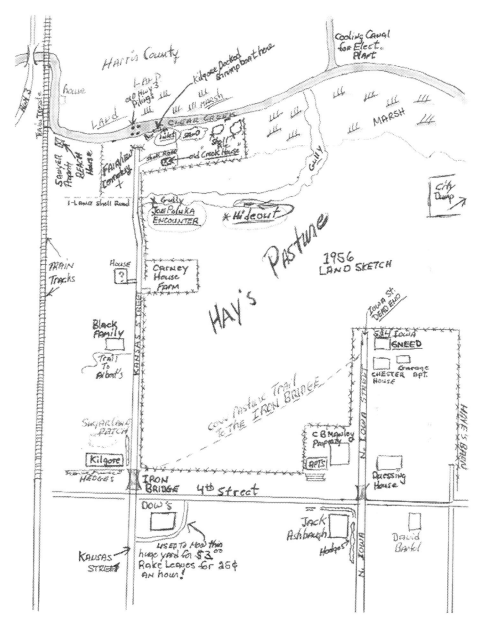

Note: This area, the T.A. Kilgore property on Clear Creek, would be humorously dubbed by Mr. Charles Kilgore on Bayou Drive as "Billy Sneed's Playground" five decades later. This would come as our paths crossed on e-mail. We continued to correspond until several weeks before he passed away. He was quite a character, that Mr. Charles Kilgore. A great man.

Kansas Street (Old Highway 3) dead-ended just short of Clear Creek. To its left was Fairview Cemetery, where we knew of a grave that had a thin, cement covering. It was black-gray from age, and it had a hole in one side a bit bigger than my little finger. We would bet one another who would stick their finger down the hole and keep it there for a full minute. We would always laugh and make phony excuses, so this stunt was never attempted. To the right of the wooden barricade that ended Kansas Street was the crushed oyster shell drive that the dump trucks used when picking up loads of sand or shell. The small old house, dubbed the "creek house," was on the right, before the trucks went through the gate. From my view up the long inclined bank, I could see perhaps half of the house, from the middle of its windows to the roof. Vacant and neglected for the past two years or more, the elements and vandals had taken their toll on the paint-peeling structure. Rotted boards hung at odd angles on all sides,

Looking west from the shell pile. The "beach house" is seen in the upper mid-background.

Shell pile upper right. Note land across the land in left background, which is no longer there, and the Hwy 3 bridge pilling, slightly to the left of the boat. Do I remember who is in the boat? You bet. It's Smitty of Smith's Pharmacy and Mr. E.T. King, one of his hundreds of friends!

No, it wasn't the boxer Joe Poluka like in the Sunday newspaper comic strip. This Joe Poluka was a 2200 pound Brahama bull.

Picture source unknown

Mean and ugly with a huge black hump that always had flies swarming around it, Joe Poluka guarded the 50 cows that roamed and grazed on Hay's pasture. This land bordered our house on two sides on Iowa Street. Joe Poluka hated kids, especially Albert, Nono and me. We would stand on Kansas Street across from the cemetery and throw dirt clods at Joe Poluka. He'd snort and swing his head, throwing mouth slobber in all directions, and look at us real hateful, his huge flabby chest pressed against the five strands of barbed-wire fencing. We'd laugh and run toward the creek. The day came, however, when none of us were laughing.

We were down in the big gully that cut across Hay's pasture from Kansas Street. With jagged walls from six to eight feet high on either side, the gully extended another half mile before leveling with the marsh land beside Clear Creek. (*see hand sketch again*)

We were building a hideout under a partially washed out oak tree that leaned away from the gully. It was going to be the biggest and best secret place we ever built. Digging and carving the dirt, I told the guys it was time to check on the whereabouts of Joe Poluka, though we felt safe with the tall gully cliffs above our heads. Nono locked his hands together like a stirrup and hoisted me to pasture level. I heaved my body up and on to the ground.

"See 'em?" Nono asked pensively.

"Wait. Gimme time," I replied. Indian fashion, I shaded my eyes from the bright sun and scanned the endless acreage. Nope, they must be up at the barn. Opps, wait. There they were grazing, maybe a mile away, heads to the ground. Yeah, there was that idiot, Joe Poluka.

Joe Poluka raised his head, still chewing. He looked around, taking in the scenery like he was bored. His head stopped when he spotted me.

I waved, feeling safe with the distance and the deep gully behind me.

Joe Poluka's ears perked, then they flopped back beside his big head.

I jumped up and down and made ugly faces at him, wiggling my tongue and looking cross-eyed.

"NA-NA-NA-NA-NA-NA!" I sang.

I really didn't think he would venture this distance from the herd, but Joe Poluka needed no second invite. He pawed the ground, eyes locked on me, and charged!

Still, I laughed, then jumped down the eight feet into the gully. Rolling like a paratrooper, I got up unharmed.

"Got big company coming," I said, thumbing the air over my head.

Madre de Dios," Nono said, quickly making the sign of the cross like he was at the Catholic church on Main Street by the big oak trees.

"Now?" Albert asked, hating to stop his sculpturing.

"Yesterday," I replied, feeling the ground starting to shake.

"Go!" Albert said, dropping his hatchet.

We took off running toward Kansas Street a quarter of a mile away. Nono was already way ahead of us.

Spotty, my English setter, came charging into the gully and ran with us. It was all fun and games to him. If he'd known Joe Poluka was hot on our trail, he would have stopped and run after him. Spotty loved to nip at Joe Poluka's hoofs.

We hooted and hollered as we ran through the canyon-like gully, jumping over pools of water and dodging the various sized dirt islands. We dashed across the herd's trail that sloped gradually into and out of the gully. The cow's had two such crossings. The main one located near the fence next to Kansas Street. Dust flying from our heels, we were almost there.

With twenty yards to spare, we scrambled under the barbed-wire fence, safe as always. Spotty turned when the bull came up, went back inside the pasture, and started snapping at Joe Poluka's feet. We laughed and threw a few dirt clots and ran down Kansas Street. But that had all happened weeks ago. Now there was no excitement---just the wait for Albert.

"Want some, Bee-lee?" Nono asked, bringing my mind back to the present. He was cutting on a three-foot stalk of sugar cane. He laughed at pronouncing Billy like Albert's sister, Mary, always did.

"Sure," I replied, reaching down inside the boat. I looked at the cane. It was streaked with purple, a good sign of sweet sugar cane.

"Old lady Kilgore almost got me this time," Nono said, carving a piece of cane to put into his mouth. He laughed. "But I ran like a scared rabbit, but, boy, yum, yum, I knew I had a good piece of cane for our camping trip. No way was I gonna drop it, no matter how much buckshot she put my way."

"She didn't really shoot at you," I said, hands on my hips.

"I swear she did," Nono said, his right hand up to God.

"Yeah, yeah." I stuck the cane in my mouth and sucked on the end. It was great.

"Well, I heard something that sounded like a gun. I swear."

I sighed.

"When's he gonna get here?" I looked up the slope again.

Nothing.

I grunted, gnawing on the sugar cane. It was getting stringy, but it was still sweet. This helped my feelings. I turned and looked toward the sand pile, then the shell pile. A crane was parked on the short, heavily piled pier. A barge, still half loaded with shell, was snugged against the crane pier. No workers or vehicles were present. While the barge was large, there was still plenty of room left on the creek for a boat to pass it safely, even one with a water skier in tow. Thank goodness it wasn't the weekend.

I hated Saturdays and Sundays on Clear Creek. Yachts from the Kemah and Seabrook area would speed up the creek, throwing up waves galore. Houston people would launch their boats from their trailers at the *Galveston County Park*, located in our town. It was easy to get swamped or capsized if the oncoming waves were not navigated correctly.

While there was a definite shape and direction to Clear Creek, the waves from the hundreds of weekend boats slowly dissolved its banks, eating at the low lands and bordering marshes like a terrible cancer. Four decades later, I would return to the "creek house" area and view Clear Creek's shapeless form with awe and sadness.

Scratching my sweaty chest, I looked at my boat, trying to think of something else besides Albert being late. My boat, yes, it was unlike any other, far and wide.

The well-constructed craft was 14 feet long with a lawn mower-type inboard engine. The boat cost me $200, a staggering amount in 1956. I was paying it off at $25 a month. Unlike my old boat, which I steered using oars,

I navigated this baby with a real ship's "miniature" wheel that was mounted on the bow. It was neat to see the little cables moving inside the boat on either side, controlling a rudder at the stern. The engine was bolted on rubber grommets centerline in the boat's middle. It had a gear shift which was actually a belt and pulleys. A small steel handle allowed the boat to go forward when shifted from the neutral position, or to go astern when the handle was shifted in the other direction. While the little gas-powered engine only pushed the boat between six and eight knots, it was the neatest thing I had ever seen. Albert, Nono and I used to laugh when people ashore saw us scooting on down the creek, bubbles in the water at the stern, a small wake following. The people would scratch their heads, seeing no outboard engine or a sail or any oars powering the boat. It was the envy of every boy who frequented Clear Creek, even the older boys and bullies, but they generally left us alone.

While I didn't miss my old row boat, I had to admit that the past two years of rowing it up and down the miles and miles of Clear Creek had really developed my upper body, especially my arms and chest muscles. A fighter or a bully I wasn't, but I could out-do most of the other boys in P.E. class, especially with chin-ups, rope climbing or any other sport that involved heavy exertion of the upper body. But I was no tough guy, looking for trouble. Generally quiet, except when I was with Albert and Nono, I took my anger out in rowing my boat whenever it occurred, which was not often.

Looking closer inside the boat, I tried to find my harpoon. Rats! I grimaced, remembering I had left it in the gully at our hideout. I had wedged it inside a heat and erosion crack on one of the sun-baked cliffs at the secret place. No one would ever find it, I felt sure. On impulse, I glanced at the setting sun, trying to judge if there was enough time left for me to run to the hideout and get the harpoon before it got dark. Nope, the orange orb was already below the horizon. Snakes came out at night. On occasion we had spotted water moccasins in the pools of water scattered throughout the gully's bottom.

"Darn," I said softly to myself.

I sure hated to leave without the eight-foot steel harpoon that Mr. Camp had given to me as a bonus, when I bought my new boat from him two months ago. The ten pound harpoon was fun to use to stab at the alligator gars that splashed near the boat. You could also never tell what you might run into in the woods ashore, maybe a wolf or even a bear. Who knows? I grinned, recalling I had a 'possum cornered once with the heavy weapon.

"Kill it! Kill it!" Ralph Welsh had said. He was a friend who lived with his dad in a trailer house beside the creek.

I stepped back from the hissing 'possum, showing his mouthful of razor-sharp teeth at me. I just couldn't bring myself to stab a defenseless little animal.

"Gimme that!" Ralph commanded. He grabbed the steel rod, with its sharp half-arrow pointed end, from my hands.

I turned and walked away, unable to watch Ralph harpoon the little animal. Although my merchant marine dad was not a hunter either, like me, he always stressed: *"Never, but never kill for the fun of it. Kill only if you're starving, your life, or someone else's life is in danger."*

I wiped the 'possum vision from my mind like erasing chalk from a blackboard as I looked up the slope again for Albert.

"Now I'm really gettin' mad!" I said, rubbing my wet chest in frustration. I looked back at Nono, standing in water up to his knees. His face suddenly lit up, looking past me.

"Here he comes," he said, tromping through the 85 degree water to the bank.

"'Bout time," I said, looking up the slope. Sure enough---Oh, no, Albert had that stupid chicken snake coiled around his neck! No way, I thought, was he bringing that thing on our camping trip! I folded my arms across my chest and stood defiant.

Herman *Pabalno* was the snake's name. Spanish. Albert and Nono were going to teach me Spanish, but I just did not understand how words could be divided between a man and a woman. While I wasn't no 1956 Forrest Gump, I just couldn't understand this ah..."ginger", I think that's what Albert called it. Said something about verb "congenation" or something like that, too. Well, I did poorly enough in Mrs. Flores' English class at League City Elementary School, so I gave up on Spanish and failed this, too!

Albert had cornered Herman at a yard customer of his dad's. Much to his dad's dislike, he brought the snake home in a box. He built a makeshift cage out of scrap screen wire. When he reached for Herman the snake bit him, but, still, he kept it, his father rattling in Spanish that he ought to let it go.

I hated snakes, even garter snakes. I'd walk 400 miles around one just to avoid it. To touch one was out of the question. No way. To me they were slimy, evil creatures.

"Guy's ready?" Albert asked. He looked at Nono. "Sure you got all my stuff?"

"You ain't takin' no stupid snake with us," I said.

"Everything by the door like you said," Nono chimed, smiling at Albert. Man, they weren't even paying any mind to me!

"I even asked Mary," Nono continued, "She said that was all your camping gear. Put some food with it, too." Nono indicated the sleeping bag and backpack in the forward part of the boat.

Albert Perez was a pro-camper. He always brought along waterproof matches that he'd made himself by dipping them in hot wax. Having read and memorized the *Boy Scout Handbook* from cover to cover, he was also the Senior Patrol Leader of Boy Scout Troop 29 of League City, Texas. Mr. E.D. Blanchard was our scoutmaster.

With both hands, Albert uncoiled Herman from around his neck.

I winced, stepping back a bit.

Albert straightened Herman out like a stiff, fat rope, and squatted. He placed the snake on the ground gently, then let go.

I almost jumped all the way to the shell pile. Wasn't no snake gonna leap on me and squeeze me to death! And while I was too big for Herman to swallow, I wasn't gonna give the sonofagun the chance to try!

"*Madre da Dios!*" Nono said, crossing himself.

"He bit me again a while ago," Albert said. "Dad wants me to get rid of him before he bites one of the little kids, so that's why I brought him."

We watched as Herman slithered along the bank a while, then disappeared into the tall weeds and shrubs of the slope.

"That's the way I like to see a snake," I said "Leaving!"

"Or dead," Nono added.

"*Mucho,*" I replied.

Albert looked at us slyly, then spat. He turned and started back up toward the shell drive.

"Where're ya going? We're ready to shove off," I said, sticking the sugar cane stalk in my rear pocket.

"Hang on a minute," Albert said over his shoulder.

Nono and I exchanged blank stares.

"Now what," I said. "More waiting?" I looked at the darkening sky.

"*Se, se, senior,*" Nono said. He laughed, high-pitched as usual.

While both Albert Perez and Raul "Nono" de los Santos had black hair and dark eyes, they were as different as an apple and a pick-up truck. Albert's eyes were penetrating, studious and calculating; Nono's danced with humor and wit. Albert was tall and lanky, while Nono, like myself, was of average height and weight for his age. Nono had wavy hair on top of his head; Albert's was long, straight, and he combed frequently, but the wave combed above his forehead seemed fixed. In school, they were always neatly dressed, usually in jeans, loafers, and pressed shirts. And they definitely had a humorous side:

Albert Nono

Albert and I loved to wear leather moccasins, which we both had on our feet with no socks. Who needed socks in mid July? Nono wore a pair of frayed tennis shoes, with no socks, of course.

"Zegot what I think?" Nono asked, looking up the slope.

My brow wrinkled, looking at the small, galvanized bucket Albert was carrying back. He must have left it up by the drive. To surprise us. Yeah, that was it. The only person who carried a similar, but much larger, bucket in League City was Mr. Guzman, who made hot tamales. He sold them beside the highway in front of Herbie's Drive-In Grocery.

"Say, Albert, Old Buddy," Nono said in a sing-song voice, running to meet Albert halfway down the slope. He draped an arm over Albert's shoulders. "Buddy, let me help you with that." He laughed.

"Get back," Albert said, feigning anger.

"I smell 'em from here," I said. "Can't hide 'em, Albert."

"But it ain't Saturday," Nono said. "How'd you get Mr. Guzman to..."

"Mona and Mary made them last night," Albert said as they neared the boat.

"Mona and Mary?" I said. Albert's older sisters. "Wow, that's even better than old Mr. Guzman."

Unless a person had special friends like I did, authentic Mexican food could only be had in very few restaurants in Houston or Galveston. Mr. Guzman only made tamales, and you had to get to his bucket early because he sold out usually within an hour.

"How many?" Nono asked.

"Three dozen," Albert said.

"What're you guys gonna eat?" Nono said, taking the bucket and pulling it to his side. He laughed, and then placed the container of newspaper-wrapped tamales under the bow platform.

"Okay," I said. "Let's get going."

We all heard the sound of a speeding boat coming around the bend in the creek by Ralph Walsh's. We stared as it came into view. Holy-molly, it was pulling a skier, and it was almost dark! Big boat, too. Big wake. I saw waves peeling over the marsh behind the railroad trestle.

"Idiots," Albert mumbled.

The boat zoomed past us in the creek's center. Holding on to the bow rope, I pushed my boat away so it wouldn't bang the pier when the waves hit. I looked at the boat. It was an inboard Chris Craft with a straight bow. Probably built in the late 30s or 40s. It had a dark, highly polished hull. The skier swung our way, jumping the waves nicely. He came in close, but didn't spray us with water. I hated it when they did that. Smarty jerks from Houston. My boat heaved and tossed with the waves, then settled down. I pulled it back to the pier and held it steady as Albert and Nono boarded carefully. Glancing across the creek to a spot I knew was dry land surrounded by marsh, I saw a huge piece of under-washed land fall into the creek. Then the air became laden with the boat's exhaust fumes mixed with the water, a type of odor found only when oily motors mixed with salt water.

Suddenly I heard a dog barking.

No, I thought with a grin. I had locked him on the back porch before I left the house. Mom said she wouldn't let him out for at least an hour.

Spotty, my English setter of over three years, came charging down from the "creek house," having obviously cut across Hay's pasture. No doubt he checked our hideout in the gully for me first.

"Here comes your buddy, Billy," Nono said, looking up, holding the engine's gas cap in his right hand.

"You ought to know by now you can't sneak off to the creek without him" Albert said, laughing.

Spotty leaped on the pier, and dove into my arms.

"Heyyy," I said, happily, grabbing a post to keep from falling into the water. "Where'd you come from?"

"Eat em up, Spotty," Nono goaded with a laugh.

Albert looked on, grinning in wonder as he nodded.

I felt Spotty's smooth, pink tongue all over my face, even on my lips and teeth. I didn't care. Spotty was my chum, my ever-faithful friend. He wasn't a dog. Spotty was family. He was the pride our whole household. He even had his own chair in the house...and he knew it! On occasion my mother took Spotty on town trips, but he went everywhere with me, especially to Clear Creek.

"I tell you," my mother boasted to friends, "that Spotty boy knows when Billy's even *thinking* of going to the creek!"

Hunting and swimming were innate characteristics of his breed. Unlike the usual "hunting dog" of the south, referred to as a *hound*, which was tall and skinny with long drooping ears, sad eyes, ran in a long, loping stride and howled and barked continually, the English setter—at least "ours"–was a medium sized dog with black spots blotched on a white coat that was as smooth and soft as fleece. The right side of his face, including his ear, was black, giving Spotty a bandit-like appearance. The bulk of the right side of his head and face was white, but peppered with more black spots than the rest of his white body. Friendly-looking brown eyes and a perpetually wagging tail made him a favorite of all who met him. The comments were endless:

Spotty in his chair at 524 N. Iowa Street
League City, Texas

19

"He's so soft and cute."

"Really beautiful."

"He's a dog lover's honey."

"A show champ for sure."

"Wanna sell 'em?"

An uncle in Marlin, Texas often said that a dog wasn't nothing but a human beings with four legs. He himself had five bulldogs.

"Tank's full," Nono said, replacing the gas cap on the boat engine. "Ready to start it?" Nono was the engineer, taking the stern seat so he could adjust the throttle when I told him.

"Wait," I said, hand up as Albert, the navigator, took position on the bow seat. He also helped me steer.

"I'm all set," Albert said. He reached behind him and removed the *MAD Magazine* folded in his back pocket. While he loved and laughed at everything he read in it, I couldn't see wasting a dime like that every month. The front cover had that odd-looking Newman character on it, whoever he was. Strange. He tossed the magazine under the bow platform with the tamales.

I nodded, then picked up Spotty, already anticipating my move, and placed him gently on top of some folded blankets behind Albert. He barked his thanks, ears perked, eyes alert, and ready to move.

Untying the bow line, I scanned our camping gear, hoping we weren't forgetting anything. I felt sick about having to leave my harpoon behind, but I'd get it tomorrow on the way back to the house. Let's see...blankets, Albert's sleeping bag, water jugs, gas, my box of food and cooking utensils, Nono's things... *oars* in place. I never forgot *them.* They were a must, in case the little engine conked out. But then sometimes I'd row a mile or two just to keep in practice. There was a definite art to rowing a boat in a straight line—keeping the oars together, feet braced, and pulling the oars in exact precision together in the water.

Okay, let's see, I thought, completing my brief inventory. Ice chest. Yes, there behind the middle seat. It was a nice, metal Coca Cola ice container with a waterproof galvanized tin interior. Bottle drinks inside, with eggs in a paper carton, bacon, bologna and Nono's three punch drinks in their wax bottles. They were new on the market. You could chew the cap off, drink the liquid, then eat the bottle. They weren't as tasty as glass-bottled drinks, and to chew the wax, when it came out of the icebox, was like eating saw dust, until the particles became soft and blended together with the body's heat. They were yucky. On top of the five trays of ice cubes I had gotten at home were two other items belonging to Nono the Comedian: 2 sets of big wax lips, the fronts colored deep red. Similar to the bottles, the lips could be chewed like gum.

Under the bow platform below the steering wheel, there was an anchor, spare rope, flashlights, two large pork 'n bean cans stuffed with kerosene-soaked rags for emergency lighting...oh, yes, and the bucket of hot tamales. All set.

"Okay, amigos," I said, tossing the bow rope into the boat. "Let's hit the trail." I reached out and pushed hard against the pier.

"YA-HOOOO," Nono sang, then said, "Want me to start the engine now?"

"Wait til we get mid-stream. Ain't got that much gas," I said. I looked west toward the Welsh property where the "beach house" was located. While it was dim at ground level, the sky was still visible, but it'd be....

Suddenly the shell drive in front of the "creek house" above exploded in white dust. A car engine raced loudly, its exhaust pipes popping. Then a door opened and slammed, then another.

"Boy, you sure showed them jerks!" someone said roared.

"Gimme another beer!" another shouted.

"EEEEE-HHHAAAAAA!" yet another voice yelled.

The car radio was so loud we could plainly hear Duane Eddy's *Rebel Rouser*.

"Drunks," Albert said.

"Sounds like Johnny Lowe and his hoods," Nono said.

Spotty growled.

I hated Johnny Lowe. He was a year older that I was. Several times he had tried to get me to fight him, but I wouldn't. He pushed me, saying I was chicken. My brother, Charles, showed up and told him to knock it off. Charles was tough, much tougher, than Johnny. Johnny knew it and backed off.

"Glad we're out here now," I said.

The boat continued to drift toward the creek's middle. We watched the older boys come down the slope. They were laughing and cutting up, beer bottles in their hands, cigarettes dangling from their lips. All wore jeans low on their hips with no belt, white T-shirts tucked inside their trousers. Sleeves were folded up to reveal their muscles. Johnny Lowe had a pack of *Luckies* rolled up in his left sleeve. His hair was combed with a big wave on top, a few strands hanging down in his face. The sides were combed back into a greasy ducktail. I didn't recognize the other two boys. One had a very short crew-cut haircut; the other wore a pair of 3-D movie glasses, thinking he was a cool cat, like that latest rising star, Elvis Presley.

"Well, well," Johnny Lowe said loudly at the water's edge, "would you looky out there at them punks in the boat now? Bring that yacht up here, son. Now!" He blew smoke out his nose and mouth. "Hey, hey," he added with sudden surprise and a sly grin. "It's my old buddy, Billy Sneed and his... *amigos*. C'mon back up here so I can kick all your rears to the moon!"

We were mid-stream now, a good ways from shore. I stood up.

"Why don't you just go, Johnny, and leave us alone?" I said loudly

"Why don't you just come up here and make me, punk!" Johnny roared.

"Ahh, bite me!"

"Whadda you just say?" Johnny threw down his bottle, beer spilling out.

"Start it, Nono," I said.

"You get that boat back up here. NOW!" Johnny shouted. "I'm gonna push all your noses to the back of your stupid heads. Git here, now!" He pointed at the ground, his penny loafer tips at the water's edge.

The little engine started, smoke issuing from the exhaust for a moment. I sat back down and turned the wheel as the boat started moving.

"You ain't nothing like your big brother!" Johnny roared. "You ain't nothing but a little dork with a few muscles that you don't even know how to use!"

I steered the boat west, the engine at full throttle as tiny wake formed off our stern. Mouth closed, I grinned and gave Johnny Lowe the hand sign, which I still wasn't that well coordinated to do.

"Billy," Albert said, a bit embarrassed. "You used the wrong finger."

"Well," I responded without thought, "Ah…it…he ain't the right sex either!"

"Why you little twerp!" he roared. "I'll see you again, don't worry. I'll cream your little bodies! All of you!" He picked up his beer bottle and threw it at us. The other two hoods joined in with rocks and pieces of shell, but the distance was too great now. They all fell short into the creek.

"I'll see you again, you little freak!" Johnny shouted. "Mark my word. Maybe even tonight!"

"In your dreams," I mumbled.

"Maybe they're gonna camp in the "creek house," Nono said.

"Yeah," Albert added. "There's a couple of dresses hanging in a closet that's just their size."

Albert Perez in 1955 on East Railroad Avenue. Chicken coop houses they lived in are partly visible middle of photo, far background.

We laughed, then turned our attention to the dark creek in front of us.

"Cut the throttle to half," I told Nono.

We cruised past the rusty steel pillars of what used to be part of the bridge, when Highway 3 was here before Columbus discovered America. There were two pairs of bridge pilings: one set near the bank on the Galveston County side, and another pair across the creek on the Harris County side. Then, to our left, far up the bank on sloping land was Fairmont Cemetery.

Almost dark now, I could still see Ralph Walsh's slivery mobile home where he and his dad lived. Further down the hill was a roofed, screened-in "beach house", where we camped often. I made out some people from two cars unloading things into the "beach house." I didn't recognize Ralph among them. I guess they were going to camp in the "beach house." I waved, but the people were too far away, and it was too dark.

Steering the boat right, we turned, the "beach house" on our stern now, the train tracks running parallel to our course. The wooden trestle appeared to be a multi-legged monster, its hundreds of feet stuck in the mud and water of the marsh.

"Boy, that sure looks spooky and snake infested," Nono said, indicating the trestle pilings and swamp. He must have read my thoughts. "It's a wonder we ain't been snake bit at least four-hundred times wading in all that liquid mush."

"There's alligators in there, too," Albert said, combing his hair back on the sides of his head, his dark face serious.

"You're kiddin'!" Nono yelped. He crossed himself quickly. "*Madre da Dios*," he said. "I ain't ever going in them swamps no more."

Albert and I laughed.

"Yeah," I said. "I heard there was alligators in there too, but I ain't never seen one."

"Hope we don't, either," Nono replied, dark eyes scanning the water in every direction.

Albert grinned, looking at me and nodding.

Nono was right. We'd been lucky. The creek shores were like a jungle, full of wild life. At night it was dark and eerie. You could smell its mystery. Lightening bugs orchestrated the sounds of buzzing locusts, hooting owls, croaking frogs, screeching hawks, and other strange sounds we could not identify. Gray moss hung from tree branches like old men's beards. Hundreds of eyes stared back when a flashlight beam disturbed their privacy. Roots clung to the under washed creek banks; trees bent into the water on both sides, fighting desperately to stay alive. You could almost hear their cries. It was like being back in a prehistoric era; you could feel the presence of snakes, turtles, lizards, and frogs along the banks and in the tree branches.

"Drink?" Nono asked, pulling out a wax bottle of yucky-tasting liquid. I shook my head.

"Why not?" Albert took the chilled drink. He bit the top off and spit it overboard. Reaching under the bow platform, he pulled out the prized bucket. "Guy's want some tamales?"

"Silly question, *amigo,*" I said.

"Don't have to ask me twice," Nono said, shifting in the seat to get closer. "Matter of fact, you don't even have to ask me at all. Hurry up, Albert." He laughed, hand out.

Now, this was living, I thought, the boat cruising the creek as moonlight danced on the water, and eating Perez-made tamales with two of the best friends a boy could ever have. We were carefree and full of banter.

"Say," Albert said. "You heard about Moe and Joe going fishing?"

"Moe and Joe," I replied, pretending ho-hum boredom.

"Who's Moe, and who's Joe?" Nono asked, his mouth full. "Never met em." Tamale bits flew from his mouth.

"They live in League City?" I chimed.

Albert sighed, pulling the bucket of tamales back. "Guess I'm gonna have to put these..."

"No, no, no, no!" Nono and I said together. We pulled the container back.

"Go ahead, we're listening," I said.

"Yeah," Nono pleaded. "Cut off my legs, but don't take the tamales."

"Okay, here's the boat deal," Albert said. "Moe and Joe." He stopped and looked at us.

Nope, we weren't about to interrupt again.

"Moe and Joe rents this boat, and they go fishing out in the lake. They catch fish right and left, enough to feed our whole boy scout troop, twice. Joe says to Moe, 'Hey, this is a great spot. Be sure and mark it.'"

"'Okay,'" replies Moe.

"They get back to the boat dock and Joe asks Moe, 'Hey did you mark the spot?'"

"'Sure,' Moe says. 'I put a big X on the side of the boat.'"

"'Why you stupid idiot!' Joe explodes, slapping Moe about the shoulders."

"'What, wait, why'd you, ah...' Moe says."

"'You dumb clod. Now what if we get a different boat tomorrow?'"

Me and Nono looked at one another dumbly, then suddenly we got the joke. We cracked up, tamale bits spraying the air. I almost got chocked. Suddenly, I whirled the wheel, barely missing some trees. Branches scraped the side of the boat.

"Hope no snakes jump in," giggled Nono, trying to control his mirth. He picked up an oar to defend himself.

"Me, too," I said, hating that my boat was getting scratched.

Spotty barked.

"Keep it up, boy. That'll scare em away," Nono said, fanning the branches with the oar.

Back in mid-channel, I indicated the wheel, and Albert took control as I turned in my seat. I poured some water from the glass one-gallon jug into my bailing can. I put the tin down in front of Spotty. He drank eagerly. The hot tamale bits we'd given him earlier made him thirsty. He looked at me with appreciative eyes. I patted his head and rubbed his soft tummy.

Author, Billy Sneed, age 15, on Clear Creek, League City, Texas

"Good pup, Spotty," I said.

"Maybe he wants some *chot-ho-ko*," Nono said, and laughed.

Albert and I did, too.

Chot-ho-ko had been Nono's mispronunciation of "hot chocolate" one morning last winter, when we had awaken to freezing weather on a camping trip. Teeth chattering and vapor coming from his mouth, he had wanted to fix some...some...*chot-ho-ko!* That's all the word he could muster in the blistery cold air.

Chot-ho-ko had also been adapted as our secret club word to stand against anyone, or any dangerous situation, *together*. Whoever spoke the word, the other two were supposed to repeat it, meaning we would tackle and defend one another against anyone, or anything, *together*. We had never been challenged thus far. The Johnny Lowe thing didn't count because I wasn't ashore having to face him. Like all boys with club secrets, it was fun to know that only we knew the meaning of *chot-ho-ko*.

Death to the end, I thought with a proud smile. *Chot-ho-ko.*

Albert steered steady on a westernly course that would ease us under the towering trestle that stretched across Clear Creek between Galveston County and Harris County. Then we all heard it:

Air horns howling, coming from the Houston direction.

A deep rumble vibrated the air as diesel engines came our way.

"Hurry, Albert," Nono said as raising the motor throttle.

"Wastin' gas, Nono. Ain't got that much," I said, and reached back and eased the throttle back.

"*Madre de Dios!*" Nono said, crossing himself. "We're gonna be right under the bridge and all that weight over our heads!"

I stood up, bare chest out. "*Chot-ho-ko!*" I said, raising a fist to the air toward the coming train.

"*Chot-ho-ko!*" Albert said, standing, too.

Nono appeared pensive a moment, then rose. He grabbed our hands.

"*Chot-ho-ko!*" he screamed above the noise.

The vast tonnage rumbled and shook above our heads as we passed under the trestle. It was eerie and scary, but we wouldn't admit it. The freight train screeched and groaned, sporadic sparks coming from the wheels. The air vibrated, the noise drowning out everything, including the boat engine and Spotty's incessant barking.

"Holy cow!" I shouted, but no one heard. I jerked the wheel left, steering away from the barnacle-infested cement pilings of Highway 3. We slipped under the other bridge silently, the clickie-clacking of the train wheels snubbing the boat engine noise.

Minutes later, the Humble Oil Company building and tanks on our right slipped past as the train faded in the background. Moonlight waltzed on the ripples of creek water ahead as we made the slow bend in the creek and headed south. To our left was *Galveston County Park*. I looked into the secluded trees for any parked cars, but there were none to be seen. Nono had the same idea as he beamed a flashlight among the trees.

"No lovers tonight," Nono said. "Shooooot. I was gonna mess em all up with this light."

"Albert," I said, letting the wheel go on its steady course. "Was we brave back there under the train bridge?" We always looked to Albert for answers, beings he was an avid reader, the brains of our club. Man, he was smarter than both me and Nono put together.

Albert was silent a moment. He rubbed his chin.

"*Ignorant* is more like it," Nono said.

"Not really," Albert replied.

"Okay, then," I said. "What is *courage?*"

"Courage," Albert said in thought.

I passed Nono a tamale, then removed the corn husk from another and ate most of it. I gave the last bit to Spotty. I patted his head, then scratched him behind an ear.

"Courage," Albert said again.

"Yes?" I replied, brows raised.

"Courage is when a person loses his fear of death," Albert said.

"Like what and when?"

"Like...like the people on the Titanic, like the servicemen in Pearl Harbor...like Audie Murphy. History is full of people who performed well in the face of death."

"Okay, then what makes..." I was confused. I looked ahead and turned the wheel slightly. "I mean they gotta be mad, angry, or hurt. Know what I mean, you know, to do this thing without fear of death."

"What if a three-hundred pound man comes into your house," Albert said, "and he..."

"I'd run," Nono chimed in with a laugh.

"Shuddup," Albert said in a serious tone. He looked at me. "This big man starts beating up on your mother..."

"What?" I said, feeling my body becoming rigid. "I'd jump on him. Nobody beats up on my sweet mother!"

"Yeah, but you're only a fifteen year old boy. Strong perhaps, yes," Albert said, "but this guy is six foot tall, along with his three-hundred pounds. He's a wrestler, too. I forgot to say that."

"Makes no difference I'd still jump him or hit him with whatever I could find first." I opened and closed my fist on the steering wheel.

"You just answered your own question," Albert said, patting me on a shoulder.

"What? I mean..."

"You just lost your fear of death. That's courage."

I stared at him blankly, still confused.

"Man, them tamales sure make you thirsty," Nono said as he pulled another wax bottle from the cooler. "Guys, want one?"

"Coke this time," Albert said.

"Me, too," I said.

Nono used an opener and popped the caps off. He passed the drinks to us.

Observing the empty park, vacant tables and no barbeque grills glowing with hot coals, we continued our jaunt in silence. A car drove slowly on the upper road but did not stop anywhere. Maybe they saw us and changed their minds. Tomorrow would be Friday and matters would liven up both in the park and on the creek. But, it was nice right now. Quiet, tranquil. Just me, my friends, and my creek chum, Spotty, my forever companion.

With the water calm, except for the occasional wind-generated ripples in the wide areas of the creek, I turned in my seat, and picked up Spotty. Without protest, I turned back and set him on the bow platform in front of the steering wheel. He licked my face and whined. It was his favorite place on the boat. He could see everywhere. He was like a seeing-eye hood ornament.

"Now, if that don't beat all," Nono said, talking like a real Texas cowboy. He laughed his high-pitched tone.

"He's like a barking headlight," Albert said.

We all laughed. Then I thought of Albert and his dog, Red, and my *Butterfinger* candy bar. Boy, how could I ever forget this? But after tonight it would be four decades later before I remembered the prize product! The event unfolded again in my mind. Boy, was it ever so funny:

We were at the city park across from the old train depot, roller skating on the big cement slab that was supposed to be a basketball court, but I rarely saw it used for this purpose. We hadn't been there too long, but I was already frustrated with my dumb skates. One kept coming off my shoe because I had long ago lost the key that tightened the hooks onto the sole of my shoes. I used a pair of pliers, but could never get them quite snug enough. What I really wanted was a pair of real shoe skates, but, man, those things were $30 and up. That was a whole week's salary at Jimmie Walker's Edgewater Restaurant in Kemah, Texas for me. No way! I worked too hard as a busboy cleaning those stupid tables to spend my whole weeks salary all at once.

**EDGEWATER
RESTAURANT**

Phone 3660

Kemah

Texas

"Seen Red?" Albert asked as he came up from behind.

I was sitting on the grass beside the court, a few feet from what we called the "Dust Bowl," which was nothing but a worn dirt area where we would slide our bicycle brakes to see how must dust we could raise. Red? Red was Albert's dog, a type of hunting dog. Albert said that one of his dad's yard customers had given him the animal, stressing that it was an expensive and very intelligent breed.

"Over there," I said, pointing with the pliers to some oak trees. The whole block was lined with huge oak trees on all sides. I slipped the pliers inside my jacket on the ground, careful not to squash the Butterfinger candy bar that I was saving for when we quit skating.

Albert spat, then whistled, using his tongue, teeth, and lips in a way I never could, much as I tried.

I looked around for Spotty, my English setter. "Humm," I grumbled, then turned. There he was, right behind me. He looked at me like I was nuts.

"Good boy," I said, patting his head. Spotty generally stayed close to me, unless he saw a cat. He hated cats.

"Bet I have more money than you, Billy," Albert said as Red came tromping up to his side. Albert laughed, turning his toes outward and skating in a small circle, making the big dog jump at some imaginary food he held out high with his right hand. He loved teasing the dog this way. He said Red could do tricks, but I never saw one.

"Prove it," I replied, the usual words we said whenever we accepted the wager. I pulled out my wallet. With our part-time jobs, we always had a buck or two.

Albert stopped skating and dropped to his knees in front of me. He whipped out his billfold smartly. With a sly smile, he peeled out a crisp five dollar bill... then, one, two...three, four...five ones.

I waited.

Finally, I said, "That's it?"

"You can beat it?"

"Why not?" I said gleefully. I, too, followed with a $5 bill, worn, yes...then one, two, three, four, five...si...si...si.... Man, where was that extra one dollar bill I had? It was just in my wallet. I knew it was here; then I remembered the Butterfinger. I had spent the dollar at Kilgore's Grocery Store: two Milky Ways, some Frietos, a Coke and the Butterfinger candy bar, which was still in my shirt pocket. Rats! No! I felt my glory go to my toes. Why did life have to be so mean?

"What, you don't have another bill, Billy? Gee, that's too bad. Murphy's law, huh?"

"Whattcha mean 'Murphy'? I don't know no Murphy, except Audie. He's on at the picture show now." I loved Audie Murphy. War hero, and tough cowboy now.

"No, no." Albert laughed. "Murphy's Law. Means if something's gonna go wrong and the conditions are right, then it's gonna go wrong."

"You read too much, Albert. Books. They're gonna warp your skull."

"And the conditions are right...right now," Albert said, slipping a bill from a hidden slot in his wallet.

"What? You..."

"I win, I win!" Albert said, showing that it was a $5 bill. He laughed happily and held the money out at arms length, almost in my nose.

Like a flash, Red leaped in the air and snatched the money from Albert's hand, thinking it was food.

Albert glanced at me, mouth agape, face both surprised and horror-stricken at once.

Then I started laughing. Holy cow, that was a beautiful trick. I fell over and rolled on the ground.

Albert grabbed Red in a bear hug. They hit the grass in a tumble, feet over paws. Man or beast, no one took Albert's money.

"Get some food, quick!" Albert yelled as boy and dog fell smack dab into the dust bowl. "I see the five!" he shouted through the thick cloud that rose from the ground. "He's got it clamped in the back of his mouth. Part of it's sticking out. Get some food, anything!"

I eased up, stomach hurting from laughing. Wow! I thought as I watched them disappear in the dust storm. An arm or leg or paw appeared now and then, but vanished again in the powdery thickness.

"You nuts? Gonna stick your hand in that dog's mouth over money?" I asked.

Over the growling and snarling, Albert managed to speak. "'C'mon, Billy, help me, huh?"

Red snorted and huffed under Albert's weight, but Albert was strong, you know, from all the lawnmower pushing. I could never beat him in wrestling.

"Okay, okay," I said. I reached for my shirt on the ground beside me, and pulled out the Butterfinger. I quickly unwrapped it, dropping it twice. Then I passed it to Albert's out-stretched hand, just as they fell back to the grass in sight again. In a flash, Albert grabbed the candy.

"Red! Red! Take it easy. Here, this is for you. Now open your mouth and drop the money," Albert said. He rubbed the chocolate on Red's nose, then let the dog loose, keeping the candy bar back so Red couldn't get it.

"He'll grab anything," Albert added. "Forgot about that. But he'll drop it for food." He got to his knees, Red inches away, eyes wild and eager in anticipation.

"Guess this makes us even," I said, on the verge of laughing.

"Not if I get it back...and I will!"

"Make it so, Mr. Murphy."

"Here, Red. Here, Red," Albert said, quickly passing the candy across the dog's mouth. "He'll drop the money in a second, watch and see. Works every time."

"Yeah, but the conditions gotta be right, right?" I said.

Albert glanced at me just as Red snatched the candy from his hand. He jerked his head back to the dog.

"No, you son-of-a-gun. Loco perro!"

We both saw Red swallow.

GULP!

There went my Butterfinger, and the $5 bill!

"Stupid dog!" Albert said. He kicked off his skates, and looked around for a stick...anything. He picked up a branch.

Red took off running.

"You're right, Albert," I shouted. "Dog's pretty smart." I laughed and laughed.

That was the last I saw of Albert and Red that week. Dust flying from their bodies, they ran in the direction of Egypt.

When we finally met again, Albert told me how he never let Red out of his sight for a whole week. He even tied the dog to a tree beside their chicken coop house, and slept outside, waiting for the dog to pass the five dollar bill. It never happened.

"Well," I said. "You did say he was an expensive dog."

Albert spat, scowling at me. "Not funny. Not funny at all."

"Say," I pressed. "I think you owe me a Butterfinger, amigo."

I grinned at the memory again as I looked blankly ashore.

At the roofed pier of the County Park, near the bend where we would ease to the right, I peered at the rather steep hill where boaters backed their trailers down into Clear Creek and grinned as I recalled seeing a few cars and trucks slide down the bank into the water. It served those Houston nuts right.

"Boy, we've come a long way in such short a time," Nono said, munching on a tamale as he took in the last of the park area.

"Yeah, little engine does okay," I said, easing the boat in a wide right turn. "Beats rowing, that's for sure."

"Wonder why they don't just tear down that thing," Nono said, indicating the abandoned train trestle ahead.

"A waste of money," Albert said.

"That old thing will still be here when I'm a hunnered years old," Nono said.

"Not likely," Albert said. "Things, places, and people change over time."

I laughed. "Now, for once, you don't know what you're talking about."

"Enjoy it," Albert said with the sweep of a hand. "Twenty, thirty, forty years from now you won't even recognize any of this."

"Well, that's all the tamales you get," I said. "They all went to your head."

Nono and I laughed.

"I'm serious," Albert said. "I'm reading Thomas Wolfe's, *Look Homeward Angel*. It's about..."

"About how you're losing all your brains with all that reading you do," I said. "First you tell me I have to lose all my cool to know what courage is, and now you're telling me I'll change...this whole place will change." I laughed. "I'll always be me, so will Nono and so will you. And this will always be like this," I said with a mock sweep of a hand. "It'll never change!"

Albert looked at me strangely, then shook his head.

"'Nother one?" Nono asked, getting into the cooler again.

"Yeah. *GP*," I said, remembering *Grand Prize* used to be my dad's favorite brand of beer.

"No *Grand Prize beer* tonight, sir. Coke'll have to do," Nono said.

Thirty minutes later we were about a hundred yards from what was known as the "Super Highway." Laughing, we had just finished singing the Boy Scout song, "*Trail The Eagle*." All but one bottle of the drinks had been consumed, and the three dozen tamales were history.

"Ah," Albert said, seeing headlights above on the bridge. "Civilization again."

Spotty barked at the distant whizzing of cars and trucks passing on the big bridge.

I reached into the cooler and got a tiny ice cube and put it in my dry mouth. Rivulets of sweat ran down the center of my back and chest.

"What say we pull up under the bridge and go to the *Thunderbird Inn* and get some more drinks," I said, reaching into my pocket.

"You mean that beer joint up toward Webster?" Nono asked.

"Sure, why not? They sell cold drinks, too." I handed two crumbled dollars to Albert as he pulled out some money. Nono shook his head, giving Albert some money, too.

"Me and Spotty'll stay with the boat. Shouldn't take you guys long. If you have any money left, get a few bags of potato chips, huh?"

"Fritos, too," Albert said.

I nodded, steering toward the cement bridge pillars to the right. Easing between the columns, I guided the boat under the bridge to bank on the Harris County side. The din of cars and trucks sounded above our heads, echoing slightly. Albert and Spotty jumped off the boat. The bow lightened and came ashore with a light thud.

*　*　*　*

"Want to sell that nice boat?"

Twenty minutes had passed and Albert and Nono had not returned. I was getting worried. Maybe it was a longer walk to the *Thunderbird Inn* than I thought. I sighed, sitting on the boat bow, my feet on the damp bank. Something stunk now and then. It had to be fish bait, shrimp, probably, from the foul odor. With the Super Highway above, I was also keeping an eye on Spotty. He was on the cement slope under the bridge end, not too far away. Although it was dark, I could still see his white body darting about, nose to the ground. To keep him near, I called his name and whistled now and then.

That's all I needed was for something to happen to the family pet. No, it was unheard of. Nothing could happen to Spotty. The mere thought horrified me. I whistled and called his name again.

"I say, 'you want to sell that boat'?" the voice said again.

I heard the man the first time, when he was coming my way, but avoided him. It was dark under the big bridge, but I could make out the road that came down and crossed under the littered ground up the short slope from where I stood. The man had on trousers and a long-sleeved shirt. Odd, when it was so blasted hot. Here I was in rolled up jeans and no shirt. Holding the bow rope, I got to my feet, twitching my nose at that awful smell coming my way again.

"Nice boat," the man said, stopping closer to me than I wanted.

"No, sir, it's not for sale," I said, glancing to see Spotty coming my way.

"Say," the man said. "My sister's got a nice car. I bet I could get her to sell it to you real cheap. Maybe for twenty-five dollars." The man folded his arms across his chest, studying my boat.

What? This guy's gotta be some kind of nut.

"I'm not old enough to get a driver's license." I said. "But I will be next year. I'll be sixteen then." Spotty came to my side. I squatted and patted his head, then put an arm over his shoulders as he sat and eyed the stranger.

"It's a nice car, my sister's. Like this here boat. That's just what I need."

I swallowed, not knowing what to do or say. This guy was a definite nut case.

Suddenly, headlights came down the slope from the highway, bouncing on the rough road. A spotlight came on and beamed under the bridge where Spotty had been, then started to scan between the graffiti-slopped cement pillars. The dirt road turned under the bridge about twenty yards from where I stood, and rose up a slight incline.

At the sight of the lights on top of the Highway Patrol car, I felt both relief and apprehension.

Why is their spotlight on? What are they looking for? Is it okay for me to be docked under the bridge? Oh, no, I must have broken the law. I'll go to jail!

The spotlight reached us and stopped. I felt my heart pounding in my chest. The stranger glanced at the brightness as though bored, then continued to look at my boat more closely with light on it now. The patrol car turned sharply and came under the bridge, the bright beam never leaving us. I felt like I was on a stage. The vehicle slid to a stop, dust flying.

"Hold it right there. Don't move!" a male voice commanded.

"Yessir," I replied, feeling my heart drop to my toes.

The stranger turned and stopped, looking like he'd been treated this way before.

The cop got out of the patrol car, leaving the door open. The radio crackled and a voice said something I could not understand. A second officer joined the driver. They came our way down the incline, eyes never off of us, their right hands poised above pistols on their hips.

Spotty growled.

"Shhhhh!" I said, holding his mouth closed. *Surely they wouldn't shoot a fifteen year old boy...would they?*

"Hey," the driver said, and laughed. "That you, Mr. Weaver?" The officer was young and dark-headed.

The officers stopped by the boat; their tension relaxed at the sight of a known person. They looked neat and spiffy in their blue creased uniforms.

"Hello, Mr. Billy Crook," Mr. Weaver said. "'Evenin', Sergeant Gilmore." Mr. Weaver nodded as he slowly extended his arms out like airplane wings.

"Going to have to take you home again, Mr. Weaver," Billy Crook said, walking up behind him. He patted the man's sides, then down both legs.

I saw the stripes on Sergeant Gilmore's sleeve. He looked at me and smiled thinly. Hey, I recognized them both now. Billy Crook and Sergeant Gilmore. Yes. They were in Smith's Pharmacy frequently; the same guys that "Smitty" was always in coohoots with on his pranks he pulled on people he favored. But I knew they weren't here on a joke errand, that's for sure. Also, Albert worked part time at Smitty's every day after school.

"What's your name, son?" Sergeant Gilmore asked kindly.

"Billy. Billy Sneed." I stood up straight, Spotty eyeing us.

"Live near? Pretty dog you have."

"524 Iowa Street, sir. League City. Sir, I've seen you at Smitty's drug store a lot, sir. I'm with Albert Perez. He works there, too. Smitty's, I mean." I said. "Albert...he and my other friend, Nono, they went up the road to get us some cold drinks."

"I know Albert," Sergeant Gilmore said. He glanced inside the boat. Guy's going camping, I see."

"Yessir. That way." I thumbed west. "'Bout two, maybe three miles to go yet. It's on the Goode property."

"That's fine, Billy. You..."

"You officers find that escaped convict yet?" Mr. Weaver volunteered. "Heard about it on the radio. Sugar Land ain't too far from here, you know."

"Mr. Weaver," Billy Crook said. "I think you should be quiet." He glanced back at the sergeant, then me.

"But, Mr. Crook," Mr. Weaver said. "I was just trying to trade my aunt's car for this here nice boat. Ain't she a beaut?"

Billy Crook looked at me and winked. He a made a circular motion with a finger beside his right ear.

I was right. The man was cuckoo. They were going to take him back to wherever he walked off from. Escaped convict? How'd Mr. Weaver know about the prison in Sugar Land? But wait. Mr. Crook indicated he was nuts. So let him talk about escaped prisoners all he wanted. Right? No problem. League City never had any problems with escaped convicts from Sugar Land, anyway.

"You take care, Billy," Sergeant Gilmore said, helping Mr. Crook guide the handcuffed Mr. Weaver up the slope toward the patrol car.

"Yessir," I replied, smiling.

"Two-fifty-four," the car radio crackled. "Please be advised that the eighty-three was last seen heading toward Pearland. Use ten-oh if sighted."

Beside the black and white unit now, Billy Crook reached in and pulled the mike outside the car. He held it close to his mouth.

"Two-fifty-four. Ten-four. We have the usual ninety-six. We'll be ten-seventy-six to drop him off in a moment, then ten-seventy-six to five-eighteen."

"Ten-four," the radio blared.

Talking with numbers. How'd they do all that and understand everything? I was never any good in arithmetic. There went any hope of ever being a Texas Highway Patrolman.

They put Mr. Weaver in the back seat and shut the door.

"You guys be careful," Sergeant Gilmore said. "Awful dark up that creek. Say hi to Albert for me."

I laughed. "Been up it when it was darker than this , sir."

The officers smiled and got back into the squad car. The spotlight suddenly went out and it was dark again.

* * * *

"Escaped prisoner?" Albert laughed.

"Honest, that's what he said," I replied, right hand up with the three-fingered Boy Scout honor sign. I didn't tell them the guy was nuts. *A little joke never hurt anyone, right? Who would ever know but me?*

"I think we ought to turn back, at least camp closer to home," Nono said, voice concerned. "You know, like maybe at Ralph's beach house or the shell pile."

We were five minutes west of the Super Highway Bridge, cruising the dark creek, the boat engine running smoothly. Spotty was the usual look-out, sitting on the bow platform. I reached up and patted the soft coat. He turned and looked at me affectionately.

"I still can't believe you guys were gone so long," I said.

"It was farther that we thought," Albert said. "I told you. And the guy wasn't going to wait on us. Pushed us back out the door. Sure made me mad. He had no right to do that. I ought to tell Smitty. He knows Billy Crook and Sergeant Gilmore."

"He charged us triple for the drinks!" Nono said. "Fifty cents each. Highway robbery. We ain't never going there again, even if we're dying of thirst!"

"Okay, okay, okay," I said, right hand up. I didn't know what else to say. *They are right. Five dollars for a few Cokes was a lot of money.*

"How much further? I gotta go to the bathroom," Nono said.

"Why didn't you go back there?"

"You kiddin'? Guy wouldn't even let us come in. Just wanted our money, when we showed it to him. And there was too many cars, you know, to do anything beside the road. Besides, I ain't talkin' about peeing."

"Who was this guy the highway patrol picked up again?" Albert asked.

"Danged if I know," I said, playing a good part. "Some bum, drifter, but a real mean-looking person. Boy, I was scared there for a while." I sighed in relief. Although dark, I could still make out their surprised faces. It was my secret. I had to sound tough. "Here I was," I added, "sitting under the darn Super Highway bridge, and this scary-looking guy comes up to me. Wants... wants...to trade me my boat for his car. He..."

"Where was his car?" Albert asked.

"It...I never saw it. Guess it was...yeah, parked up by the highway. Guy reaches into his back pocket. Thought for sure he was gonna pull out a knife or a gun or something!" This was getting real good. "Then the "fuzz" shows up, red lights flashing. Guy didn't do nothing but stand there, looking lost, ya know?" I laughed. "Well, wasn't no place for him to go 'fore the cops got there, except in the water. Guess he figured they were just too close for him to run. Man, I was gonna grab him if he did," I said proudly.

"Sure you were, Billy," Albert said doubtfully.

"I was. I was. Honest. Ain't that like some of the courage we talked about earlier?"

"You need to see the witch doctor," Nono cut in, laughing.

"Which one?" I laughed, slapping my leg. Boy, sometimes I surprised my own self with my witty words.   "Get it? Get it? Witch and which." I laughed again.

"Funny, funny," Albert said, dead pan. "See Jane run. See Spot go. Go, Spot, go."

"Man," Nono said, squirming. "We'd better get to our camp soon. I gotta go bad!"

"Hold your horses. No...put a finger in it," I said.

Albert and I laughed.

"You know," I said seriously, moments later. "I think that guy was the escaped convict. See, there wasn't no radio around. How could he have heard it without a radio, huh?"

"Billy Crook and Sergeant Gilmore just took him away?" Albert asked. He spat overboard.

"Handcuffed! Honest. Ask em about it next time you see em at the drug store."

"Man, is it dark up this side of the Super Highway," Nono said. He slapped one arm, then at his shoulders. "Skeeters are bad here, too. Say, hand me one of them cans with the kerosene rags. That'll keep them boogers away, all that smoke and smell."

I reached under the bow platform and got one of the pork n' bean cans. I passed it back to Nono. "Wet a rag and set it on the stern seat before you light it. Don't want my boat to burn up."

"So you think the guy was just making it up about the escaped convict from Sugar Land?" Albert asked.

"Sure. Don't think there's ever been a prison break from there. You reckon?"

Albert rubbed his chin. "Naw, ain't ever heard of one."

I looked back to see Nono as he struck a match and cautiously stuck it inside the bean can. A yellow flame slowly lighted the stern area. With the still hot air, smoke went everywhere. Nono coughed and fanned the air with a hand.

"That's all we need," I told Nono. "We'll draw the attention of every animal and bum on the banks with that fire and smoke."

"Ain't no body in them woods on either side. This place is blacker than hell itself," Nono said, looking around blindly. He coughed and waved the air again.

Nono was right. West of the Super Highway bridge on the creek always appeared frightening. It was tar black in every direction, really eerie and spooky. It was as though death stalked our every move. Maybe it was because the creek started getting narrower, making the overhanging trees seem even more menacing. But, we were all alive and *together*. This unity made the difference.

"You hear that?" Albert asked, voice tense.

"What?" Nono yelped, eyes wide scanning the darkness.

I looked at Albert as he turned his head, stifling a grin.

The only noise was the puttering engine and an occasional owl hooting. Even the din of highway traffic had long disappeared.

Suddenly something hit the boat under the keel.

Nono screamed.

I laughed, nudging Albert with an elbow. I sure wished I had my harpoon now. It served absolutely no purpose where it was hidden in our gully hideout. If I only had it in my hands right now!

"It's just an alligator gar, Nono. They're all over up here," I said. "'Member the one we saw up by the camp? Gotta been eight foot long!"

"Shhh! Hear that?" Albert whispered loudly. He grabbed my arm and froze.

"I ain't fallin' for that again," Nono said. "But I do have to go to the bathroom, Billy. We stop soon so I can?"

Albert and I laughed.

"Okay, okay," I said, squinting at the dark creek ahead. "Wait til we get round the next bend. It's getting late. We might just go ahead and pitch camp. Whatcha think, Albert?"

"That's the best idea you've had all night," Albert said, pushing his hair back.

"Who's land, Billy?" Nono asked, yellow-orange flame dancing on his dark face.

"Oh...why? Does it matter? Ain't nobody around for miles."

"What if there's a Joe Poluka where we camp? What if there's two Joe Poluka's?" Nono moaned.

"Oh, Nono," Albert said. "Just be quiet. You know cattle go to the barn at night. Anyway, we'll get a fire going. That'll keep any cows and mosquitos away." Albert spat overboard.

I rolled my eyes in the dark. Why'd he always have to spit?

"Who're you in love with at school, Billy?" Nono asked, popping a cap on a Coke. He passed it to me. I passed it to Albert.

"Oh, I got three or four I'd marry tonight if they'd let me," I replied, taking another proffered cold drink.

"Like who?"

"Oh, ah...you guys gonna laugh?"

"Naw," Albert said.

"Not me," Nono chimed.

"Okay," I said, love visions filling my heart. "Jane Harmon..."

"You kiddin'? She wouldn't give you the time of day. Her being big wig, pretty, and a cheerleader," Nono said.

"I know that," I said a bit too sadly, and embarrassed. "I said I was in love with them, not they were in love with me."

"Okay, who else?"

"Lillie Longbrook. Been in love with her side the sixth grade. Her and Cookie Lynchman."

"Boy, you know how to pick em," Nono said.

"But who I really like, and always have, is Pat Smithers. But she would never let me carry her books, even back in elementary school. What about you guys? Hey, Albert, I hear you got a big liking for Kay Stramwell and Sherry..."

Suddenly a gunshot sounded from somewhere. It reverberated in the woods and on the creek, lingering as it died echoing down the creek.

"Whoa!" I said. "Kill the engine, Nono."

The boat went silent and slid through the water nicely.

"Snub the fire, too," I added.

Nono grabbed a wet rag and stuffed it into the flaming pork n' bean can.

Instant darkness.

The odor of white kerosene smoke filled the air as the boat slowed. Like Spotty, we froze in alertness, listening, looking, and trying to feel what was beyond.

There was nothing but darkness and total silence, not even a speck of light anywhere for miles around.

"Let's go back to the shell pile," Nono whispered.

"Shhhh!"

"Even the "creek house" would be better that this," Nono whined.

"Shhhh!" Both Albert and I stressed, fingers to our lips.

Except for the crickets, it was spooky silent. I grabbed an oar and pushed away from some trees we were gliding by. Limbs scrapped the side of the boat. I winced at the possible scratches on the boat.

"Albert," I said, taking the other oar and positioning them both in the oar locks. I turned and took the rowing position. "Take that spare rope and tie Spotty. Don't want him to jump ashore and disappear hunting like he always does."

Albert nodded and proceeded with the task.

"See anything, guys?" I asked as I took command of the boat movement, turning it back toward the creek middle. Then I back-treaded twice with the oars, stopping the boat.

"Nothing," Nono said in a whisper.

"Hunters," I said. "Has to be hunters. How far away was the shot? Mile... two miles?"

"You kiddin'?" Nono whined. "Close. Real close. Like right on the shore, coupla hunnerd feet!"

"Naw, no way," Albert said. "Good boy." He patted Spotty's head.

"Okay. How far, Albert?" I trusted Albert's judgment.

"Don't know. Hard to say," he replied. "You know how sound travels in the woods, especially at night. But I'd say less than a mile.

I stood up, holding the oars deep in the water. Squinting, I scanned the bank and woods on the right. There was a twenty foot open space between two overhanging trees. I turned, quickly swapping hands on the oars and started rowing little by little, the bow easing toward the root-infested bank.

"Don't see a darn thing, not even a speck of light," I said. "Some farmer or rancher must have shot out his back door. Okay, this is where we camp. Albert, get ready to jump and tie us up."

"Here?" Nono cried.

I laughed.

"Whattsa matter? Ain't you got none of that courage Albert talked about? Anyway, you have to go to the bathroom so bad, right?" I said, eyes on the moonlit bank.

"Easy," Albert said, then jumped to shore, rope in one hand, a flashlight in the other. The under-washed bank was about two feet higher than the bow.

Fifteen minutes later, we had our camp set up nicely under the moss-laden trees. Except for the ice chest, several rags, the gasoline can and a few other small items, the boat was empty. With the pork n' bean can flickering its yellow-orange color, Albert was ready to light the small pile of wood sticks that he had fashioned teepee style for the campfire. Like the good Eagle Boy Scout he was, he had cleared a wide area to bare dirt in case the fire got out of hand. Nono was out of sight someplace doing his private business. Searching under the bow platform earlier, I had found Spotty's black harness and strapped it on him, thankful I could get rid of the rope around his neck. My mother loved to see him with the harness on. She said he looked "sweet" and "all dressed up;" thought he was Mr. Aster himself, whoever Mr. Aster was.

"Gonna gas up the boat," I said, as Albert stuck a lit match under his teepee. "C'mon, Pup," I said with a light pull on the rope-leash. I hated keeping Spotty tied, but it was the only means to keep him with me without him running off to hunt all night. Being this far from home, I feared he'd get lost or someone would steal him. I stopped, got to my knees, and put my arms around Spotty. I gave him a hug til he grunted, then pulled his snout to my face. I kissed him, laughing, as he licked my face. I got to my feet, and we walked to the boat.

"Hey, Albert," I said over my shoulder.

"Yeah?" Albert replied, head down. He blew on a red glow within the teepee.

"I hope you ain't thinking about cooking pinto beans again. We're only gonna be here overnight, not a week." I laughed loudly.

"Guess you'll never forget that one, huh?" He laughed pleasantly.

"Yep," I said with a slow sweep of my hand, mocking Albert earlier, *"When all this is gone...changed, you know, like you said about the book that guy wrote..."*

"Thomas Wolf. *Look Homeward Angel...*"

"Yeah, that one, too," I said with a laugh. "When it's all gone, and we *can't* go home no more, I'll still remember your stupid beans, twenty, thirty, forty years from now."

"In your dreams," Albert replied, leaning thicker sticks on his flaming teepee as the camp site started to brighten.

At the under-washed bank, I stopped and looked down at the moonlit boat. I spotted a curved root protruding from the ground and tied the leash to it. I held Spotty's soft snout with one hand and stroked his face several times with the other.

"You sit here, booger dog, while I gas up. I'll get you some water when we get back to the camp. Some groceries, too, huh?" I had all sorts of pet names for Spotty when no one was within ear shot. I loved him so much, he was part of my soul. Spotty and I was the perfect example of a boy and his dog. We were *friends forever*. Our fun and adventures on Clear Creek spanned over three years. Thus far, we had camped over one hundred days and nights up and down the creek. Actually, I lost count at one-hundred-and-ten overnighters. That was what, about three months ago? Yes, thereabouts. And there would be many more trips, too, I thought as I carefully stepped down the two foot drop to the bow platform. The bow tilted slightly in the mud and water but I held my balance like a pro.

"Shoot!" I grumbled, picking up the one-gallon gas can. There wasn't enough gas left to even fill the tank. I sighed. Good thing we stopped when we did. Shaking the metal can, I guessed there was enough to barely get us back to the shell pile, that is, if we kept the throttle at half speed. I checked the gas shut-off valve under the tank. It was open. I closed it. I unscrewed the cap and started pouring the gas into the engine tank.

Suddenly a gunshot exploded. The noise was so intense that I jumped and ducked at the same time, dropping the fuel can. Raw gasoline gurgled into the bilge. Spontaneously I set the can upright, eyes toward the camp, mouth agape.

Spotty growled and barked, ears perked.

"Easy, boy," I whispered, crawling onto the bow platform. I jumped to the bank. I pulled Spotty to me, arm over his shoulders.

"Shhh," I said softly, looking toward the camp.

Albert was not in sight.

What happened? Where'd he go? Did he get shot? And where was Nono? He hadn't even screamed.

Heart pounding in my chest, I crouched and crept closer to the camp. Albert's teepee was ablaze, lighting the small campsite. I wiped the sweat from my forehead. Spotty whined and licked my hand.

"Easy, pup," I whispered, rubbing his head, my eyes glued to the camp. The only noise was the popping and crackling of the fire. Even the crickets ceased their racket.

"Pssst. Albert, you there?" I said in a tight whisper.

The fire cracked and popped. Sparks fluttered upward. A full minute passed as I took in the camp again, then tried to look beyond the trees into the darkness.

"Albert," I said in a normal tone. "You there? Answer up!"

"Over here," Albert replied, coming from behind the pup tent Nono had put up. "I dove behind here the second I heard the shot." He brushed the leaves and dirt from his arms and T-shirt as he walked near the fire where I stood.

"You okay?" I asked.

"Sure, you?"

"Fine. Whatta heck's going on?"

"Don't know, but we gotta find Nono."

"NONO, NONO! " I shouted. "WHERE ARE YOU?"

"Nono, *venga aqui. Ahora mismo, me amigo!*" Albert shouted, hands cupped to his mouth.

"NONO, NONO!" we roared together.

We listened, staring with frightened eyes at one another.

The only sound came from the fire and the crickets starting their nocturnal noise again.

"Let's get torches from the fire," Albert said, squatting. "We'll comb one end..."

Suddenly, Nono was pushed into sight, a hand over his mouth, by someone behind him. His torso glistened with sweat. His jeans were wet in the crotch. Terror-stricken dark eyes looked at us, and the biggest silver-coated pistol I had ever seen was pointed at his head.

"You boys jus take it easy now," a southern male voice drawled, "and nobody's gonna git hurt!"

Nono was shoved forward. He collapsed at our feet, gasping for air. We squatted to help him.

Spotty bared his teeth, growling.

"Keep the mutt cool, or he's dead!" the man said, pointing the pistol at Spotty. He cocked the hammer back.

Still thunderstruck, I nervously motioned a hand at the man, pulling Spotty to my side, a hand over his mouth. I prayed the man wouldn't shoot.

"I...I...I have him...sir. Spotty ain't gonna be no problem, sir. Please, not my puppy, sir," I cried.

"You be mighty sure, boy, or I swear I'll kill him!" The man released the hammer slowly. It clicked audibly. He held the gun at his waist as he paced the camp taking everything in. He breathed heavily as though he'd ran a mile without stopping.

"He won't be no bother, sir. I promise," I replied nervously, hugging my pet as I watched the stranger.

He was a little bit taller than Albert, filled out more, but he looked real young, maybe twenty-one, twenty-two. Beady eyes looked out from a small head and a pockmarked face with a short pointed nose. From the flickering light, he looked brown-headed, the hair crew-cut and shaved high above the ears. Yellow crooked teeth showed from a small mouth curled downward in a perpetual pout, like he could never smile, or didn't want to. His voice was raspy-sounding as though his vocal cords were made out of gravel. A shiny scar looped the lower part of his neck from shoulder to shoulder like a lavaliere. He wore work boots that laced up past the ankles, a loose-fitting pair of denim trousers and a blue, sweat-soaked chambray shirt with the tail out.

"Can I get my friend a drink of water?" Albert asked.

The stranger stopped, looked at Albert, then the water jug nearby, then Albert again. He walked to the jug and looked around. He kicked the blankets and sleeping bag, glancing back at us frequently.

"You boys got any guns, you better tell me right here and now about where they are. I find one later, you all die right on the spot. Clear?"

"No guns, sir. None whatsoever. We're not on a hunting trip. Just out camping, that's all," I said, holding Spotty close.

"Better be!" He looked at Albert, helping Nono to his feet. "Getcher water, Poncho." The man then looked at me. "Y'all in a boat? I need a boat real quick." He glanced back at the direction he had came in from the woods.

I swallowed. He was going to steal my boat! I looked where the boat was tied below the bank, out of sight. If I lied, and he found out, he'd kill us and Spotty, too. Maybe I could talk him out of taking it. I could offer to take him where he wanted to go. Yes, that was even better.

"Yessir," I said, pointing. "I'll be glad to take you to the place you want to go. See, the creek at night is real tricky. Hundreds of waterways to go in if you wanna get lost. But I know em all, sir."

"Name's...ah...Roy," the convict said, adding, "None of that 'Sir' crap again. And don't call me 'Mister' either. I'm sick of it, hear, all of you?" Roy banished the gun at us.

"Sure, sure. No problem, si..." I gulped. "Ah, Roy. Roy, yeah." I forced a smile.

"You Meskins got that, too?"

While Nono nodded, Albert glared at Roy. I saw a loathing in Albert's eyes I had never seen before.

"Roy," I said forcing a laugh. "Albert and Nono are my friends. We live near..."

"Shuddup!" Roy said, scowling at Albert.

I swallowed, watching Roy's fingers twitch on the gun. He moved it to aim at Albert.

"Roy, Roy," I pleaded. "I..ah, I can get you to the Super Highway in twenty minutes. Honest," I said, hands waving in a slow down gesture. "Nice boat. Tied over there by that big tree. Go check it out. You'll see."

Silence.

The fire cracked and popped. Sparks fluttered upward.

Roy slowly lowered the gun, glancing at me, the tree, then back at Albert and Nono.

"You two, out this way!" Roy said to Albert and Nono, pointing with the gun. "We're all gonna take a trip together."

"We'll get there faster if there's only two of us," I said. "With the camping gear out and only us two..."

"Shuddup! Roy said loudly. "You think I'm dumb enough to leave these two here so they can run up to that dead...that farmer's house and call the law? You're a pretty stupid kid to be a white boy if you think that!"

Mouth agape, I just stood there. *Holy cow! He killed those people, that man, probably the owner of this property we're on now. That was the first shot we heard earlier!*

"Alright, everybody go over by the boat. NOW!" Roy waved the gun.

I swallowed, holding Spotty's leash, looking at Albert, who nodded ever so slightly. I could see that he was angry. We moved slowly toward the creek.

"MOVE! MOVE!" Roy screamed. "I ain't kiddin'! Believe me, I ain't got nothin' to lose by killin' you three! Nothin' whatsoever!"

We moved quicker. I recognized Albert's anger. He kept watching Roy's every move.

"Hold it right there!" Roy said when we were standing by the bank.

I pulled Spotty into the darkness behind me.

"Now, here's what we're gonna do, boys." Roy held his hands on his hips, the gun positioned awkwardly. "Y'all is just kids. I may kill, but I don't kill babies." Suddenly he waved a finger at us. "But I will if you screw up, try to be Mister Big Shot, or the world's worst hero, so don't be gettin' no fancy ideas. Okay, let's get in the boat."

We started to move.

"Hold it! Hold it!" Roy commanded loudly.

We froze, but I saw Albert's eyes flashing.

"Here's what we're gonna go, kiddies." Roy crossed his arms over his chest, the gun held firmly and finger on the trigger. "This here's a gym class. You're all out in the yard exercising, see. And what do you do in the locker room afterwards, huh? Why you get naked and take a shower. Okay, you guys, strip down!"

I let out a gasp. "What? You serious?"

"As the electric chair!" Roy spit out. "See, none of you will go running to the law after I get off at the highway. At least not right away, til you come back here to get your clothes. By then I'll be long gone...Houston, Galveston... maybe even Dallas. Who Knows? Now...get out of those clothes. Move it!" He pointed the gun at us. There was a loud click of metal on metal as he cocked the pistol.

Clothes in a pile, we stood naked in the darkness less than two minutes later.

"Okay, kid, you and the dog first." Roy stood aside.

I glanced at Albert and Nono, sighing. Giving slack on the leash, I jumped the two feet onto the bow platform. The bow tilted downward, then hit the soft mud. I turned and picked up Spotty, whining and waiting in anticipation. Roy motioned with the pistol for me to move to the stern.

"You next," he told Nono. Nono trembled, his knees shaking as he stepped down onto the boat. Again the bow tilted. Nono almost lost his balance, dropping to his knees to keep from going overboard.

From the stern seat, I watched Albert's silhouette. Even though it was dark, I knew he had on his calculating face, judging, watching, and scheming. And he was angry.

"You, ignorant Meskin kid!" Roy said, gun on Albert. "I'm gonna jump on now. No funny tricks or your amigos are dead! You come behind me when

I tell you, then jump in the mud and shove us off." Roy wagged the gun in front of Albert's face. "Whattsa matta, you no speakada da English? Sure you do. You don't fool me one bit. Seen plenty of your kind in the pen. Now do what I say...step back and untie us while I get on the boat!"

Albert stared at Roy a moment, then turned. So did Roy. Just as Roy's weight made the bow tilt and bottom on the mud, Albert sprang.

"CHOT-HO-KO! CHOT-HO-KO!" Albert shouted.

"What the..." Roy only managed a half turn.

Albert's weight hit Roy like a football player. Roy's back arched, throwing his gun hand up. The pistol fired in the air. They fell overboard into the waist-deep water.

Mouth's open, Nono and I stared at one another too galvanized with fear and surprise.

Albert and Roy surfaced, locked in a fury of strength. The gun was between them, pointing up and down at the bank. It fired again. Bark flew from the trunk of the big tree.

"I'll kill you! I'll kill you!" Roy shouted, twisting the gun muzzle.

"CHOT-HO-KO! CHOT-HO-KO!" Albert pleaded, teeth clamped.

Holy cow! I thought. "CHOT-HO-KO!" I said, standing. "Stay, boy, stay!" I quickly told Spotty.

"CHOT-HO-KO!" Nono repeated.

I dove overboard, tackling Roy's waist. Nono was on his shoulders. Roy grunted and groaned and staggered under our weight.

"The gun!" Albert managed to shout.

Roy dropped to his knees. Nono and I stuck to him like leeches, fighting to get the gun. Roy got to his feet again. I couldn't believe it. Albert stood. He swung his fist back and hit Roy as hard as he could in the face. Roy fell against the boat. His hand hit the gunnel. The pistol fell into the boat. I turned and heaved myself up half way into the boat. I grabbed the barrel and pulled it to me. I pushed back into the muddy water. I swung my arm back and threw the gun out into deep water.

Nono screamed.

I turned to see him in the air above Roy's head. He threw Nono against the tree. Stunned, Nono slid down the trunk on the bank above. Albert kicked Roy in the groin. Roy yelled, grabbing himself. I jumped on Roy's back. He reached up and grabbed my head. He flipped me over his shoulders, body-slamming me on the muddy shore. Sludge and water flew everywhere. He snatched Albert by the neck and pushed him under water. On my elbows, I watched in horror.

"No!" I mumbled. I struggled to get to my feet as Nono came flying over my body and landed beside Roy. He reared back with a two-inch thick branch and slammed it across Roy's teeth. Roy yelled, grabbing his bleeding mouth. He staggered.

Albert surfaced, coughing and sputtering. Face resolute, he quickly regained his senses. Roy dropped to his knees. Albert jumped behind him and wrapped an arm around Roy's neck, locking his arms together. He squeezed, putting the wrestler sleeper hold on Roy. When Albert did this, there was no escape. We had all learned the horror of this hold while watching Friday night wrestling on TV in Houston, hosted by Paul Bosh. Albert had pulled this on us lots of times, but always stopped for fear of chocking us to death.

"In the boat! Get in!" Albert managed.

"Not...not without you!" I gasped.

"Be right...behind...you! Now...do it!"

Roy's hands strained to pull Albert's arms down. He gagged and sputtered. He slowly went limp.

Nono had already leaped back on the bank. He untied the rope and jumped on the bow platform.

I looked at Albert's determined face, then at Nono. Nono nodded. I turned and shoved the boat off the bank into deeper water.

"C'mon, Albert, that's enough! He's out," I said. I heaved my naked body inside the boat. I nodded to Nono, waiting for the cue to start the engine. I grabbed the oars and stopped the boat.

Albert let Roy go. He slid from Albert's body onto the muddy bank. Albert got to his feet. He combed his hair back with his hands, face dripping with mud, water and sweat. He glanced down at Roy, then started walking toward the boat.

"C'mon! C'mon!" I goaded.

Roy's head moved. An arm lifted slowly. The left eye opened, then the right.

"Billy! Billy!" Nono screamed. "It won't start! It won't start!"

Albert dove in the water and started swimming toward the boat.

"Open the gas valve under the tank!" I said, glancing back at Nono. "Then choke it some."

Roy pulled himself half up with a overhanging root and shook his head. He took in several deep breaths, then his head jerked our way. Face contorted, he got to his feet and charged out into the water.

"Hurry, Albert!" I said as he grabbed the side of the boat. I dropped the oars and helped him aboard.

"Little punks! I'll kill you with my bare hands!" Roy said, spitting water.

Nono pulled and pulled on the engine cord, but it wouldn't start. He had choked it too much.

"Sit down guys!" I said, taking the rowing position just as Roy's hand grabbed the side of the boat.

Nono screamed.

"You're dead little boys now! You're mine!" For the first time Roy laughed.

I made two long and hard pulls on the oars, feeling Roy's weight slowing the boat, causing it to swing to starboard. My heart pounded, almost exploding out of my chest.

With both hands, Roy heaved himself upward just as Albert's fist punched his nose.

"AAAAAHHHH!" Roy yelled, falling backwards into the water.

I saw our only chance. I mustered all the muscle power in my arms and took long, hard, deliberate strokes, propelling the boat forward with such force that a bubbly wake was created instantly. All I could think about was Albert's punch on Roy. Just like in the movies, he had actually socked the convict. In rare conflicts, I was still in the pushing and shoving stage. I didn't even remember slugging Roy as we struggled for the gun.

"Come back here, you little punks!" Roy yelled, treading water. "I'll kill you!"

Thirty yards away, I stood up, the boat gliding still further away.

"Sorry, *Mister* Roy, *Sir*! We just can't do that," I said loudly just as Nono got the engine started.

"And aawwwwaaay we go!" Nono said, imitating Jackie Gleason on television. He even did the arm and foot routine. He laughed, then reached down and put the throttle at full power.

Roy yelled and yelled, shaking a fist, but we didn't hear him, or care. We had escaped death. We were free again and the feeling was exhilarating. We stood laughing and jumping, shaking hands and slapping one another on the back, even hugging, oblivious to our nakedness.

Although jubilant, I could tell by the look in Albert's dark eyes that something was still wrong. Maybe it was just the excitement of it all, or maybe he had changed. Could be he was still scared, too, but I didn't really believe this.

At full power, we were making the bend, that would put the Super Highway bridge in sight. No one had spoken a word. Spotty was on the bow platform, ears picking up the distant din of occasional vehicle noise.

"We gotta call the sheriff," Nono said loudly

"I'll just..." I reached back and cut the engine throttle to half power. "Why don't I just let you off, all naked and all, and you run up and flag down Billy Crook and Sergeant Gilmore, huh?" I snapped.

Our jubilance had passed. The night was ruined. We had no camping gear, except—thankfully—the cooler with drinks and water in melted ice, and no clothes. If anyone saw us, they'd call the law and report us as indecent. And who would believe three naked boys with some foolish tale about fighting a convict in the woods on the creek? No, there was nothing else to do but to try and make it home without being seen.

Nono looked at his body and grimaced. Like Albert and me, he was sitting on the deck below the seat, keeping the bulk of his body out of sight from anyone that might be looking from the banks.

We made the bend, the Super Highway bridge dead ahead. I steered the boat straight toward the middle, looking up at the infrequent traffic. I estimated it to be about 2 a.m. It was a blessing to hear and see and *feel* the passing vehicles. People. Civilization. We were back in real life.

Spotty barked as we went under the bridge. I grinned, trying to catch his wagging tail. He appeared as though he was smiling, too, thankful like the rest of us to be fine and alive.

When the lights and the bridge disappeared on our stern, Albert pulled out from under the seat and stood. He stretched a bit, then reached down and killed the engine.

"Whatter' you doing, Albert?" I asked, surprised. With his hair down on both sides and naked in the moonlight, he looked like and Indian.

"What I want to know," he said, hands on his hips, "is why you guys...my secret club members, didn't respond right away when I yelled 'CHOT-HO-KO.' You should have come at him, slugging with your fists, immediately!"

"But, Albert, we didn't know what you were up to," Nono said.

"Billy did. He was watching me." Albert looked down at me. "Didn't you?"

I swallowed. "Yeah, but, Albert, you jumped him so fast I just didn't know what to do right then."

"Your fists! You should both have used your fists right away at the signal. That was our secret agreement, right?"

Nono and I nodded.

"It ever happens again, you come in slugging! Got it? And I hope we're as lucky as we were tonight."

Nono and I nodded again.

Albert sighed. He looked at us, then smiled kindly.

"Thanks. You guys did great, really great. I mean it. I'm proud of you," he said nodding. He reached out and shook our hands. "We're all lucky to be alive. Maybe I was the one who did the stupid thing by jumping...Roy, which I doubt is his real name,"

"I think he would have killed us anyway," I said.

"Yeah," Nono said. "Why would he leave three witnesses behind..."

"Witness to what?" I asked.

"He did admit to killing somebody, when..."

"Oh-yeah, he did. I remember now," I said, interrupting.

"Well, it's all over," Albert said. "Nobody would believe us now---" he looked at his naked body---"anyway. Let's just get on home. We'll regroup tomorrow and discuss the matter further. Everybody agree?"

"Amen," I said.

"No problem," Nono answered.

Albert nodded, then folded his arms across his shiny, moonlit chest. He looked up at the stars a while, appearing like a great praying Indian chief. But he *was* Indian, right? Wasn't the Spanish race a type of full-blooded Indian like the Aztecs in Mexico? Sure they were. Being Boy Scouts, we had studied and learned Indian customs, hunting and stalking skills, and even Indian apparel. In my mind, it was the secret wish of every boy that he had some trace of Indian blood in him. It was considered a great honor. To have this meant you were even more American than the early settlers. You were a brave, an Indian warrior, no different than beans and *frijoles*.

I closed my eyes a moment. When I opened them, there stood Albert, tall and erect, arms folded across his expanded chest. He wore a loin cloth, and on his head was a great feathered war bonnet, the biggest, most colorful one I had ever seen, the tail hanging down his back to the deck. I blinked my eyes and the vision vanished.

"Okay," Albert finally said, dropping his arms. "Let's get back to the promised land."

My jaws dropped. It was as though he had been reading my mind.

"We ain't there yet?" Nono beamed.

We laughed.

Albert squatted and put his hand on the engine pull cord. He stopped.

"I ever tell you guys about Moe and Joe? See, they..."

Nono threw an oily, wet rag at him while I tossed water on him from the bailing can.

We laughed and laughed.

"My friends," Albert said in mock sadness, shaking his head. "My *amigos.*" He started the engine, put it in gear, and away we went.

"Be nice to get back to my "chicken coop" house," Nono said, adding with a laugh, "I might even start liking that rat hole."

Both Albert and Nono lived within earshot of the fig plant where his dad worked during the harvest season. In between, he worked at the Kilgore Grocery Store and mowed lawns. Talk about a heavy-duty worker... And despite their complaints about the chicken coop homes, I rather liked them, Albert said they were always hot in the summer and cold in the winter. The single-boarded walls were only covered inside with tar paper and cardboard. Worn carpet and rug scraps covered the floors, but you could still feel the wind between the cracks with your bare feet.

Exposed electrical wiring ran to various wall plugs. With no air conditioning, the big flap windows were raised. It was then that one could recognize that, yes, these paint-peeling, old boarded buildings had once been chicken coop structures.

Albert (glasses). Taken in 1980 prior to our first 1960 high school class reunion. Both Albert and I had retired from the military. The chicken coop houses are no longer there.

The major inconveniences of the coop houses were that they had no bathrooms or showers. A community restroom was located behind the structures, and a shower was a walk toward the outside rear of the fig plant on the west side. Anyone for a shower, or a toilet call at 3 a.m. on a freezing day?

As we got closer to home, we felt better. We reached the County Park, where the Houston boaters launched their craft, when the little engine started sputtering, almost stopping several times "Crappola!" I snapped, jerking my head at the motor. In an instant I knew what it was. We were out of gas! My glee changed to gloom in a heartbeat. That meant only one thing.

Rowing.

Since it was my boat, and I was the expert with the oars, it was automatic that I perform the task. Nono could row like a chicken could play baseball, and, while Albert wasn't bad with the sticks, no on could push the boat like I could.

"There's still a bit left," Nono said, shaking the gas can.

"Not enough to get us fifty yards," I said, taking the oars and putting each one in a oar lock. I turned my back toward the bow and sat on the wooden seat, trying to position my rear properly for the force I knew would be exerted when I worked the oars. I spread my naked legs, bracing a foot on a rib on each side of the boat. Leverage. This was important. Most landlubbers thought a person just sat in a boat and rowed. Not so. Like everything else in life I would later learn, there was a system to everything, even the so-called simplicity of rowing a boat.

"Well, we ain't really got that far to go," Albert said encouragingly. "Round the bend ahead, under the highway and train bridges, another several turns and we're at the "creek house".

"Man," Nono said, "Sure hope no train is coming this time."

"Wattsa matter, scared of a little rumble above your head?" I asked. I laughed.

"Remember the word *courage*, guys," Albert said.

We nodded, sweat slicking my whole body as it gleamed in the moonlight.

"Hey," I said as I tested the oar-locks with a slight pull of the oars.

"Gene Autry," Nono said.

"Roy Rogers!" I replied.

"Dick West," Albert said.

"Who…oh, yeah," I said. "*The Range Rider*. Good show."

"Wild Bill Elliott," Nono responded. "Comes on Sunday afternoon after church."

"Personally," Albert said seriously, "I like *Rooty Kazooty.*"

"*Rooty Kazooty?*" Nono and I said collectively.

Albert laughed, then added even more seriously, "*Howdy Doody?*"

Nono and I exchanged confused looks.

Albert laughed, then said, looking at me, "'bout ready, Billy?"

"Yep."

"Put about a hunnered horsepower on them arms, Billy," Nono said.

"Make that a hundred-and-fifty," Albert added with a laugh.

"You got it," I said.

"We ain't at the *creek house* yet?" Nono cried.

"Keep your teeth in your nose, we'll get there," I said.

"Teeth in my…what?" Nono quizzed.

Albert laughed.

Gripping the oar handles, I looked aft, then turned and looked ahead, getting my bearings. In the bright moonlight I could see one of the huge oil tanks of the Humble Oil Tank Farm.

Clear Creek, looking north from the Galveston Country
Park toward the Humble Oil Tank Farm

I steadied the boat, then looked astern again. The moonlight between two trees became my bearing. Sweat ran in beads down my sides, chest and back. I positioned the oars equally and took several deep breaths, feet braced, eyes on my mark. I glanced at the engine, then started a steady rhythm of long, easy strokes. I tried not to feel the engine's heat between my legs at the calves...and elsewhere! The main thing right then was to get back to my wobbly pier down from the "creek house."

"You make it look so easy," Nono said a quarter of a mile later. "Why can't I do it like you?"

"Practice. Takes...practice," I said. "Pop us a Coke, huh?"

Boat on course, we eased under the Highway 3 bridge, then the creepy train trestle.

"Sure glad there ain't no train coming this time," Nono confessed.

Albert and I laughed.

I paused, oars balanced equally on my legs as I took a long pull of Coke. Boy, was I thirsty. Sweat drenched my body like I had been dipped in water.

"Whattsa matter, Nono, you lost your courage now?" I teased, then resumed my labors.

"No," Nono said rather proudly. "I'd do it again...for you guys."

I stopped rowing. No words could express my feelings right then. "I..." but that's all I could say. I felt Albert place a hand on my shoulder. The boat coasted through the water silently as our friendship bonded more closely. It would be five decades later that I would determine that those days at age fifteen would be the most memorable times of my life, with two of the best friends a teen could have.

Finally, I said, "You guys..."

Then I propelled the boat even faster as it made the turn and headed straight toward the next mark for reference—the Welsh "beach house" a quarter of a mile away.

I welcomed the even more familiar territory; we were almost home. Spotty barked at the familiar sights and smells. He knew we were near, too.

Sweat drenching my whole body, I pulled the oars even faster. Spotty jumped from the bow platform, passed under my rowing arms without making me miss a stroke, and sat on the stern seat with Nono.

"He's ready to get home to momma," Nono said, an arm draped over Spotty's shoulders.

We laughed.

Spotty was our pal, our champion camping companion, our friend, our soft, fur-coated amigo. He would always be at our sides on the creek to defend us. Had I not held him in check back with that Roy character...well, I didn't want to think about it.

Nono picked up the bailing can and poured fresh water in it from the gallon glass jug. Spotty was lapping before he could set the can on the seat. He looked up long enough to give Nono a thank you lick right across his mouth.

"Blaaah," Nono said with a stifled grin.

We laughed.

"Hey, Al," Nono said. Maybe the Collin's are still up and we can watch Television, huh?"

"Nono, you yo-yo, it's probably two a.m. Everybody's in bed this time of morning," Albert replied, shaking his head.

With no television in either chicken coop house, Albert and Nono always went to the Collins' house up near the "Iron Bridge" on Fourth Street to watch TV, especially on Saturday's when the three only TV stations aired nothing but cartoons. If they went early and everyone was still asleep, Mr. Collins would get up, let them in, turn on the TV, and go back to bed, leaving the boys alone. While they were always welcome at our house on Iowa Street, the Collins' house was closer so that was where they usually wound up at. Shorter walk!

"Hey," Nono beamed. "Friday night wrestling will have Rito Romero fighting. Gotta see that one. He's my favorite. He's gonna stomp that Danny Savage for sure this time. The announcer Paul Bosh thinks so too. I agree."

"In your dreams. Ricky Starr's my favorite" I puffed between rowing. "Still the best show is *Ed Sullivan*."

"I like *Red Skelton* and *I Love Lucy*," Albert chimed in.

"Yeah? What about *Wagon Train* and *The Hit Parade*?" I said.

"*Jackie Gleason's* got them all whupped." Nono said.

We all agreed, then fell silent. We were all tired, that was for sure.

I glanced at the Welsh "beach house" ahead. Still another six or eight minutes left before we turned left for the final stretch to my rickety pier. Mouth clamped, I continued my strenuous rhythm, feeling my chest and stomach muscles tightening and relaxing with each pull and pause of the oars. I shook the sweat from my head almost continuously. I was like a boxer warming up for the championship fight, only I didn't know how true this was at that moment!

"Spotty, you're a cute little mess," Nono said, rubbing his back.

I grinned, watching the two, wishing time would pass quicker as I thought about Spotty and several of our creek adventures.

Two summers ago, a barge was docked at the crane pier by the shell pile, restricting, as usual, the creek width. We were in my old boat, trying to make the passage to get back to the pier. Being Saturday, the creek was alive with careless boaters, giving no right of way to my small, motor-less boat. I waited near the shore for the speeders to pass, my boat rocking and pitching heavily in the waves. Braced in the boat bottom, his head showing above the gunnels, Spotty barked at the rude people. I stood carefully, looking in both directions. While I could hear loud motors, I didn't see any in either direction. I quickly sat and began rowing, fighting the rebounding waves.

Between the barge and far bank, there was no systematic flow of waves. There were white-capped waves rebounding off one another, like being in the worst rapids on the Colorado River. I fumed and muttered as I struggled awkwardly with the oars, trying to get a few good strokes to keep us going. The air was heavy with the odor of oily outboard engines and water. I grimaced, hearing a boat coming from the Clear Lake area. The Chris Craft emerged in sight. I stopped rowing to wait its passage. I frowned, seeing its bow high in the air, the muffler gurgling a low noise. Coming through the narrow passage at half speed meant bigger waves. What an idiot. Didn't he see me ahead? If the driver did, it was obvious he didn't care. Then I heard an outboard coming from the "beach house" direction, the opposite way!

Spotty barked as though warning me.

"I see em, pup. Hang on!"

But Spotty jumped up to the bow seat and continued his vocal protest at the coming boats.

The Chris Craft plowed through; its wake four feet high. The driver raised a beer can at me and laughed, glancing back, knowing full well the havoc his wake was going to cause. Clearing the passage, he throttled fully and the boat took off. The oncoming outboard turned into the turbulence and jumped the waves, its bow pounding the water. It rocketed past us before the huge waves rebounded off the side of the barge

"Jerks!" I shouted, shaking a fist.

I was almost thrown overboard as water hit us from every direction. The bow lifted out of the water. Another foamy wave flipped it almost completely around as still another one slammed the stern. Water poured into the boat.

Spotty yelped.

My head jerked his way. My heart seemed to stop as I saw him thrown in the air. He disappeared overboard.

"Spotty, Spotty!" I cried desperately.

He was not in sight. Feet wide apart, I stood up, frantically looking around. There he was, head barely above the water, front feet splashing the surface. Caught in the turbulence, he was confused.

"C'mon, boy, you can do it!" I shouted, but he didn't seem to hear my voice. I felt like crying at both the lost and the desperate expression his little face. He was looking for his master.

"Get..."

I jerked my head toward an even lower muffler bubbling sound in the distance.

I felt my jaws drop at the twenty-five foot yacht barreling toward the passage.

Oh, my God, No! I thought.

I looked at Spotty, head bobbing and still trying to get a sense of direction. I snapped my eyes back at the approaching monster. Didn't that driver high on that bridge see my dog in the water?

NO!

I dove overboard and swam like crazy.

"Here, boy! Here, boy!" I shouted spitting water. I heard the yacht but didn't see it. I reached Spotty and grabbed him. I felt his little heart pounding in his body. I was treading water, my head going under now and then. The clashing waves appeared like rolling mountains. I started toward the marsh land, where I knew my boat would probably wash up.

Suddenly, a white bow materialized. It must have been ten feet high. I gaped as the yacht slid past me, inches away. More waves bouncing off its gleaming hull. I heard the low drone of diesel engines, then the rumbling and bubbling of the twin exhaust pipes on the stern as it continued its trip down the creek.

I didn't stop swimming until I felt the muddy marsh bottom with my hand. Gasping, my knees in the mud, I hugged Spotty as he licked my face in repeated thanks.

Mind back in the present now, I was glad it was dark and my face sweat-drenched. It hid my tears as I rowed the boat, Nono staring off in the distance. Well, I didn't want to think about this incident any longer.

"How much further to the "beach house" turn?" I asked Albert, not turning his way as I kept a steady pace rowing.

"'Bout four minutes," Albert replied.

"'Kay," I answered. I looked at Spotty sitting beside Nono. Some dog, I thought. My mind drifted again, this time to our sailing days.

Sailing days?

I laughed inwardly.

While it was the dumbest looking rig on Clear Creek, it nonetheless worked. It had been the brainstorm of Mr. Albert Einstein, Teddy Kilgore. Teddy was a genius. I would have never dreamed of such a contraption. With Teddy's father building a large shrimp boat in his resident shop, Teddy had access to ample wood and *wiring*.

Teddy shrewdly used electrical wiring for the mast stays, the sail supports, the sail guide wires and to bind the sail supports to the mast so they could be turned at least 45 degrees. In order to tack up wind, he built what he called a "leeboard". We had to put in the water on one side of the boat. Because it went deep into the water, it took both of us to push it down and hold it until Teddy could nail it to the boat. Boy, I thought, if that leeboard ever popped loose and your face was in the way, there goes your teeth! For a sail, my mother gave us a chenille bedspread that was Pepto-Bismol pink with a circle of hideously colored flowers in the center. Yuck! It had several holes and tears in it, but we used it. All said and done, when it was all set up on the boat, it looked like a jury-rigged, Robinson Crusoe piece of junk. We were the laughing stock of every boat that slowed and passed us on the creek. Some people even turned around and circled us, taking photos! Imagine that. It was awful. Here I was on the stern seat, trying to hold a wad of wiring that controlled the turning of this dumb-looking sheet-sail 12 feet in the air.

Spotty barked, loving the attention this "boy-boat-dog" attracted. Often he would sit on the middle seat, looking with his cute bandit-looking face in the wind, ears blowing. No wonder everyone turned abound.

This was the picture.

"Okay, Billy, pay attention!" Albert said, snapping my mind back to the present.

Funny, rowing a boat was like mowing a yard. Once you got the routine down, you could do it automatically, by rote, and daydream all you wanted.

"Yeah?"

"You gonna turn us tonight or is it next week?" Albert and Nono laughed.

I jerked my head to see. "Whoa!" I said. We were near the bank below the Welsh "beach house." I quickly rowed in reverse, then did a opposite direction maneuver to the left.

On the home stretch, I had the beach house in view as I rowed. A gas lantern burned brightly inside the screened-in building and several people milled about. Good, I thought. They hadn't seen us. Amen.

I breathed deeply, then exhaled, thinking about that Roy guy...*Roy Convict*. Yes, that was a good name for him. Gripping the oars tighter, I wished we could do it over again. Words flashed in my mind like neon signs:

USE YOUR FISTS! SOCK HIM! HIT HIM!

YOUR FISTS!

USE YOUR FISTS!

I had never hit anyone with my fists. I didn't really know how. Was there a special technique to it? Then again, I had never been angry enough at anyone to hit them with my fists. With Roy Convict, I had been scared to death, not angry. I remembered how Albert had hit Roy when he tried to climb into the boat. I envied Albert's courage. Maybe that's what it took to hit someone with your fists: courage *and* anger. Were they related? I didn't know. I was getting confused again. Maybe I should ask Albert, but this was no time to be engaging in talk about courage, anger, fear or how, or what, it takes to use my fists.

"Hey," Nono said as we approached my shoddy little pier. "Which way we going home?"

"The road. Kansas," Albert replied.

"Whattsa matter with the tracks? It's shorter for us. Lucky Billy just has to cut across the pasture up by his house."

"Snakes," Albert said, taking the bow rope and getting ready to jump on the pier. "You know how they like to lay on the warm gravel between the railroad ties. Can't see them too well. Might step on one."

"Oh, yeah," Nono replied. "Forgot about that. I say we take the road then." He said it like it had been his idea.

"What if a car comes?" I asked.

"We jump in the big ditch til it's gone," Albert replied.

"See any lights or cars parked up by the "creek house"?". Don't sound like anybody's using the house as a target. No guns or bullets flying," I said, easing the boat in a right glide towards the pier.

Silence.

Finally, Albert said, "Nope. Nothing."

"Thank God this night's almost over," Nono said. "All we gotta do now is get home...unseen."

The boat bumped the pier. Albert jumped ashore to tie the bow line.

"Gonna leave your boat and all this stuff?" Nono asked, looking at our camping gear.

"My dad promised he'd come with me early in the morning with the trailer," I said. "We're gonna take it home and work on it. Maybe paint the hull. Nobody should bother it. It'll be okay."

Spotty jumped on the pier, his face beaming to be on familiar ground. He seemed cocky wearing his shoulder harness. I grinned. He thought he was *it*. No, he was *Mr. Aster*. I scratched my head, confused. Just *who* was this Mr. Aster my mother talked about? When she chatted with her friends on the telephone and one of them said something surprising or shocking, mom would always reply, "Well, I'll swanny!" Just what did *swanny* mean? More confusion.

Oh, well, it was great to be this close to home, even if we were...naked. We all felt relieved. I know I did. Another saying of my mother's rang in my ears: 'It's always good to get away a while, but it's always good to get back home, too.' She was right.

Stepping from the boat, I watched Spotty as he ran up the slope toward the "creek house." He darted left in the direction of the sand pile. I started to shout at him, but we were on familiar ground. He'd come running later and follow me home.

Boat tied, we crouched, easing up the slope in single file beside the wooden fence, listening for the sound of any noise coming down Kansas Street. Albert was leading.

"See anything?" I asked from the rear.

"Clear."

We were at the gate when headlights came down Kansas.

"Back..." Albert said. "No, no, we can be seen down by the boat if they get out of the car." He looked around quickly.

"Quick!" he said. "The "creek house"!"

"Oh, God!" Nono cried.

"Don't go, then. Stay here and let them see you," Albert replied. He turned and ran toward the "creek house."

We quickly followed.

"Careful," Albert said when we were inside. "Glass on the floor." He walked gingerly on his toes in the darkness. "The rear bedroom beside the kitchen. There's less trash in there. We can see out the window, too."

Moonlight streamed through the bedroom window, almost like it was daylight outside. We bundled in a squatting position looking out. I glanced around quickly, noticing the light coming in through tiny holes in the wall facing the shell drive. I realized that they were bullet holes, remembering that the house was used as target practice by careless teenagers...even some adults.

As expected, the car slowed, but turned left into Fairmont Cemetery.

"I ain't walking up Kansas Street buck naked. We'll be seen for sure!" Nono said, eyes on the distant headlights.

"'Fraid of your birthday suit, Nono?" I asked, nudging Albert with an elbow. "Albert?"

He was gone!

"Albert! Albert!" I said in a loud whisper.

"Huh, ooooh!" Nono cried.

"Don't you dare scream!" I told Nono.

"Over here, guys," Albert said in a normal tone, pulling something out of the closet. His silhouette moved around in the darkness.

"Whatta..."

"Take it, Nono," Albert said. "Put it on. At least you won't be naked."

Nono caught the object and held it in the moonlight near the window. Suddenly he laughed.

"I gotta put this dress on?" He laughed again, then his expression turned serious. "Fine. Fine. Won't be showing my butt. Anything's better than nothing. We won't be in them long anyway."

"Only thing left, Billy, is this light jacket, minus half a sleeve," Albert said. "You can put it at your waist and tie the sleeve ends together."

I caught the jacket with one hand. I looked at it and nodded with a grimace. "Just what I need!"

"Well, it's better than nothing," Nono said, pulling the oversized dress down at his waist. The bottom draped on the floor, the upper part exposed his chest, sagging almost to his waist.

"Nono's right. Beats exposing our rear ends. Better to be seen like this at a distance than up close and bare-butted," Albert said, coming into the moonlit window, a knee-length dress bulging on his frame. It had shoulder straps like a sun dress, and the chest material flopped down, making it appear even more ridiculous.

I tied the sleeves of the jacket around my waist, still exposing most of my body. I looked at Albert, then Nono, then Albert. I tried my best to hold back a belly laugh, but it came up, and I spit and howled with laughter.

"Shh..." Nono started to say, then he, too, exploded in mirth, followed by Albert.

We laughed til tears streamed our dirty faces. This was just too much. We laughed more and more.

"You..."

"I..."

"But..." we said, pointing to one another, wheezing, stomachs hurting. We leaned against the bullet-riddled wall, patted the window sill, or leaned forward, hands on our knees...anything that would ease the laugh pains knotting our middles.

Finally, I put a hand on Nono's shoulder.

"You..."

He slapped my hand away, his face trying in a useless effort to look dead serious.

"Jus...jus," he stuttered, using a high-pitched girlish-sounding voice. "Keep..." Then he got it out: "You keep your hands off of me. Just because we got a date for the prom don't mean you can touch me anywhere, Billy Sneed. I'm not that type of girl!"

Oh, brother, the mirth kicked in even harder. We beat the floor on hands and knees, kicked the walls, anything. I had never before laughed so hard in my fifteen year old life.

"Shhh!" Albert finally said, looking out the window. "Car coming. Get back down and out of sight!"

We did, but Nono and I kept snickering.

"Shhh! It's turning our way. Quiet!"

Lights played across the wall as we hunkered down closer. The sound of a car engine got closer and closer. The vehicle stopped at the gate, motor idling. The din of music came from its open windows, then the engine quit.

We glanced at one another with oh-no expressions.

The car lights went dark.

"I don't like this place, Gerald," a girl's voice said. "It's creepy."

"Ain't so, Sandra," Gerald said. "C'mon, let's get out and go down by the water."

I blew an audible sigh. "Good thing we left there when we did," I whispered. I recognized Sandra Williamson and Gerald Motley's voices. Gerald had a hot, red and white Chevy with a hard top. Lucky guy.

"Shhh!" came Albert's reply.

"I'll turn up the radio, if that'll help, Sandra," Gerald said. He opened his door, then reached over and turned the volume up full power on the radio as it blasted out the start of Johnny Otis singing *WILLIE AND THE HAND JIVE.*

Music filled and reverberated within the old house. A gunshot couldn't have been heard.

I peeked out and saw two heads disappearing down the slope toward the creek.

"Get up, Albert!" Nono said, standing.

"What?" Albert replied, then grinned.

I looked back, and, low and behold, Nono was dancing to the *Hand Jive*, kicking his legs and arms in a perfect rhythm. I couldn't believe it. It was easy to see why he was voted best dancer at school, and would be for the next five years. His talent would earn him in the future, 26 wins at dance contests in every county on the Gulf coast. I envied Nono's innate talent and was often jealous of it, too. When it came to dancing, my legs were rubber bands and my feet were cinder blocks!

I laughed and clapped my hands as Nono and Albert danced happily. Albert was pretty good, too, but that Nono...

Gee, I suddenly thought: Here we had been in the dark woods earlier, fighting a convict, coming back down the creek naked and out of gas, and now we were in women's dresses, dancing and carrying on like nothing had happened. It was...

Suddenly the music stopped.

"You ever touch me there again, Gerald, and I'll swear I'll never speak to you or go out with you again!" Sandra shouted.

We stopped and scrambled back to the window. Ever so slowly, we peered above the sill.

"You take me home this instant!" Sandra said. She slammed the door, then folded her arms across her chesty chest, mouth set in a firm frown.

"But it was an accident, honest, Becky, ah...I mean..."

Sandra turned the radio up full volume.

Out blurted the Platters singing, *THE GREAT PRETENDER*, the summer of 56's number one song. I loved it.

Gerald continued to plead and apologize as he got in and started the engine. He turned, backing carefully, toward the slope. When he knew he was safe, and turned completely, he spun out, white shell dust going everywhere.

"Perfect couple, huh?" I said, retying the loose sleeves at my bare right thigh.

"Yeah, the life of Riley," Albert said.

I looked through the door of the living room and out the broken front window. In a perfect picture as he stood gallantly on top of the mountainous sand pile, Spotty looked down on the "creek house." His bandit face beamed proudly, his white chest out. He stood against a star-studded background, the moon bright on his shiny white coat and black shoulder harness, giving him a majestic appearance.

That's my pup, I thought exaltedly. Then abruptly a nervous sensation went down my spine. I had never experienced such an odd feeling. I turned for a fleeting moment to ask Albert about it, but changed my mind. I looked back up the mountain of sand for Spotty, but he was gone.

Suddenly, horns blasted on Kansas. Lights beamed and bounced as one... two...three cars raced down towards the creek.

We all exchanged wide-eyed glances.

"There goes our chance of going down Kansas Street," Nono said.

Suddenly a gun fired.

With its short, distinct report, it sounded like a .22 rifle.

The three cars barely slowed enough to make the right turn on to the shell drive. Tires ground into shell as they slid, making a hurricane of white dust.

"YAAA-HHOOOOOO!" someone yelled, half their body out the window of the lead car. In his hands was a rifle.

"There goes our chances of cutting across Hay's pasture to avoid them, too," Nono cried.

Another gun fired. The bullet whizzed through the roof over our heads.

"Quick," Albert said. "Out the back door, over the fence, and run to the gully. It's our only chance now. From their angle on the house, they'll never see us."

"The gully?" Nono moaned. "Any place but there! The cows, and, oh-no, Joe Poluka. OHOOO---NOOOO!"

"Go!" Albert shoved us toward the kitchen.

"Madre de Dios!" Nono cried all the way to the barbed-wire fence out back while crossing his Catholic chest over and over.

Gun shots sounded rapidly as the house was riddled by the fun seekers. Glass shattered. Wood splintered.

I crouched at the fence as the shooting died down, I assumed they were reloading their guns. I held a foot on a strand of wire, and pulled up two with my hands, making a hole through the fence for Albert and Nono.

"C'mon, Nono!" I said, sweat beginning to drench my body.

As Nono zipped under the barbed-wire, the seat of his dress caught a barb in two places, but he kept going. The cloth tore out completely, exposing his butt.

Albert crawled through, then turned and held the wires for me as I dove through the opening, rolling on the ground like a paratrooper, then springing to my feet.

Suddenly the shooting resumed, laughter and foul language filtering through the dusty air.

I tensed to run when I saw Nono trip on his dress and go tumbling head over heels. Then Albert fell to his knees. His dress restricted his running stride.

"Lift up your skirts, lift up your skirts!" I said, holding the knot tied at my open thigh.

Hems held at waist level and exposing themselves, Albert and Nono rocketed across Hay's pasture toward the gully outlet a quarter of a mile away.

I followed, wanting to help if either fell again. Our summer-tough bare feet held up well on the cattle-chewed stubby weeds and grass as the gorge drew closer. Like the dresses, my jacket flew open, but I didn't care. We had to get away from the flying bullets, out of sight in the ravine.

The plan was to follow the gulch, safe in its confines, all the way to the fence that paralleled with Kansas Street. There we would crawl through our opening in the gully, and cross what we called the "big ditch," and then climb up to Kansas.

Presto. Home free after that. Simple plan.

I saw Albert veer right, entering the gully at ankle level. Nono and I followed. With the uneven ground, we slowed as the sides eventually became jagged walls, and the gunshots only a din in the background. We stumbled and jumped v-grooves in the ground that had been caused by erosion, We leaped over holes, water pits, and "mud bogs." Hay's pasture soon disappeared above our heads.

"Albert!" Nono huffed. "Let's stop and rest!"

Another minute passed before Albert slowed, then stopped.

I was glad for the rest too. We needed this pause.

Black hair down over his ears, Albert looked around, judging and gauging, face dripping with sweat. He nodded and sat on a small dirt island, breathing heavily.

With its rutted v-grooves in the gully bottom going every direction, and the holes, water pits, dirt islands of every shape and size, and the "mud bogs", running in the gully was like skittering on a writhing sea that had been petrified. In the dark, speed and distance were cut even further. It was like trying to run in a dream or underwater.

Breathing laboriously, we were silent for several minutes.

"Boy," I said finally. "I could sure use a gallon of water right now."

Heads nodded, moonlight gleaming on faces.

Having expended a lot of energy over the past hours, I was suddenly hungry.

"And I could sure go a big bowl of Mom's fresh-shelled purple-hull peas. That and a big piece of hot-buttered cornbread with a sliced tomato. Man, that's good groceries." I rubbed my wet stomach. I looked at Albert, trying to act serious. "And I'd complete the meal by eating one of them there *Butterfingers* you still owe me."

"Yeah-yeah," Albert said, pretending bored irritation. He wiped the sweat off his forehead with a crooked index finger and flicked it to one side.

"Where's Joe Poluka? He must be near," Nono said, not hearing a word we said. "I smell something awful, and my dress is split in back," he added, pulling the excess cloth to cover his rear.

"We got that wrestling booth at the town fair weekend after next," Albert said.

"Yeah, I know," I said, looking around, then up to pasture level at the gully's edge. It was clear. No cows looking down at us, especially that awful Joe Poluka, King of the Brahama bulls.

Talking helped settle our nerves, and to ease our fear, whether we wanted to admit it or not.

"Gonna have to show me how to do that "flying mare" bit again and not get hurt," Albert said.

"Sure," I replied.

Being avid wrestling fans, my brother and I had practiced all the holds and movements we had watched on Friday night wrestling in Houston with Paul Bosh, hosting. We could really look like we were killing one another. Our scoutmaster, Mr. E. D. Blanchard, rightly agreed, and hit on the idea that every member could participate in earning our troop some money at the town fair. To a lesser degree, wrestling with Charles, my brother, had helped the development of my muscles. But he could still beat me and body-slam me all over the place if he wanted to.

Several years later, Bobby Dean Martin and I put on a wrestling performance in the school gym during a pep rally. We really had the crowd in a laughing roar. With the fake blood made with food coloring, some of the girls were really horrified when we first used it, thinking it was real blood. Some were even on the verge of getting sick. Coach Dub Kelly was the referee, half of him visible in the photo; me on my back.

"Where's Joe Poluka? He's here some place. I just know it," Nono whined.

"Boy, today just ain't went well at all," I mused.

"Well," Albert said. "Some days are just destined to go bad, that's all."

"Confucius, or Mr. Goforth?" I asked. Mr. Art Goforth was our hard-nosed disciplinarian English teacher at Clear Creek High School.

"Neither," Albert replied. "Albert Perez."

We laughed, except Nono, who kept glancing up at pasture level.

"No, really," Albert said seriously. "There's a time for everything. Living, dying, giving birth, war, peace...even killing."

"Killing? Hey-man, don't confuse me any more that I already am, huh?" I said.

"Okay, let's get going." Albert started walking, holding his dress above his knees with one hand.

We followed, Nono holding his dress together with a hand behind his back, the other at crotch level, wadding the material so his feet showed. It was easy going, no running or dodging convicts or bullets. But we still had a ways to go, even to our gully hideout. By gosh, I thought, I'm gonna get my harpoon this time and take it home. I was dumb to have left pressed in that cliff crack in the first place.

"Yeah," Albert teased. "I know how them Brahama bulls are. Mean and completely unpredictable. They'll fool you sometimes..." He stifled a grin looking at us.

I whispered to Nono, "Don't pay him no mind. He's just trying to shake you up. Be cool. Be cool.

Nono nodded, face still skeptical.

"...saw one of the clowns at a rodeo once walk right up to a Brahama and thump him right on the nose. Bull did absolutely nothing til the clown turned his back on him," Albert said, stifling a grin as he glanced at Nono. "That's when the bull---"

"Don't hear no shootin' no more," I said interrupting. "Guess they killed the house and left." I laughed, but no one joined in.

In silence, we walked in the clearing where the pasture sloped upward at a 45 degree angle on either side. This was one of the two areas where Hay's cows, including Joe Poluka, crossed the gully. There was a single dirt trail up both slopes. The main crossing was up by the fence next to Kansas Street. It was here that we often taunted Joe Poluka, throwing dirt clods at him, making him snort, slobber flying, his chest bleeding as he pressed his flab against the five strands of barbed-wire fencing. He loved us.

Without looking in either direction, Albert crossed the trail and continued walking as the slope soon turned back to eight and ten foot high jagged walls again.

At the trail's edge, Nono and I stopped and looked both ways.

Nothing.

We hurried across and caught up with Albert, walking around what we called a "mud bog," which was nothing but a muddy hole, most of the water evaporated, leaving a thick paste of mud. It was dried and cracked around the upper edges. The cows rarely ventured into the interior of the gully, and we assumed that this was one of the reasons. To get stuck in a "mud bog" surely meant a slow and miserable death.

"Hear that?" I asked.

"What? I don't hear nothing," Nono said.

"That's it, then. The shootin's stopped. Everybody went home."

Nono grimaced, like "big deal."

It was late. Morning, actually. But there were always some teenagers still out prowling, looking, just passing the night away. Other than the "Rose" picture show, there wasn't anything to do in League City, except perhaps hang out at the Dairy Dream. But even these were closed for the night, including the Showboat Theatre and Falco's Drive-in Dickinson, the next town south, three miles away.

"Feel that?" Nono asked, stopping, pulling my arm back.

"Don't you mean, 'hear'?"

"No, the ground. I felt it move!"

Albert stopped beside an overhang in the ten foot wall. "Nono," he said. "You know cows go to the barn at night. Joe Poluka ain't no different. Now you quit imagining things."

We walked to his side and stopped. Each of us stood stock still and listened, then looked around and up and down.

Nothing.

"Okay, satisfied?"

"No," Nono said. "I want to look up in the pasture just to be sure."

"We ain't exactly got a ladder here," Albert said. I could tell he was getting tired.

I pulled Nono back from a "mud bog" behind him, just forward of the precipice above.

"So whatta we do here," Albert said, pointing to the wall, "carve you out some steps?"

"No."

"Then what?"

"You let me get on your shoulders, so I can see up in the pasture all around."

"What?" Albert's shoulders slumped. One of the dress straps fell down his arm.

"C'mon, Albert," I said. "Let em do it. Look," I confessed, "it'd make me feel better, too."

"We're completely safe down here. Ten foot walls on both sides. How's Joe Poluka gonna get down here if he's up there, which he ain't? Cows never come down here cause they can't run on the uneven ground, and they're afraid of the "mud bogs." Now, if Joe Poluka is up there, how's he gonna get down here? Jump?"

"Well," I said with a grin, "a cow jumped over the moon once, right?"

"Not funny." Then Albert looked at me and grinned, then laughed, the undersized dress on him looking even sillier. "Good pun, Billy," he said. "Didn't think you had it in you. You're improving."

"What?" I mumbled, scratching my head. *Just what did he mean by that, or was it a compliment?*

"Lean over and let Nono step on your back," Albert said. He turned and faced the side of the overhang. He leaned forward a bit, raising his arms. He braced his hands against the cliff for added support. "Okay, hop up when ready, Nono," he said.

I leaned forward, bracing my palms on my knees, and bent my legs, dropping so Nono could get on my back easier. Closer to the ground, I saw the deep ruts better. Albert was right as usual. It would be difficult for a large, four-legged animal to run in the gully. The poor thing would probably break a leg racing to find an outlet.

I winced, feeling Nono's toes dig into my back.

"Okay," Albert said. "Heave up. Grab a root or something and pull yourself up."

I felt Nono's weight come off my back. Standing straight again, I folded my arms across my sweaty chest and turned to view this feet-on-shoulder process.

Nono gingerly balanced himself, his left hand grabbing at anything on the cliff. He let loose of his dress wad in his right hand. The cloth fell, covering Albert's head and shoulders.

"Haaay!" Albert protested.

"Can't help it," Nono said. "It'll only be for a minute. Hold on."

"Better be less than that!"

I laughed as Nono started raising his body toward the top of the cliff. Opps, wait. I needed a better view of this. I turned and jumped over a big "V" rut large enough to lay down inside.

Cool.

I turned back to the master feat being conducted right before my eyes. I grinned. Well...

Suddenly my smile ceased. I felt my blood run cold and my scalp jump at the same instant as Nono went nose to nose with Joe Poluka!

Nono froze. "Ma...ma...ma...," was all that would come out of his mouth.

Joe Poluka snorted.

"Oh, no, you farted!" Albert cried from under the dress.

Nono tried to make the sign of the cross, but his eyes rolled up inside his head. He fainted, his body slumping down the wall like a dead snake.

"What is going on?" Albert demanded, falling away from the cliff as he struggled under Nono's weight. He fought to get the dress out of his face as they hit the ground.

Joe Poluka glared down at us with vehement eyes as black as thunder. He snorted.

I picked up a dirt clod and threw it at him, hitting his shoulder. He let out a war-like bellow and reared up.

"Oh, no. Stupid me!" I said. I had really made him angry now.

Joe Poluka's front feet came back down on the ground with a thud.

What happened next was so fast I couldn't believe my eyes.   The cliff edge cracked and gave way. Three tons of dirt fell into the gully, along with two-thousand-two-hundred pounds of pure hate in live hide. Joe Poluka went head over heels, landing in a "mud bog" on his feet! Water and mud exploded everywhere from under his mammoth belly.

Too galvanized with both fear and horror, I couldn't move or speak.

"What the..." Albert fell inside a v-groove, rolling Nono to one side. His head popped out from under Nono's dress.

"Al...Al, Al...Albert," I said slowly and softly. "We're...in really...big trouble now!"

"Oh, my God!" Albert replied, seeing the behemoth bull.

Joe Poluka grunted loudly, swinging his head, his feet squishy-squashy in the mud as he fought to get out of the "mud bog."

"Nono! Nono! Wake up!" Albert said, eyes never off the bull. He found Nono's face under the wad of cloth. He shook his chin.

"Huuuhhh," Nono moaned, slowly opening his eyes.

I eased over to help my friends to their feet.

Joe Poluka tromped and kicked, muddy water flying. He bellowed loudly, bestial black eyes baleful.

"*Madre de Dios*!" Nono said, eyes wide on the Brahama. He crossed himself, slowly getting to his feet.

"Pull your dresses up and let's make tracks!" I said softly, holding the knotted sleeve at my open thigh. "He'll be outta there 'fore long." I looked at Albert, then Nono.

"Ready?" I asked.

"Go!" Albert said.

We shot up the gorge like bullets.

The *blitzkrieg* had started!

We jumped and dodged "mud bogs", holes, craters, islands of all heights and sizes, and v-grooves, large and small. It was like running in jello.

We heard the din of Joe Poluka as he wailed.

Nono screamed.

We knew there was no keeping him stranded in a "mug bog." With his noxious and caustic nature, he was bound to escape.

Legs aching, we pushed even harder as the gully finally started veering to the right.

Good, I thought. Kansas Street wasn't too far away.

"Aaahh!"

Running side by side, Albert and I glanced at one another. We looked back to see Nono tumbling in a v-groove, feet in the air.

In an instant, we stopped, whirled and darted back to help him.

"Okay?" I asked, holding Nono's arm.

"Uh...huh," he gasped.

"Ready?"

Nono nodded.

"Go!" Albert commanded.

We all took off at the same instant.

More crooks, turns, inlands, bogs, holes, and those forever gapping v-grooves in the rock-hard earth. Another turn or two and we would be at our hideout. That meant only a quarter of a mile to go to Kansas Street.

"Ze...Ze...Ze behind us yet?" Nono managed.

"No...not...yet...", I huffed

"But he will be. Bet that!" Albert added.

At a waist-high embankment that was a waterfall when the gully filled during rains, we stopped.

I paused a moment, then jumped up, bracing my hand on the ground. Albert followed. Tensed to blast off again, we saw Nono slip and fall backwards. He screamed.

I jumped back down.

"Gimme your hand!" Albert told Nono, poised to grab.

Nono reached up and gripped Albert's hand.

With my shoulder, I pushed Nono above the fall. I looked back. It was all quiet back there.

Whew! That was a really...whoa! Was that the ground shaking?

My eyes jerked to my friends above and their out-stretched hands. I grabbed them and they wrenched me upward.

"Okay?" Nono asked.

I nodded.

"Go!" Albert commanded.

In unison, side by side, we scampered at full force again. Boy, this was going easier than I had thought. Our hideout was just ah---

The rope caught us at the necks. There wasn't even time to yell. It was so sudden. The ploy was just like in the cowboy movies: rope taut between two trees. When the posse thundered through on the way to the pass, they were knocked off their horses.

Suddenly looking up at the stars, I blinked several times, trying to figure why we'd left a dumb rope across the gully. Nothing came to mind.

Someone was laughing. No, it was more than one person.

"Look at the little girls!" a voice said snidely.

More laughter.

"Think they been doing anything, ah...you know...like messin' around?" the tone teased.

More mirth.

I got to my elbows, focusing my eyes on the tall frame standing at my feet. Oh, God...

It was the one person who might just be meaner than Joe Poluka—Johnny Lowe!

"Whattsa matter, twerp? We can't visit your little boy hideout?" Johnny said with mock interest. "Nice place. Nice place. I have to admit," he added, smiling wryly.

I grimaced and started to get to my feet, when Johnny's buddies walked up and stood by his side, grinning sarcastically. I almost gasped out loud at the sight of my eight-foot harpoon in one of the idiot's hands. They must have really searched our camp carefully. Almost invisible, the harpoon had been stuffed inside one of the many wall cracks.

"What're y'all doing here?" I asked, getting to my feet. Albert and Nono followed. Nono rubbed his neck and rolled his head from side to side.

"Whattcha mean? This here your property, man?" Johnny said, pulling something from his back pocket.

"Look," Albert said, laughing lightly, "we really have to be going." He glanced at me and Nono. "Don't we, guys?"

We nodded quickly.

"You ain't going nowhere! That's a bunch of bull!"

"Man, have you got that right," I said.

"What's this, some kind of game with you...girls?" Johnny flicked out a hand. Something clicked, then an eight-inch switchblade knife gleamed in the moonlight.

"Look, Johnny," I said, stepping forward. "We...I mean, *we all* got a big problem. Back..."

"No, no, no, no. *You* got that wrong, ah, Miss...Nancy, yeah, Miss Nancy," he laughed ruefully. "Yeah," he added, running the blade tip lightly across my sweaty bare chest.

"*The skirt with all the useless muscles.*" He laughed again, looking at his stooges, who appeared surprised at his overt movement with the knife.

"Funny, huh, guys? Funny!"

The flunkies nodded, then picked up the hint and started laughing. The one with the harpoon still looked ignorant, wearing the same pair of 3-D glasses as before. I doubted that he even knew what it was he was holding, much less how to use it.

While Johnny paced back and forth in front of us, trying to think of some other smart garbage to tell us, I looked the camp over briefly.

The rope.

It was still stretched across the gully. A few beer bottles lay on the ground. One was sitting on top of the waist-high island behind the three thugs, who—in turn—faced each of us like this was a one-on-one deal. Naturally, I was Johnny's target.

God, if Joe Poluka comes charging in the same as we had, he'll enter on the side of the island where we're standing. Why couldn't Johnny and his cohorts be on the other side of the island?

I looked over at the nice steps Albert had sculpted in the wall, but Lowe's gang had harpooned them beyond recognition. My blood began to boil. Jerks!

"Hey, girl muscles," Johnny said, flashing the knife under my nose. "You said something earlier this evening that I didn't like, when I told you to come back, but you and your, ah...amigos took off in that there yacht you were in. Boy, next time I tell you..."

Joe Poluka bellowed, the noise echoing in the big gully.

"Whatta' hebbie-jebbies was that awful noise?" Johnny snapped, looking both ways.

Exchanging concerned glances with Albert and Nono, I noticed the stooges swallow noticeably. The ground started shaking. Something had to be done. Now!

"CHOT-HO-KO!" Albert said loudly.

"Hunnh?" the thugs said collectively.

"CHOT-HO-KO!" Nono said.

"CHOT-HO-KO!" I said quickly.

Without hesitation, the three of us swung our elbows back and...

SMACK!

Right across the chins of three totally stunned faces. Johnny and his gang tumbled backwards over the island behind them, the beer bottle rolling with them.

"Go!" Albert commanded, pulling up his dress.

We turned and started running.

"Wait!" I yelled ten steps later.

"What?" Albert said in confusion.

I had already turned and was almost back at the island when Joe Poluka busted in on the side where we had stood only moments before. He stumbled, then slammed into the wall, the rope tangled in his horns.

I grabbed my harpoon, only feet from his two-thousand-two-hundred pound body. My heart almost exploded out of my chest. "Yipes!" I moaned, jumping over the island where three surprised and suddenly frightened faces looked at me.

"The rope's tangled in his horns!" I said quickly. "The other end's gonna break loose soon. Follow me!" I glanced at each one to make sure they had heard. "Run like the dickins and don't stop!"

All three nodded.

"Go!" I said and took off, the heavy harpoon in my right arm. I wasn't about to lose it again.

"Whattsa matter with you?" Albert asked as I matched their stride like an Olympic relay runner.

Huffing, I held the harpoon above my head.

Joe Poluka howled.

Nono screamed.

We strained every muscle harder, jumping ruts, holes, bogs and pits. Johnny's gang was right on our tail.

"Whoaaa!" Nono cried. He flipped and tumbled into another v-groove.

Albert and I stopped and darted back.

"Leave 'em be!" Johnny said, as he ran past us. "Save yourselves!"

"Darn you, Nono," I said. "You're gonna have to hold your dress up."

"I ain't no girl," Nono cried. "I keep forgetting."

"Ready now?" Albert asked.

Nono nodded, breathing heavily.

"Go!"

We all took off again with Nono holding his wadded up skirt around his middle. Joe Poluka was furious in the background, kicking, bucking and snorting.

Two minutes later we were near the barbed-wire fence where our hole was located.

"Al...almost there!" Nono blurted.

Yes, we could see it. The moon was bright, so resplendent now it almost seemed like daylight.

"Awwwhhh!"

We saw Johnny fall, his leg twisting awkwardly.

"I...I...I got him," I huffed. "Keep going." I stopped.

"Hel...help me!" Johnny cried, grabbing his leg.

"No, no," I said as my amigos stopped, too. "Keep going. Ain't far. Get to the fence!" I dropped the harpoon and squatted by Johnny. I looked up. There were Albert and Nono again.

"Go!" I said rather bitterly.

"Sure?" Albert asked.

"No problem," I said, helping Johnny to his feet. "Git!"

Albert nodded to Nono and they took off.

Joe Poluka bellowed.

The sound was different. It was different because he was loose and somewhere else in the gully, I reasoned. Headin' this way for sure!

"C'mon, Johnny!" I said, looping my arm under his arm and coming back over his shoulder.

"Tryin'," Johnny moaned, holding his right leg up.

"Not far. We can make it, you hear? All you gotta do is hop on one foot, and I'll hold you. Just hurry!"

"No problem...Billy." There were tears in Johnny's eyes. He added, trying to be cool again, "Hey, thanks...thanks, man."

I smiled. The stupid coat came untied and fell to the ground, but now was no time for modesty.

"Nice coat, Billy, but don't worry, I'll get you another one," Johnny giggled, his cool, daddy-oh wavy hair hanging in strands over his face.

"Just hush up or I'll leave you here!" I said, sweat dripping from my chin.

"Yessir, Billy." Johnny laughed lightly, patting my sweaty shoulder.

Johnny hopped quickly, leaning on me as we headed toward the fence.

I looked back at my harpoon on the ground, then down the gorge. Joe Poluka was not in sight, but we could hear him.

Out stretched hands at the fence helped me get Johnny through our hole safely. I looked back in the gully, judging, thinking.

"No, Billy," Albert said. "It ain't worth it."

How did Albert know what I was thinking? I grimaced, then turned and ran back.

"No, Billy!" Albert shouted.

"Guy's crazy!" one of the stooges said.

"Looney tunes!" the other added.

"Shuddup you two. Any more lip and you're gonna eat another knuckle sandwich!" Nono said, a fist raised.

The instant I grabbed my harpoon, Joe Poluka materalized. He was closer than I had thought. I looked back at the fence, then back at Joe Poluka's muddy body. He was closer than the fence. I'd never make it. Joe Poluka stopped, looked at me, and he, too, knew I couldn't make it.

"Billy!" Albert screamed.

Joe Poluka shook his head, slobber and sweat flying, and slowly rumbled toward me.

I dropped the harpoon. It'd only slow me when I had the chance to turn and run. *Chance?*

Joe Poluka threw his head back and bellowed as though taunting me. Years of carefully aimed dirt clods flashed in his eyes.

I turned to run and tripped. I fell to the ground on my face, but quickly rolled over. I tried scooting backwards on my elbows, pushing with my heels.

Shouting and hollering came from the fence, but nothing scared the bull. His flashing eyes were locked on me, his head down. It was too late for me to do anything but pray. I tried, but nothing came out. I had always believed in Jesus Christ, but rarely prayed. It was hard.

"God, help me," I finally pleaded, crying.

Suddenly there was barking to my right. Spotty appeared running in a dead heat toward Joe Poluka. The bull gave no notice to the dog. His hostile eyes only saw me.

"Get 'em, Spotty! C'mon, Billy!" someone said.

Just as I started to get up, Spotty dove into Joe Poluka's face. The bull stopped and slung Spotty to one side, but he rolled unhurt and got up.

"No, Spotty. Back!" I said, worried now over Spotty's safety as much as my own.

"Billy, get over here!" Albert shouted.

On my feet, I eased back as I saw Spotty charge again, barking furiously. He bit at Joe Poluka's face, then the feet, dodging Joe Poluka's swooping horns.

"C'mon, Billy!"

I picked up a dirt clod and threw it, hitting the bull's neck, hoping to distract him. Again, this only goaded his anger. Stupid me.

Joe Poluka raised his head and snorted, strings of thick saliva hanging from both sides of his mouth.

I was almost to the fence when the bull came toward me in a trot, head down.

Suddenly Spotty tore into the bull's face, his teeth gashing the thick hide. The Brahama bull howled, stopping. His head swooped down and picked up Spotty. He slung Spotty upward, throwing him against the gully wall. Spotty yelped and slid down the embankment and got up again. He looked around, trying to regain his senses. He held up a front paw. As he started to walk, he limped, whimpering. He looked my way as though making sure I was safe on the other side of the fence. I wasn't. He head jerked back toward the bull and he charged again, growling furiously and limping.

Joe Poluka's head swooped downward, then up. The horn stabbed Spotty just behind the shoulder. He never let out a cry. Then a horn caught on Spotty's harness. He was slung up high and shaken like a rag doll.

Mouth open, I stood mesmerized.

"No! No!" I finally cried.

My pet's body came whirling through the air and landed between me and the Brahama bull.

A chorus of voices screaming, crying, yelling followed me as I moved toward Spotty...and the enraged bull.

"Billy...come back!"

"No, Billy, No!"

"Don't be stupid!"

All life and hope seemed to drain out of my being, right onto the ground as I looked at Spotty's lifeless form.

Joe Poluka stood stock still, arrogant, head up, huge flabby chest out.

I walked slowly toward Spotty, looking down. I melted to my knees, my throat so tight I could hardly breath. I put a sweaty hand on Spotty's soft white coat. *He..he was...was, still alive. He wouldn't die. Couldn't die. Not my Spotty, not my little Booger dog. Impossible. No! This wasn't happening. It was just a dream. He'd get up in a moment. C'mon, baby, move for me, huh? You ain't dead!*

Suddenly a fury, a hatred so strong inside of me, it felt like molten lava mushroomed upward. The world moved in slow motion as I turned and looked blankly at the stunned faces by the fence, then at the taunting Joe Poluka.

As I got to me feet, I started to breathe in short, ragged breaths, my lips trembling. Sweat poured from my naked body.

"You!" I spit.

Face white with rage, neck corded, I walked toward the two-ton bull.

"You!" Uncontrolled saliva ran down my lips and off my chin.

The bull whipped his head back and forth as though he was mocking me.

Knuckles white in a fists, I walked up to Joe Poluka's face.

Eyes obsidian-hard, he glared back with all his raw power.

"You!" I said, lips tremulous.

Face resolute, I yanked my right arm back. With every ounce of strength in my rowing arm, I socked the bull right in the soft part of his nose. I felt gristle, then teeth.

Joe Poluka roared like never before. He slung his head in the air, flinging snot and blood everywhere.

"C'mon!" I said, fist ready again.

The bull's head descended, horns outward. The snout came between my legs. I grabbed the horns with both hands. Joe Poluka scooped me up as I straddled his nose and face. I locked my legs together under the massive jaws and gripped the horns tighter. He whipped his head in the air, snorting. The odor alone made me feel giddy and faint.

Joe Poluka twisted and shook his head vigorously, but I held on. I was hoping I would exhaust him, make him keel over from total exertion. He was already bone-weary from having run the uneven gully floor. Maybe, if I could just...

Suddenly the bull put his nose to the ground. I thought I had won. I started to release my grip when he abruptly threw up his head with such force that I was thrown off into the air, head over heels. I didn't know where the ground was so it was impossible to try to land on my feet. I closed my eyes, bracing for the impact and broken bones to follow.

In an instant, I landed unhurt on solid ground. Wait. What happened?

I raised up on my stomach and looked around. I was ten feet above the gully! No wonder there wasn't a long downward fall. I was up at pasture level!

I peered over the edge of the gully.

There stood Albert and Nono, shouting and throwing clots at Joe Poluka's back. They were standing on my side of the pasture, trying to lure the bull away from me. Joe Poluka paid them no mind. He was looking around for me!

"Up here, jerk!" I shouted, shaking a fist as I got to my feet.

"Billy, no!" Albert said.

"*Madre de Dios,*" Nono said, crossing himself.

Johnny Lowe and his gang watched in mute horror, bodies paralyzed with fear.

In an instant, Joe Poluka turned and ran up the slope to pasture level.

I shook my head, still a bit stunned. Then I saw the bull stop and turn only yards from me. I looked over my shoulder down into the gully. I could jump, yes, but I'd probably break a leg. I looked back at the bull. He was nodding as if to say, *Yes, this is it, Mr. Billy Sneed. Prepare to die!*

"C'mon!" I said, fists ready.

The bull didn't charge. Instead, he walked up to me strangely, like he was teasing before the kill. He snorted, blood oozing from a nostril.

Looking at the ugly face, my anger and grief intensified. Teeth bared, I started shaking uncontrollably. I pulled back my foot and kicked at the face. The bull jerked its head aside just in time. I backed to the cliff's edge, hands frozen claw-like.

The bull followed. He swung his head just as I grabbed his horns. My feet slipped off the edge. The sudden weight on the Brahama's head again made his feet shift uncontrollably. He took two steps forward to balance my weight. I guess he didn't realize how close to the gorge we were. Maybe, at this point, he didn't care. His feet slipped over the edge of the cliff. With my weight, the tonnage slowly started to slide over the brink. I hung on, dangling briefly in space.

"Me and you both, huh?" I said in his ear. I drew my head back and spit in his face.

It appeared as though I gave Joe Poluka a "flying mare" as we tumbled past the edge, the bull going over my shoulder so easily that it was actually a miracle. I was thrown to one side near a v-groove on the gully floor. Joe Poluka was pitched to a large ground split in the center, famous for what we called a v-groove. He grunted and groaned. He rolled on to his side, then kicked furiously, trying to stand.

"Aaahh!" I moaned, feeling the pain of scratches and cuts on my back. I winced getting to my feet. Face contorted, I looked around slowly.

Joe Poluka was between the fence and me. I was against a gully wall. To run to the fence would be suicide. I couldn't climb either wall, and to run back down the gully...who was really faster, boy or beast?

I looked around for something to throw, a rock, a...then I spotted it three feet in front of me.

The harpoon.

Lips quivering uncontrollably, my face set, I eased into a crouch and slipped slowly toward the heavy weapon. Joe Poluka watched me, pawing the ground, slobbery blood drooling from his nose.

Albert and Nono circled from behind, one on either side of the gully. They picked up anything heavy, rocks or sun-hardened clots of clay. The Brahama never even looked at them. His insane rage was directed at one thing.

Me!

I slowly picked up the harpoon. With my right hand over the rear of the spear, my left hand under it in front, I poised the javelin at the bull.

"C'mon!"

"Billy, no, no!" Albert pleaded.

"C'mon!" I brandished the harpoon.

Albert and Nono threw their ammo at Joe Poluka. All of it bounced off harmlessly, but it further angered the bull.

I stayed close to the cracked wall, shifting slowly to my right, the 8 foot harpoon sticking up at a 40 degree angle. I dropped it to 30, then 20.

Joe Poluka charged, head down, horns ready.

Muscles taut, the blood veins bulged like spider webs on my arms. Sweat dripped from my chin, fingers and elbows. I licked my parched lips, tasting the salt, eyes locked on the giant behemoth. I moved slowly to the right.

"Aaaahhh!" I groaned, losing my balance in a rut. I fell down and the harpoon flew from my hands.

I quickly got to my feet just as Joe Poluka lunged at me. I pressed my body inside a wall groove the same instant horns buried themselves in the dirt on both sides of my chest! The bull's head pressed against my middle like a vice. With all my might, I brought my knee up, smashing his damaged nose.

Joe Poluka wailed in agony. He jerked his head back and bucked and kicked with insane rage. Then he swayed in stupefaction. He stepped in a hole and tripped. He fell over on his back inside a V-groove, legs up in the air like a turtle on its back.

I grabbed the harpoon and turned, ready to charge him, but stopped. Joe Poluka bellowed repeatedly. He was stuck helplessly , but, no doubt, he'd be free in no time. There was no way I could stab Joe Poluka deep enough to stop him. The harpoon had to penetrate his thick hide and go deep enough to kill him, hopefully hitting a vital organ.

But how?

My strength was ebbing fast. I had to think quick and move fast. I looked up the gully wall, then back down at the bull. It was a straight shot from the cliff top to the bull below. It couldn't miss...if I didn't mess it up! Gripping the harpoon, I ran up the cow trail above the gully. I turned and dashed to the cliff edge, and looked down. Joe Poluka was still kicking frantically, but had gone nowhere. He'd be free, though. Soon!

Toes on the gully edge, I held the harpoon out over the gully edge as far as I dared, Joe Poluka directly below. I gulped in several lungfuls of air. Face resolute, I leaped out and quickly straddled the javelin like climbing a flag pole.

WHHOOOSSH!

Down I flew riding the heavy steel rod.

I felt the harpoon as it penetrated the underside of the bull's tough hide. I gritted my teeth as a fountain of blood shot upward. On impact, I was slammed against Joe Poluka's heaving belly. I rolled on the ground for several yards, winding up inside a V-groove, looking up at the stars.

"Billy, where are you? You okay?" Albert's voice floated on the air from somewhere.

Here, I thought, thinking that I had said it aloud. The dying wails of Joe Poluka echoed off the gully walls.

I remained still as though I was lying inside a coffin. Tears welled in my eyes, then ran down the sides of my blood-splattered face. *It's over. It was over...but Spotty...oh, Spotty.* My face contorted just as Joe Poluka looked down at me!

"Ooaahh!" I wheezed, eyes wide. I cringed. How had he gotten to his feet?

Wait. Did he really see me? His eyes were glazed like he was in another world. The harpoon stuck out six foot from his underside. Had it not been that he was straddling the v-groove, it would have dragged on the ground. The movement would have caused more damage to Joe Poluka.

Joe Poluka staggered, then slowly walked my way. He lowed in pain, his head down.

Hands pressed at my sides like I was flat in a coffin, I froze as he stopped at my feet.

The bull looked down, his eyes became abruptly alert. He raised his head and snorted, blood, stringy saliva and white foam from his mouth and nose went everywhere.

"Go away and die!" I yelled.

Joe Poluka advanced directly above me, dragging the harpoon end between my legs. I felt his body heat, then the hot blood flowing from the gaping wound as it splattered on my bare chest.

Suddenly the bull reared up on his back legs, yanking the lance upward. He howled like I had never heard before. I closed my eyes, then opened them.

There stood Joe Poluka on his hind legs right above me, getting ready to come down! I couldn't move, jump or go anywhere. I gritted my teeth as the two-ton body descended, the spear end pointed directly at my chest.

"Aaaahhh!" I yelled.

Two-thousand-two-hundred pounds of Brahama bull slammed down on the v-groove, covering my body. The harpoon plowed into the ground inches from my stomach and stopped. As the bull fell, the harpoon stabbed through his body with a god-awful grinding sound. I was certain the point came out his back.

In shock and fear, I jerked my head up hitting Joe Poluka's chest. Then the huge head plopped down inside the groove, the nose expelling the last awful breath as dust flew. The body stench, sweat and last breath almost made me vomit.

"Billy! Billy!" someone yelled frantically.

But it was dark and I was out of sight, hidden from view down inside this ground erosion groove with 2,200 pounds of Brahama bull on top of me! And what was that...hot and liquid and sticky?

Blood!

It was flowing like a river from Joe Poluka's body all over me, filling the v-groove!

"Billy! Billy!"

God, I had to do something before I drowned. Blood was everywhere, pooling on both sides of my naked body. I raised my head to keep it out of my ears.

"Billy! Billy!" Albert said, lifting the bull's head by the horns.

"You okay?" Albert cried. "Say something, amigo. Please?"

"Please help me get out of here!" I screamed.

"Ooohh, praise the Lord! You're okay," Albert said. Then, more concerned, he added, "You are okay, right? No broken bones?"

"Don't think so. Hold the head up and I'll try to scoot out. It's a little muddy and messy under here."

"Nono..."

"Got it," Nono said quickly.

"Okay, Billy!" Albert commanded. "Go!"

I dug my heels into the bloody mud. I pushed and wiggled and squirmed. Soon my hands were free and I pulled myself up in the moonlight, my amigos helping.

Madre de Dios!" Nono cried, looking at my blood-soaked naked body.

Blood dripped off my chin, elbows...everywhere. It was God-awful smelly and sticky, too. I lifted Nono's skirt and wiped my eyes out.

"Man alive!" Albert said, looking at me then the dead bull. "Unbelievable!"

I nodded slightly, trying to catch my breath.

"You..." Albert started to say.

I held my hand up for silence as I saw Spotty's little body not too far away. Grief overcame me again as I felt a void in my middle, a total emptiness I couldn't describe. My throat got tight as I slowly stood, eyes locked on my loving pet. How was I ever going to explain this to Mom, Charles...and Dad?

"Billy, Billy," Nono said softly. "Don't..."

"Nono!" Albert said sternly, motioning for silence with a hand.

I glanced at my friends, and saw pity and compassion in their faces. I turned in the bright moonlight, my whole body gleaming red, and walked slowly toward Spotty. I barely noticed Johnny and his gang on the other side of the fence, their faces petrified, mouths open.

I dropped to my knees beside Spotty and went limp with grief, gazing woefully at the little lifeless form. My lips trembled as tears streaked my blood-splotched face. I held a hand above his shoulder. Blood dripped from my finger tips on to his pretty white coat.

"Oh, God," I said, looking up at the bright sky, my voice soft and quavering. "Why, why, why, why?"

Years of memories flooded my mind.

Spotty and me on the creek in my boat, his bandit face in the wind, ears blowing.

Spotty sitting on the bow platform, eyes alert, ready to bark at speeding boaters.

Spotty at my side on the creek bank as I fish, waiting curiously for the cork to sink.

Spotty in his chair at home, his brown eyes appreciative and kind.

Spotty running in Hay's pasture barking after a rabbit he'd never catch.

Spotty licking my face happily with me laughing and trying to hold him back.

Spotty and me jumping off the crane pier at the creek into the water; holding his tail and laughing while he swims, pulling me to shore.

Spotty licking his chops at a campfire, waiting for the can of pork n' beans I hold over the fire in a forked branch; me laughing as I ruffle his head.

Spotty and me side by side sitting on the mountainous sand pile, my arm over his shoulder as we wait for the morning sun to rise.

Spotty's face in the wind as he sits below the mast of that awful-looking sail boat of me and Teddy Kilgore's.

That was the picture!

I looked at Spotty's body. Even lifeless, he was so pretty. I stroked his coat several times, then, ever so gently, I scooped him up in my arms. His head went limp over my left elbow.

"Spotty," I cried, trying to will him back to life with every ounce of power I could summon.

Nothing happened.

I started to rock him gently, bringing his head to my face. I wept and hugged him and kissed his face and snout.

Well, I had loved him in life. Surely, I could hug him in death.

* * * *

EPILOGUE

We never told anyone or talked about that awful night again. No newspaper or town gossip ever surfaced about the killing of Mr. Hay's prize bull. The harpoon disappeared. Alone, my dad went and picked up the boat the next day. It was months before I ventured to the creek again. When I did, it all seemed so different. Once everything seemed so big. Now it appeared small.

What happened to me?

Maybe it was because I sold my boat. I was a landlubber like everyone else now. Even if I still had the boat nothing seemed the same. The thrill, the excitement, the fun of being on the creek vanished. It was just…gone.

Johnny Lowe lent me his '57 Chevy when I had my first date. Good with his gully words about the ragged coat I had worn and dropped, he bought me a new one. "With sleeves this time!" he said, laughing. Like my brother, Charles, Johnny was there to defend me when others picked on me. Visions of a lifetime friendship ended when both he and Charles were killed in a car accident. Strange now, it was so long ago, yet the memory is still so vivid.

There were many lessons learned that awful night. It would take years to realize what all of them were. I know I trusted law enforcement officers, like Billy Crook and Sergeant Gilmore, more. They were all there to help the public, not to shoot them. And Mr. Weaver, the man they handcuffed and took away, he was nice in his own way and meant no harm to me. I should have sold him my boat, then we would have never gotten involved with Roy Convict, where that night went downhill from there.

Courage. The meaning surfaced again in the murky inland waters of Vietnam in '66 and '67. Agent orange, prostate cancer and having to wear a catheter until I die now. Then there was one of my good buddies who was seriously wounded. He, ah…well, never mind. 'Nuff said here, please.

Albert went on to get a college degree while serving a career in the Air Force. He retired as a major and is a CPA, owns several motels and stays forever busy on his ten-acre property in Lockhart, Texas. He's quite an enterprising individual, and a very generous person. As always, he's still the leader of our pack.

Nono, partly retired, continues ranching and working with animals. While color blindness kept him out of the military, he signed up for the next best thing: the Peace Corps. He served in the Philippines and later attained a college degree and worked with the mayor of Houston before shifting to ranching. He lives one block from the ever expanding University of Houston.

Like Albert, I am also totally retired, having served a twenty year Navy career, retiring in 1980 and a "chief". I also served in the Navy's *Military Sealift Command* during *Desert Shield* and *Desert Storm*. I retired from Texas State Technical College where I was a police officer, having attended night school for nine months to get my state license. I was fifty-seven years old at the time. Like Albert said on that night back on the creek when I made a sly remark about a cow once jumping over the moon, I was improving, huh? Although retired, I am active in the Harrison County Sheriff's Office where I am captain of the sheriff's Reserve Division.

Yes, me, Albert and Nono get together now and then. We laugh, act up like kids, drink a few suds and reminisce about the days of old, then we fight over who is going to pay the tab, and most of the time Albert wins, or pays whether we like it or not.

It wasn't until fifty-two years later, when I returned to the shell pile and creek house area, that Albert's words rang in my ears from that night so long ago as we passed the county park where the old train trestle had stood. Even this was gone.

"All this," Albert said with the sweep of a hand, *"will change twenty, thirty, forty years from now. You won't even recognize it."*

At the very end of Kansas Street, turn right where the old shell road used to be. This turn to the right no longer exists as it is blocked off.

Albert had been right.

I was just too stupid not to have seen his future vision.

Now, looking at the area where the mountainous sand pile used to be, I abruptly recalled my vision of Spotty that night when I had looked through a window of the "creek house."

In the moonlight, he stood dauntless, head up, eyes and ears alert. Now I understood it had been God's way of allowing me one last view of my pet before the gully engagement with Joe Poluka

End of Kansas Street, looking toward Fairview Cemetery in the year 2000

While I could never return to the old days on Clear Creek, I can never forget it either, nor League City, Texas; the "iron bridge" at the corner of Kansas and Fourth Streets, where we used to sit on the top rail and tell how we were going to rule the world when we grew up; the Dow house across the street, where we used to labor all day to mow the huge lawn for $3 dollars , and was paid 25 cents an hour to rake the leaves . And why do I remember that there are 7 big oak trees from the driveway side on Kansas Street to the 4th Street corner? Odd. (I heard a rumor that a movie had been made on this property) ; and roller skating at the city park, and riding our souped-up bicycles around the cement area, braking our tires to hear the sound and to see who could make the longest skid mark on the surface.

League City Park near the old train depot. Oak trees lined all sides of the park.

This was also where I had lost that $5 bet with Albert and his dog, Red, when he swallowed Albert's $5 bill.

Mr. Art Goforth (deceased now) and Nono in the year 2000 standing
on the shell road (it no longer exist) by Kansas Street. Mr. Goforth
became keenly interested in this area after reading Naked Run To
Morning, and wanted to see the land where it all happened. Being
our high school English teacher, I was honored that he praised my
novella, especially since I had been a low grade student of his!

And the old, cream-colored train depot that was trying to appear a
yellowish color, and across the main street by the railroad tracks was T.A.
Kilgore grocery store and lumber yard. And the Rose Theatre, the Tea Garden
Cafe with its good smells across the small alley from the filling station on
Highway 3; I even remember the garbage odor in that little alley. And Smith's
Pharmacy, the Dairy Dream, across the street from Snell's Grocery. I grinned,
remembering the old, squeaky wooden floor and the smells inside Snell's
store. The Buckhorn Inn on Highway 3. Ah, yes, the memories.

With full intention of videoing my old stomping grounds for my
grandchildren, I gazed at the sand pile and creek area with sadness weighing
my heart. There was nothing but weeds and shrubs.

Where the sand and shell piles were once located. Nothing now!

Absolutely nothing of the sand or shell piles was recognizable. No road, no gate, no creek house, not even a shore hint of where I once had a wobbly pier where I tied my boat. Even the creek proper had vanished with time.

What was once land across the creek was now all under water. The Houston boaters had won after all. Of the four steel pillars in the water for old Highway 3, only two remained standing. I doubted if anyone knew what they once were. This same area, after Charles Kilgore and I started emailing years later, would be dubbed humorously by him as "Billy Sneed's Playground." I thought that neat and noble of him.

Why should I video? Only I knew what it looked like here back then.

Standing with the car door partly opened, I smiled wistfully, wishing for something, a time in my life that could never be returned to or repeated. I nodded slowly, looking at the unrecognizable surroundings. Yes, I thought, it was time I read that book Albert had boasted so much about, the one about not being able to go home again...Thomas Wolf? Ah...yeah, that's it . *Look homeward, Angel.*

Well, maybe Albert was right when he had said I was improving. I was learning quickly now.

Fifty-two years later? ?!**#!%#@*

Say, I thought, scratching my head. Didn't he still owe me...something? What was it? Oh, yeah, that's right. Wait until our next gathering. Yeah, I would tell him:

"A *Butterfinger* candy bar…with interest!"

The End

Author, Bill Sneed in summer of 1959, San Diego, Calif.
Hey, who you calling "Boot camp?"

SNIPS

It started out right but ended wrong. Good thing I was on liberty the whole weekend. By Saturday evening, my skull was fried with beer. Oh well, what the hell, I was just a young sailor of 23, lonely in a big city like Boston.

Beantown was actually the homeport of my ship--*U.S.S. Compton DD 705*--so I knew parts of the city, especially over in Cambridge. My shipmate Johnny and his wife, Carolyn, lived in Cambridge, within walking distance from the subway station on Massachusetts Avenue, a busy four-lane street.

I felt the warm glow of two boilermakers I had slugged fifteen minutes ago. It was George Washington's birthday weekend, and I was going to get stewed, whether he liked it or not.

The *Hillbilly Ranch* where I was anchored was a favorite bar of Navy men whose ships were in the Charlestown Naval Shipyard. It was also a watering hole for Marines. They still pulled guard duty on the Navy's gates and at other military establishments. There were quite a few servicemen in uniform, but this wasn't unusual for the year 1964.

The bar was getting crowded and the usual din of voices filled the air with the clanging of glasses and beer bottles. I heard a few wisecracks, the usual banter between sailors and marines.

"Yeah," a marine said, "if it weren't for the Navy, shit wouldn't float!"

"No, no," a sailor shot back. "The best sight of a Marine is when you flush it down the toilet!"

A roar of laughter.

I smiled a little, then tilted the beer glass to my lips. Guzzling the yellow liquid, I tried to summon my usual humor, the camaraderie I had grown so used to in the military. Somehow it just wouldn't come.

Loneliness was all I felt. Maybe depressed is a better word. But what was the difference, huh? Rotten is rotten, no matter which way you look at it. I sighed heavily and looked over the crowd, trying to find Lillie, the cutie pie waitress that I really liked. Ah, yess, there she was, picking up her tray of orders at the center of the bar. What a doll. Cute, not pretty, just dolly cute. There's a difference, you know. Even at 23 I recognized this. Pretty smart, huh?

But, see, Lillie didn't give me no notice. She was 27 years old. Divorced. Three kids. Yes, we had talked several times. Told her my life's history in two minutes. Being 27, well, she was over my mark. Ancient. It wasn't me; it was her. We only talked 'cause she felt sorry for me, like I was her little brother or something. All I ever do when I look at her is drool. Too bad she doesn't even know this.

USN Bill Sneed (right) with Navy buddy in
summer of 1959 at Green Coves Spring, Florida

Another hard pull on my beer, and I was ready to flee to my refuge, my sanctuary, Johnny and Carolyn's in Cambridge. It was some place to go that was decent ashore, more akin to home. I knew their phone number by heart. No problem ever to call Johnny and Carolyn. Could dial the number with my teeth!

I turned slightly on the swivel-type bar stool to check my uniform, which was wrapped in brown paper sack-like package and tied with twine. Grinning, I thought it resembled a hobo's bundle. All it needed was to be tied on the end of a shoulder stick. Red Skelton would love it! Freddie the Free Loader.

Lillie managed to glance my way, and our smiles locked in midair a fleeting moment, and then she dissolved into the human maze to deliver her goods. I grimaced.

Why was life so cruel?

Here I was single, 23, not bad looking and with a respectable professional job as a Navy engineer. Why didn't I have a steady girl, hell, a shack-up even? Didn't Lillie know I loved her? Sure she did. Just because she was 4 years older, did that make that big a difference? To her it did. Maybe it was her kids. I gave them no thought. End of that career, huh?

I belched, not giving a crap who heard, then ordered another shot of whiskey.

"Smooth sailing, Victor," the bartender said, pouring the coffee-colored kicker into a shot glass beside what beer I had left. Benny, I thought, focusing my eyes. Yeah, I was a frequent customer he knew.

"Thaaa--nks," I managed to reply. Man, I was really getting slicked. But, damn, did it feel rather good. An escape of sorts. A relief. A break from the shipboard routine.

An American sailor. I loved it. I was part of our Nation, a type of history I suppose. Red-blooded American. Me. It was hard to believe, since I was a nobody in high school just five years ago. And aboard my previous ship-- *U.S.S. Robert H. McCard DD 822*--we had recovered objects shot up in space above the earth. Stupid little monkeys in puffed-upped suits that came back to earth in things they called capsules with parachutes ballooned out on three sides. We were out there in the Atlantic Ocean retrieving these silly things. Useless, huh? Goofy. What would they ever prove? But I was proud to be a part of this breakthrough or whatever it was. Me, Victor Turner, United States Navy, out there with history.

Yeah.

I threw my head back, shot-glass welded to my lips and swallowed. It burned all the way down. I blew my breath out and then quickly guzzled my beer, praying for relief. What a pisser, those Boston boilermakers!

I slid off the bar stool and staggered. Whoa! Time to go to Cambridge to Johnny and Carolyn's. I buttoned up my dark trench coat. It was February and freezing outside. The tall buildings offered no relief from the winds that snaked and whipped between them. Although it wasn't snowing out, there were still plenty of icy streets and snow banked everywhere.

"Happy birthday, George," I mumbled, walking to the coat rack where my Red Skelton bundle waited. Can't leave without that.

My uniform. My life.

At the door I pulled up the collar of my coat. Blowing out 99.9 percent flammable breath, I plunged out into the frigid air. It slapped me in the face like a 2x6. Damn. I braced a hand against the building to help hold it up. Although I had a head full of brown hair, I wished I had my Dick Tracy hat for warmth, but it had blown off my skull earlier when I surfaced from a subway station. It was ripped off my head by a gust of wind and went flying, rolling and flipping and then finally flew and landed on Commonwealth Avenue. The $22 lid died instantly as it was pancaked by the usual rushing traffic.

Still holding up the building, I took several deep breaths, looking to the right at the Trailways bus station across the street. Cooking food, hamburgers, onions, eggs, soup and grilled sandwiches wafted though the air for a moment, making me suddenly hungry. No, I'd wait till I got to Cambridge. I knew there was one of them little hamburger joints there, *White Tower*, they were called. Cheap, too. The little I wasted my money on food the better! I had a better idea for using my dough.

At a liquor store I bought a pint of Russian roulette: vodka. 100 proof. The best.

On Commonwealth, I went underground as I unscrewed the cap on the bottle in its brown sack inside my trench coat pocket. Cool. The subway platform was almost empty, so I took a good pull from the flat bottle.

Ooooh, man! I thought. It was like drinking molten lava. I hit my chest several times with my fist, wishing it was a 20 pound sledge hammer. I wheezed lightly, trying not to draw attention to myself. Finally breathing short breaths through my mouth, I settled down.

A subway rumbled past, slowing to a screeching stop. The doors opened. I staggered aboard. I could have sworn it was still moving. As the train started in motion again, I found a seat on the half-empty car. I plopped down, my Freeloader bundle on my lap, my right hand holding the bottle against my chest. My collar was still pulled up. I knew they were watching at times with their surreptitious glances. On impulse, I almost reached up to pull the brim of my Dick Tracy hat down, then remembered I didn't have it anymore. It was a nice hat. I loved that hat. Made me feel more grown up. Although it was 1964, a lot of men still wore them, so they were still in fashion.

Glancing around, I slowly unscrewed the cap off the bottle of vodka, wondering how I could slip a slug without being noticed. Actually, I was at the point where I didn't give a rat's bean who saw me, but, hey man, I was cool, you know, 23 years old and all.

Pretending to notice something on my bundle, I scratched at it, then raised it to head level, vodka hand going up, too. I pulled a mouthful, hating its burn. I swallowed hard, putting the bottle and package back to my lap.

I made a terrible face at the after burn, noticing an elderly lady looking at me scornfully. I mustered my best innocent smile, swaying with the train's motion. As the subway clacked and screeched, I read her lips.

"Disgusting!"

At my stop, I emerged from the ground like a bad flower, Massachusetts Avenue in sight. The cold air shocked my skull, reviving me a bit. Snow banks were evident all over Cambridge, too. Traffic was light on the four-lane avenue.

Supper time for the beaners, I thought, smiling. Wished I had a home to go to. Well, Maybe Johnny and Carolyn would let me spend the night on their couch. It'd happened before. I needed some place to stay tonight, didn't I?

Standing on the curb of "Mass Avenue," I was tempted to dash across, not wanting to wait for the light to turn green. These Boston drivers were nuts. They'd run over you. Anyway, some cop might be watching. In my condition of stupor, being stopped by a policeman wasn't exactly on my schedule. *Jail* wasn't even in my vocabulary. Unheard of. That was for criminals, not this American Bluejacket.

Clutching my bundled uniform, vodka bottle back in my trench coat pocket, I walked across the four lanes when the light changed. I wobbled and swayed a bit, but tried to act cool. Now, where was that *White Tower* joint? I thought, looking around. Ah-yes, there, a few buildings down.

Entering the rather crowded eatery, a gust of frigid air blew up my coattail. I quickly shut the door. I stood at the counter end, bent somewhat from the waist up, my head lolling a little. I was like a tree ready to topple. All that was needed was the right breath my way and a...

TIMMMMM-BBBER!"

And either my temper or body or both would go into an uncontrollable flare or total relaxation, depending on the circumstances. In essence, my vast knowledge at age 23 knew that one should not make a drunk person angry.

Standing, swaying like I was on a subway, I looked at the rear before ordering, hoping for a vacant spot.

"Say, young man," a voice said nearby.

"Me?" I replied, pointing to my chest.

"You want a drink?" the man asked. "Got it right here." He laughed drunkenly, his words slurred. He held out a bottle of whiskey.

They didn't serve alcohol in *White Tower* eateries I knew, just burgers and soft drinks. "Sodas," the New Englanders always said. Just like they called a milk shake a "frappe". Well, maybe this guy was handicapped, too, I thought humorously. Cambridge was New England territory, right? Well, this Paul Revere wasn't going to out-do this *North American Bluejacket*. I whipped out my bottle of vodka, smiling like I had just discovered America.

"Got my own, thank you, kind sir," I said happily.

Ben E. King's melody *Stand By Me* flowed from the eatery's speakers.

"Try this. It's better," the man said.

"I doubt it," I laughed, taking the bottle. I passed him my vodka, which he took.

We toasted bottles, several customers looking askance as the bottles clinked, almost breaking.

We both slapped the jugs to our lips and slugged. What the hell, it was alcohol, right? In the John Wayne shit kickers aboard ship, didn't they always pour booze over bullet wounds before they extracted the lead? Anyway, people weren't scared of germs and disease spreading like a wildfire in 1964. This was the "modern era".

"Stupid jerks!" I heard from behind. I spun around. A tall man hurried down the aisle. Bigger than myself, he wore a black jacket. That's all I could see. My blood boiled, but I held it in check.

"Great stuff," the man said. "Whatcha got in the bag?"

"My uniform," I said. I wiped whiskey off my chin with my elbow. "Navy. I'm stationed over in South Boston."

The man's face brightened. "Aw-yes. X-Army, myself." He raised my bottle again. "To our great *Armed Forces*."

"You bet."

Our bottles banged again. Another wad of hot lava down the tube. Man, liquid suicide!

Suddenly, I was pushed from behind, the bottle top slamming my front teeth. Whiskey spilled from my mouth.

"Faggots!" the same sour voice as before said.

I spun. The tall man's eyes locked with mine.

TIMMMM-BEERRR!

I dropped the whiskey bottle and threw my bundle to the floor. Tall man recognized my fury. He whipped open the door and flew out into the cold air.

I was on his heels in a hot second. He was quick, yes, but I stayed with him, almost within grabbing distance. We ran past stores and shops. I almost had him once. He slipped between parked cars, sliding on the iced pavement, but quickly regaining balance.

People stopped to stare. Others jumped out of our way. Several cars stopped. Horns honked.

"Up yours!" the drivers yelled, eyes glued on the sidewalk action.

Tall Man side-stepped; I followed. No way this turd was going to get away. Even if he ran up the side of a ten-story building, I was gonna be on his rear, ready at the right instant to jump on him.

Suddenly a "Stop" sign on a freestanding pedestal was pulled over in my path by Tall Man. No problem. I jumped it as easily as an Olympic hurdler. Boy, I was going to push this guy's nose to the back of his skull..if...damn, almost had him. I strained, stretched, pushing myself to every limit.

"C'mon!" I yelled.

Finally, unknown to me, I made a perfect tackle on the brute right in the middle of Massachusetts Avenue!

Horns blasted. Tires squealed. A car skidded sideways toward the curb. More horns. More rubber on iced, then dry pavement. We got the whole world involved, but I didn't care. I had the jerk. Struggling, I managed to get on top of him, straddling him at the waist. I yanked him by the hair and jerked his face so that I could see...he could see...my fist as I pounded his skull. I raised my right hand to start granting me my wish, then...

Four-hundred cops descended on me. Where they came from, I don't know. Where is a cop when you don't need one?

Next thing I knew I was in the back of a padded van with a few other odd-looking characters. Hey-man, what's going on? This ain't happening to me. Impossible. No way! Hey, let me outta here!

Like a floating, unconnected bad dream, I was hustled into a building somewhere in front of a tall counter. I was ordered to empty my pockets, remove my belt, and my shoe laces. I couldn't figure out why. Did somebody there need my shoe strings? My bottle of vodka was put on the counter. I told them my name, that I was Navy and showed my ID.

"You want us to call the Shore Patrol?" I was asked.

I staggered, looking at the officer honestly. He knew I was no criminal. He...he looked at me sadly, almost embarrassed. We understood one another, but, really, I didn't understand myself as fuzzy and foggy and unconnected as my thoughts were. God, I'd never before been this so...so...damn drunk! Beer. Vodka. Whiskey.

Death was almost imminent. I'd have welcomed it if it happened.

"You got one call," the officer said.

"Huh? What? Call?" I said.

"Phone call. You want to make one?"

In ignorance, I stood, trying to study the police officer. "Ye...yeah...yessir," I finally said. "Phone, okay...sir. Yes. One, please." I almost cried.

I was lead to a pay phone and handed a dime. Standing back, I tried my best to focus on the blurry, moving object, then held it still with both hands. There. Gottcha!

Johnny and Carolyn.

Yes, their number. Easy. Piece of cake. I could dial it with my teeth, 'member? I stood back getting a better look at the little holes I had to put my finger in to dial. Gee, when did they start making them so small? Okay, okay,

okay, no problem. Gimme time, huh? I rubbed my...my chi...nec...hea...I sighed heavily.

The assisting officer shook his head sadly.

"Wait!" I said. I dialed 6...2...3...No, that wasn't it. 5...3...6...9...Damn! 2...okay, good...

The officer took the phone from my hand and hung it up. "Sorry, son, that's it. Come with me."

"Hey, hey, sir. This ain't happening, sir," I slurred. "I'm military. U. S. Government. 'Member the doggies and monkeys in space? We were out there getting them in the Atlantic. C'mon, sir, help me. I know Johnny and...Lillie's number. Gimme another shot, huh?"

"Who's Johnny, and who's Lillie?" the officer asked.

"My best friends. Oh, it's not Lillie. It's, ah, ah...Ca...Carolyn. Yeah. That's who."

"Maybe so, but no one can help you right now. You're too far gone. Let's go sleep it off>

My next memory was a 35 degree, single jail cell. Steel bed. Lidless toilet. No pillow. No blanket. Bare walls. A coldness that would scare even the devil himself. I wanted to run. But how? Impossible. God, this was a horrible dream. Had to be. I was floating, drifting. I shivered. I hugged myself, the cold, the freezing....ooohhh. Why was I here? I'll be dead before morning! Don't they have heat in this joint? My teeth chattered. I'll be frozen be... I spotted my heavy trench coat on the floor just outside the bars of my cell. Whoo...who...was the kind soul that had tossed it over the rail within reach between the bars of my cell? Someone who knew I was just a kid, caught up in adult circumstances, even though I was a tough 23 years old. Man of the world, right? Somebody understood in the *Cambridge Police Department* the human nature of common persons, the workers, the people of America who made it go. Especially, *servicemen*, be them Army, Navy, Marine, or Coast Guard. *God bless all "real" Americans who care about and support the military.*

Boiler Technician Third Class Bill Sneed. 1961 photo
taken overseas. No information available on photo.

Teeth chattering, I reached out between the bars and pulled in my trench coat. On the steel bed, I covered myself, including my head, squeezing into the smallest fetal position I could. Now, if I could go to sleep. Wonder... That's all I remember. I was out.

The next thing I knew was being awakened with a nightstick banging against the bars. Oh, my head! My mouth was as dry as Death Valley in July. I felt like throwing up. I looked around, almost gagging at the piss-sweat odor. Now I remembered. Oh, God. It was 6:30 a.m.

"What's for breakfast, guard?" a prisoner down the way said loudly.

Laughter from the cells.

Very funny, I thought sourly, my stomach feeling like battery acid.

"Everybody out of your cell and walk to the booking desk!" a voice said loudly. The cinder block walls made sound echo like in a canyon.

My head. Oooohhh, geee...

My cell door was swung open, banging heavily on the bars.

I cringed, covering my ears. A toothpick dropping a bucket of water was too much noise right now! I stood, swaying slightly, as I put on my coat. My whole body ached like I had walked the entire Atlantic from London to New York...underwater!

At the booking desk our personal items were returned. Damn, there was my Freeloader bundle. My uniform. Who...how? The guy at the *White Tower* must have brought it out. Thank goodness. I wish I could find him. Then I looked around trying to figure out which of the ten scrody-looking men standing with me was the guy I tackled in the middle of Mass Avenue. I still didn't know what he looked like, and he didn't make it known. I wonder if he remembered me.

We were transported to another building and put in a foul-smelling holding tank to wait our turn with the judge. A guard opened the door. He brought in a galvanized bucket with a dipper handle sticking up. Before he could place it in the center of the floor, a shabby-bearded bum rushed up and picked up the dipper, full of water. It dripped off his whiskers. He coughed and spit up a lugie at the floor drain. I gagged, but held it back. He then took another drink, then dropped the ladle back into the bucket.

I swallowed hard, almost losing it. While I was dying for a drink of water, no way in the hell of June would I drink from that bucket, even if it had been left alone, untouched. I sat on a long bench, as far away from the other creeps as possible. Two curled up on the dingy cement floor and went to sleep. One talked to himself, even answered his own questions.

Hugging my Red Skelton bundle, stomach churning, head pounding, I waited, staring at my concealed uniform. What a relief I wasn't wearing it. It would have embarrassed me terribly.

But now what did I have to face?

A fine, which I didn't have money for? Maybe more jail time? Maybe both? Oh, no, I'd be AWOL Monday. My Navy career would be shot. I'd be the laughing stock of the ship! Why didn't that jerk just keep his mouth shut last night? Everything would be just fine now. I'd be at Johnny and Carolyn's, probably still asleep on their old couch.

The steel door rattled, then swung open.

"Mister Victor Turner, please," a voice said.

My heart raced. This was it. I stood, clutching my worldly belongings. Walking to the door, I stepped over a snoring form on the floor.

I was led down a hall to a desk and told to be seated in a wooden chair beside the desk.

The officer in plainclothes, a detective, I guess, but surely a policeman, then sat at the desk. He was maybe 40, I suppose. Straight-faced, no smile, but he did appear to look at me in a concerned sort of way, like, I, you know, was out of place.

I heard my heart pounding in my skull like a jackhammer. I could hear it,

I swear. The officer proceeded to ask a host of physical questions, then where I was from, parents' names, etc, etc. Life history stuff. He wrote it all down on a card. I was waiting for him to say the dreaded words: *The judge will deal with you now!*

It was cold, but my palms were wet enough to soak a sheet. I needed a cigarette. A dozen of em! And 400 aspirins. And something to calm my stomach before I stared to barf soon.

"Explain last night, son. What happened," the officer asked, leaning back in his chair.

"Yessir," I replied, and proceeded to tell him about where I started. The boilermakers, the vodka, the whiskey...and the beer. The words made the bile come to my throat, but I held it back...again. That's all I needed was to blow lunch on a policeman's desk now! The officer knew this kid was hurting. Bad!

The officer sighed, picked up my card and looked like he studied it, glancing at me now and then.

I swallowed. Oh, no, death row. I just knew it. I promised myself if I ever got out of this place alive I'd never again drink boilermakers or vodka or whiskey or *any* hard liquor for that matter. Beer only, and it would be fifty years before I touched one them again. A person has to know his limitations. I had just learned mine.

"Okay," the officer said as he placed the card on the desk and tossed his pen down. "You can go now, but I don't want to ever see you in here again. Clear, kid?"

I sat silently, dumbfounded for a second or two. What? No electric chair or gas chamber? Not even a hanging? What about a fine? Parole? Finally, I spoke.

"You, you mean I can just leave, get up and walk out of here, sir?"

"That's what I said, kid." The man lit a cigarette and blew smoke toward the ceiling. He looked at me and said, "If you ain't outta here in one minute..."

I grabbed my bundle, stood and looked for the exit, a door, any outside opening. Before I made my first step, I said, "Thank you, sir. Ah, nice meeting you." I started to extend my hand for a shake, but quickly withdrew it. This was no happiness meeting!

The officer nodded, not smiling. "Stay out of trouble, huh, kid?"

"You bet, sir. No problem. You won't ever see me in here again, I promise you." I turned and headed in the direction he pointed.

Outside in the cold, I looked around quickly for privacy, then lurched toward the alley. I dropped to my knees and vomited. Did I ever! Even the thought of whiskey made me retch more. Vodka? More up-chucking. My eyes watered. I heaved again, swearing that up came a hot dog that I had eaten back in the 2nd grade. Next must have been baby formula, circa 1942. I swore again against hard liquor , but God, please let me live, or if you're gonna kill me, do it now...this instant!

Finally, breathing deeply six or eight times, my senses came to snorkel level. I stood there for several minutes, hoping I was through selling them Buicks and looking for York. Easing upright, I let the building go and stood independently a few minutes. I took several deep breaths. Yes, that was better. Maybe I was going to live after all.

Maybe.

Back on the sidewalk, I pulled my coat collar up, shifting my bundle from arm to arm so I could get it tight and close. Brother, was it cold! The sky was dark-gray. Probably snow again.

A car passed slowly, its driver window down. See, I told you these New Englanders were nuts. From the open window, the car radio played loudly The Four Seasons, *Walk Like A Man*.

Head still throbbing, I walked carefully along the snow-banked sidewalk.

Kid.

Didn't that officer keep calling me a kid? Twenty-three years old ain't exactly at boy level, right? What'd he think I was, still a growing little boy?

Hummph! Little boy! Well, snips and snails...and...

The End

Author Bill Sneed in boot camp, summer of 1959

RED, RIGHT, RETURNING

Small waves washed the lonely pier along its sideboards, threatening it into oblivion with the incoming tide. A swift wind stirred up whirlpools of white sand, then howled up the cliffs of the island. Specks of light moved among the rocks like a preying serpent as voices floated on the nocturnal summer air:

"Ain't here!"

"Here, either!"

"That dog with him?"

"Ever see the kid without that mutt?"

"Knock off the chin music, you jerks. Just keepah looking! Boss wants him back by morning. Check the usual places. He's gotta still be on the island somewhere."

From his supine position in a small row boat snugged underneath the pier by the incoming tide, sixteen year old Bobby Langley heard the muffled tones as they filtered through the narrow spaces between the boards.

"They're not gonna get us this time, Woody!" Bobby Langley whispered to the beagle he felt at his right side. "If only it wasn't so dark," he added. "This tide's just gotta stop soon or this boat just might push the old pier up! And if it doesn't, water will spill over into the boat and we'll drown, Woody!" He pulled the dog closer to his side.

"We can't let this happen, Woody. We just gotta make it back to Tugg Harbor this time. We just gotta!"

Rivulets of perspiration tickled as it ran down his bare sides. Bobby pressed his elbows against his skin temporarily stopping the sweat. "No, sir," he whispered. "Eight miles ain't that far to row to Tugg Harbor! Why with what Dad taught me before he…died, well, I could navigate clean to Galveston if I had to. You remember Pelican Island, Woody? Nah, you were just a baby then. Four years ago is a long time."

Bobby felt himself relaxing. He turned his head, listening. It was past midnight, he knew. The wind should ease up soon. And the tide should start running out.

Or would it?

Sometimes in planning this escape, he had watched the pier go under water at high tide several times, but not often. He hoped tonight wouldn't be one of those times. And the wind, he thought. Was a hurricane brewing somewhere in the Gulf? And why hadn't he grabbed a flashlight when he sneaked out of the house? Peering through a tiny space in the pier planking, he could see a star or two, but that was all.

Yuck! he thought. That awful odor. Those barnacles he knew to be only a foot away, clinging to pier piling with their razor-sharp edges. But at least he was well out of sight. He could put up with the foul odor a while longer. Anything was worth the price to get back to Tugg Harbor.

"Galveston," he said reflectively. "We'll make it there, too, soon as I'm old enough to buy a shrimper like Dad's. The Molly Jay was a good boat. Best darn shrimper in Tugg Harbor. Gosh, it'd be great to see her again." His voice became bitter. "If only mom hadn't sold her, and married that creep, Mr. Salager. He never liked us. He---

"Check that pier, Louie, a voice said loudly.

Bobby felt his blood run cold.

"But da ain't nothin' but water down there," another voice blared.

Author Bill Sneed, age 15. Used in novella "Naked Run To Morning"
and as fiction character in short story "Red, Right, Returning

"I said check it! Go out there and look!"

Bobby swallowed, hearing footsteps on the pier. "Shsssh," he breathed to the dog. He felt the animal tense, then growl lightly. "Shsssh! Not this time, boy."

"He must think I'm stupid," a voice said softly, getting closer. "Kid ain't down here!"

Light from a gas lantern begin to flicker between small slits of the pier boards. Bobby tensed, holding his breath. He heard the hissing of the gas lantern three feet above his head.

"Well, well," the voice said, surprised. "Would you looky here?"

Bobby felt tears welling in his eyes at the thought of being discovered, but, still, he didn't move.

"Hey, Ralph!" the man shouted.

"Yeah? Got something?" a rough-sounding voice replied.

"Whatta ya make of this?" The man above kicked over a can of some sort. Tiny chunks fell between the small cracks, hitting Bobby in the face.

Shrimp! Bobby thought. Rotten shrimp! But that wasn't as bad as the slimy liquid that followed. He felt his stomach churn. His jaws ballooned, but he forced it back.

"Fishin' stuff," the man growled. "Think he's been here?" he said loudly.

"You nit-wit!" the voice from shore said. "'Course, but he ain't now, is he? He was there with Tobar early yesterday, fishing. "Come on back. We still got the other side of the island to check yet."

"Oh, oh-yeah," the man said softly. He started back down the pier, the gas lantern hissing like a snake.

Everything went black again. Bobby turned his head. He gagged lightly.

The footfalls on the pier stopped.

"Humm," the voice groaned. Several moments passed, then the footsteps continued.

Bobby breathed a sigh of relief. Then the loud voices continued:

"Tole ya he wouldn't be there."

"Well, you know how Mr. Salager is. Blows his top at the slightest thing. Better to say we checked just the same."

"What about his goofy son? Wouldn't he know where the Langley boy'd be at?"

"Tobar?" The other voice laughed. "Wouldn't tell even if he knew."

"Bet Mr. Salager could git it outta em!"

"Don't be so sure. Just because Tobar looks and acts crazy don't mean he ain't got some of his senses!"

"I just can't unnerstan why the Boss beats up on the Langley kid all the time. So he knows the operation. Big deal. He can't go nowhere!"

"Jealous."

"Huh?"

"Ah, never mind. You wouldn't know about those matters."

"Ya think I'm stupid, too, jus like Tobar, huh?"

"Look, we ain't got time to argue. Let's get looking again. Hell's gonna break loose if we don't get the kid. You go up that ridge. We'll take the beach and meet you and your men on the other side of the island."

"Okay, but I don't want chew to be abossin' me!"

"Just get going. I'll tend to you later!"

Bobby wiped spittle off his mouth with the back of his right arm. Then he shifted his slim body slightly to the starboard side of the old row boat. Water spilled into the boat. He quickly resumed his other position. Water must be up to the pier boards now, he thought. He jiggled his body trying to make the boat move, but it was solid and firm, the rising sea trying to push the boat upward through the pier.

"Oh, gosh, Woody, we just gotta make it to Tugg Harbor. This is our only chance!" He held his tri-colored pet tightly. "Tide's just got to stop coming in now or we're in deep trouble, boy!"

The dog whined. Then Bobby felt Woody's smooth tongue lick his bare stomach. It was then that he thought of clothing. Everything had been planned.

But not for tonight!

If only he had taken more time before leaving the mansion. Salager had spoiled it all with the beating. That did it! Never again would he let old Salager touch him. Bobby didn't care how many times he had been told not to go down to the main pier. Salager had caught him again. Big deal. But what were those men always loading and unloading at the island's main wharf? Something strange was going on. Salager didn't want him to find out what it was. That's it. There was something illegal about that operation and Salager knew he would eventually find out.

Well, it would soon be all over for him. He was going to escape this time…for good! The twenty-eight dollars stuffed in his cut-off jeans would have to do until he could find a job. And if he could locate Mr. Gunther, well, the old fisherman would help him out, too. Mr. Gunther was a friend. His mother even considered him a part of the---

Mom, he thought suddenly. Wow, she would come flying back from Europe, or wherever she was this time, and look for him. Well, he thought bitterly, I'll just avoid her, just…just like she has me for the past…what, four years? Why had she married Mr. Salager and given up, sold, their nice waterfront home?

It was a special house built on stilts. Not all homes were constructed on pilings above water. While it was comfortable, every room reflected his Dad's presence. Model boats, shrimpers, small craft, tugboats and speedboats hung from the ceilings. Fishing nets draped the living room walls. Seashells of every color and shape decorated the nets. There were lamps made out of driftwood with shades cut from old, discarded ship navigation maps. Over the mantle was a beautifully mounted swordfish that had been caught in his dad's own fishing nets aboard the Molly Jay.

It would be great to see it again, Bobby thought. He swallowed hard trying to ease the knot in his throat. Why had mom given it all up for old Mr. Rich Pants? She had only known him for two months. After his father's boating accident where he died, his mother never went anywhere. She just sat in the house, alone; hardly ever turning on a light, even at night. Then Mr. Rich Pants comes along snooping in Tugg Harbor aboard his fancy yacht. Made everyone look his way. He saw his mother standing at the back of the house throwing bread to the seagulls. What happened then? And soon the yacht came every day.

"Why me and Nancy Walker should've run off together!" he said to Woody. He laughed lightly, but the more he thought of Nancy, the less he giggled. Somehow the memory of her made him feel good inside now. What was the matter with him? She was just a girl of twelve when he left for Salager's island. She would be sixteen now, same age as himself.

He remembered Nancy standing beside the lighthouse chapel, waving to him. Her long blonde hair blowing in the breeze, and he saw her wipe her eyes. Something…something was becoming clear to him now. Then he recalled the brass plaque. Yes, it reflected the sunlight. His father's name was engraved on the brass plaque. It…well, he would think about that later. He sighed.

Getting back to Tugg Harbor was his main objective for now. He had to think only of that.

Try as he might many times, even on the cliffs of the island, he could not see the lights of Tugg Harbor. His father had told him that the horizon one could see was about seven miles away before it curved and you could see a bit further. With the island eight miles from Tugg Harbor, he knew it would be a mile or more from the island before he would be able to see a faint glimpse of his prized goal.

Once he cleared the lagoon, where his boat was under the pier, he would use Salager's island as a reference point. It would be easy, he thought, and he would be looking at it every minute while he rowed the boat. Once he got half way, which was in the middle of the international ship channel, the lights of Tugg Harbor would really be visible. The rest was, as his father would say, "A piece of cake."

*   *   *   *

An hour later, he felt movement of the boat, and he knew then that the tide was running back to sea. Soon there would be room enough to maneuver the skiff from under the pier. Bobby listened. Not a sound. Even the wind had stopped. Then he heard distant sounds of seagulls. It was still ink black. He wished he could see something. Anything.

Bobby shifted his body gingerly so he could reach over the side of the boat. He scooped up a handful of water and quickly splashed it on his face. The awful shrimp odor was noticeable so he did it again several times. The air was terribly hot and he was sweating like crazy. He heard Woody panting. He felt around for the three-pound coffee can he used for bailing the boat. Finding his canteen, he unscrewed the cap and poured some water in the can.

"Here, boy. It's okay," he said, placing the can so the dog could drink, then he gulped water from the canteen. He winced from pain as his own sweat ran across the welts on his back from the beating Salager gave him earlier. Well, he thought, I won't have to tolerate that ever again!

He reached up the short distance to the pier boards and pushed the boat. It went the short distance of the pier. He wanted to get the skiff from under the pier, but there wasn't enough space yet between the water and the pier.

Twenty minutes later, he became impatient. The thought of the trip goaded him into action. Carefully, he shifted his weight to the bow. The boat's tip slid under the pier. With both hands against the pier planks, he pushed inch by inch while he slowly moved his body toward the stern. When the boat was half way out, he crawled back to the bow and peered out.

No lights and no voices. Good!

A gentle breeze came in from seaward. It felt cool and comfortable on his wet body. He took several deep breaths, looking toward the ocean. It appeared at rest, what he could see of it, but at least it wasn't total darkness like it had been under the pier. Even the lagoon was calm.

"Should be an easy crossing, Woody," he said. "Yes, sir, easy crossing."

The beagle whined.

"We just have to watch out for the ships in the inter-coastal shipping channel, huh, boy?" He laughed lightly, patting the dog's head.

Ten minutes later, the boat was free and rested against the pier. Bobby looked down at the big plastic bag that contained the few clothes he has grabbed on his way out of the big house. He checked the knot to ensure its tightness against water.

"There," he said. Suddenly he felt hungry. His stomach growled. Well, he'd be in Tugg Harbor by breakfast. May even have chow with old man Gunther. Yeah, that sounds super.

He looked to shore again, then at the sky. It was cloudy, moon hidden. "Everything's just super, Woody."

He grabbed an oar and pushed the boat away from the pier. Then he sat on the midship seat. He placed the oars in their locks, one on each side of the boat. He braced his feet against the bottom of the stern seat. Woody jumped onto the seat and sat facing him. With long, powerful strokes of the oars, Bobby drove the boat toward the sea. He kept the pier dead aster and knew when to rudder the right oar to slip through the narrow opening in the lagoon.

Long accustomed to rowing, swimming and climbing the cliffs of the island, Bobby's five foot, five-inch tall body was steeled with muscles, like that of a young boxer. Bronzed by the sun and quenched daily by the sea, his skin was blemish free, except for the welts and razor strap cuts on his back. These seemed to be permanent. Until now. He would never let another man touch him again. No, sir!

He scratched the jagged scar on his left temple, the result of a scrap with a coral several years ago. He thought of his nice room back at the mansion and the clothes in the closet. He hated them. His mother was always bringing new one back from her trips, dropping them off, staying for several days, then she would be off again. In two to three months she would return with more clothes.

Sometimes when they were along, he would try to explain his misery, but she would look at him, almost as if she understood, because…well, it looked like was going to cry. Then suddenly her face would brighten and she would hold his shoulders at arms length and say, "Oh, Robert Edward Langley." She always used his full name when she wanted his attention. "Come now, let's be reasonable. Now it just takes time for adjustment. You just be patient with Jerry. He's a good person. Really, he is. Now you hush this silly talk. Be a good boy." Just as sudden, she would turn and leave the room…crying, he thought.

"Just how long does it take to adjust, Woody?" Bobby gritted his teeth, grunting as he rowed toward the horizon.

Water purled rhythmically past the boat. He felt the wounds split open as his back muscles strained with every pull of the oars. Sweat rolled into the bruises and stung. Tears welled in his Mediterranean-blue eyes, but he forced them back. No, I won't cry! All that's over!

"A piece of cake, Woody. A piece of cake." His voice strained with each word. With every pull, he tossed his head back, flinging his long dark hair away from his face. He looked loathingly at the island disappearing in his wake.

The din of a ship's whistle sounded. He stopped rowing and turned. Eyes squinted as he studied the distant silhouette.

"A C-two tanker, Woody. Probably on her way to Galveston to load. She's ridding high. Looks like her screw is half out of the water, too. Wished we were closer to really see her."

He turned and looked at the island, now a speck on the horizon. There was a slight mist. Was the air a bit cooler now? He couldn't really tell. A sudden jolt of nervousness erupted in the pit of his stomach. Something was up, but he couldn't figure what it was. He let the feeling pass, bogging his mind with pleasant thoughts of Tugg Harbor, old man Gunther, and even Nancy Walker. Then he said, "We gotta make it. We just gotta make, Woody!"

Fifteen minutes later, he said, "Wouldn't it be just great if we could see the *Molly Jay* again, Woody?" He laughed lightly, remembering his father's shrimp boat, clean and spiffy.

"Remember the day you fell into the net? I thought Dad would really be mad at you, but he only laughed and scooped you out with a crab net." He laughed this time. "Yes, sir, we're gonna find the Molly Jay, and…buy her one of---"

He stopped at the sight he could no longer see. The island. It was gone. Hidden by the—

Suddenly a ship's whistle blared. Bobby whirled in his seat to look at the inter-coastal waterway. The vessel was not visible. What he had dreaded earlier now gripped the air around him.

Fog!

And it was getting thicker by the minute! Woody whimpered. Bobby stood up in the boat. He looked in every direction, face frowning. He plopped back down. He sighed heavily, then rested his elbows on his knees, his hands cupping his chin. Woody whined.

"No, we're not turning back! Besides, what if we miss the island? That's almost four miles back. No. We keep going." But he had no reference point now, he knew. He felt his heart pounding in his chest. The ship channel was very near. They had to cross it! With nothing to use as a guide, would he veer too much to starboard or to port? Where would they finally end up?

Well, either way, we have to chance it, he thought.

The fog became thicker as he rowed again. Not a sound stirred the air, except the splashing of the oars and the squeaking of the rusty oar locks. Grip, pull, feather, grip, pull, feather, he kept thinking as he rowed. Grip, pull, feather…gotta make it together. Grip, pull, feath---

Suddenly, there was a loud, solid thump. He felt the boat jar like a bolt of electricity abruptly hit it. He tumbled backwards, head over shoulders into the boat's bow. His head struck a cleat. Woody slid off the stern seat and rolled to a stop, then gripped the wooden bilge as though expecting another hit. He whined and looked around.

A green light dimly flashed in the fog. The animal barked at it, then jumped over the seat. He stood beside Bobby and looked at his face. The youth didn't move. The beagle whimpered, moved closer, then barked several times. Wagging its tail, the dog licked the boy's face. Bobby moaned and slowly moved his head from side to side.

"Oooh," Bobby said softly. He tried to rise, but fell back. Something was in his eyes. His head pounded. With his right hand, he knuckled an eye. He eased it open. Blood! He felt the small gash on his forehead, just below the hairline. He eased up and rested, leaning his back on the port side of the boat. He felt dizzy. Woody started barking at the disappearing green light.

"Okay, okay, I'm fine, boy." But the animal kept barking.

Grimacing, Bobby got to his knees and felt for the side of the boat. The blood seemed to be fusing his eyes shut. He stuck his head over the side and dunked it several times in the salt water. He shook his head, water flinging everywhere. "Oooooooh," he moaned from the salt water in the gash on his head. He eased back to his seat. The beagle barked at the green fog to starboard.

"What is it, boy?" Bobby wiped his eyes. He looked in the direction of the light. It didn't register in his mind for a moment, then he suddenly said, "A bouy! A buoy! We're at the channel!" he said loudly. "Green. Port side!"

He grabbed the oars. Using the light as a guide, he started across the shipping lane.

"Stay up in the bow, Woody. There should be a red one a few hundred yards ahead," he said, thrusting the skiff forward. The dog barked once, then stood facing the channel, its head just visible above the boat.

The guide light and just disappeared when Bobby felt something. At first he didn't know what. It was like being in a dark room and feeling the presence of someone.

Or some object.

He stopped and feathered the oars. He listened, cocking his head first one way then another. He pulled in the oars slowly. Wide-eyed, he turned to his dog. "Woo…Woody," he said nervously. The dog jumped and sat cowering next to his master. They looked at one another, confused.

"Where is it, boy?" he whispered. The dog whined, looked at the fog, then back up at the boy.

It was deathly quiet, except for a low muffled sound somewhere. And… now the soft flowing of water. Suddenly to port, it loomed through the fog.

A ship!

Bobby gasped. He fumbled for the oars. The steel monster towered above them, the steel hull disappearing in the fog.

The freighter hit the boat just under its starboard anchor. Wood cracked. Water gushed into the boat. Like a magnet, the skiff clung to the giant's side. Then, wedge-like, started moving aft. Bobby tried to push away from the ship with an oar, but it was useless.

As they neared the stern, Bobby heard the ship's propeller, thud, thump, and slice at the water. He briefly noticed that the ship was riding high, unloaded. He had to push the boat away before the ship's hull narrowed down to the slicing propeller and the rudder. He stood and rammed an oar against the side of the ship, pushing with all his strength. He groaned and strained. Several times he almost lost his balance. He plopped down on the boat's middle seat as he kept pushing.

Finally, too numb to think, he shut his eyes, ready for the final blow. Visions of his father, the Molly Jay, his mother, and even Tobar, that short-necked, bulgy-eyed son of his stepfather, flashed through his mind. He saw his father on the Molly Jay, holding Woody when he was a puppy. He laughed, then held the dog to his face and kissed its nose. He---

Suddenly, the stern of the boat lifted several feet out of the water. Bobby held his breath. The top portion on the port side of his boat was sliced opened by the monstrous propeller. He cried, trying to shield himself from the spraying water and wind generated by the ten-ton propeller. He felt its power and hugeness for a fleeting moment.

THUD, THUMP, SHWISSH roared the five-bladed brass screw. THUD, THUP, SHWISSH! THUD, THUMP, SHWISSH!

Then the death sounds began to fade. Bobby opened his eyes. Dazed he watched the slicing propeller dissolve in the thick fog.

"Oh, God, thank you," he said softly. He sighed heavily. When he could no longer hear the noise, he suddenly felt water up to his shins! The coffee can was not in sight. He dropped to his knees and crawled around, feeling for the bailing can. He found it. He quickly started bailing. But it was useless. The boat would soon sink.

He studied the damage. The port side was split. Calk it, his brain kept saying. But with what, his clothes? Yes…wait. He quickly removed his cut-off jeans. He rolled them on the seat like a short fat snake. With a foot, he pried the crack open, then wedged the jeans between the split. When he let go, the wood snapped back like jagged teeth. In seconds the pouring water was down to a dribble.

"Good. That ought to hold her," he said, standing up. Water and perspiration streamed down his naked body. Woody barked his obvious approval.

Ten minutes of bailing left about an inch of water in the boat. Bobby wiped his brow, looking for the oars,

They were gone!

He felt his heart throb. Oh, no, he thought. This can't be! His insides felt hollow and a lump formed in his throat. Squinting, he peered out over the water. Fog! Fog! Forever fog!

Wait. He thought he saw something.

Yes, he thought. It's gotta be!

He dropped to his knees at the bow. With both hands, he tried to paddle. He splashed and splashed, but the boat hardly advanced toward the object. Breathing heavily, sweating profusely, he stood up. He looked at the dog.

"Stay, boy! Stay! he said, pointing at the animal.

The beagle whined as though resenting the command. He watched his master jump into the water. Standing on its hind legs, front paws hanging over the edge of the boat, Woody barked, eyes locked on Bobby.

Spitting water, Bobby reached the flotsam. Yes, it was an oar. But it was broken in half. Shoot, he thought, it's better than nothing. He started back. He looked, straining his eyes to the left, to the right…

The boat was gone!

"Woody! Woody!" he shouted, panic filling his body.

The dog barked.

For several seconds, Bobby treaded water, trying to sense the direction. "Keep it up, boy! Keep it up!" he shouted.

He looked around again, then started swimming, holding the partial oar tightly.

Suddenly he was at the boat. It seemed to pop out of nowhere. He grabbed it tightly. Woody whined happily. Bobby felt the smooth tongue licking his hand.

"Good boy," he said, breathing heavily. He tossed the stub-oar into the boat, then climbed in. He paused to regain his wind, then felt the water up past his ankles. Grabbing the can, he started bailing.

"Guess it's about three or four a.m., boy," he said, flinging the last bit of water overboard several minutes later. He grabbed the oar, which was a paddle now, and sat on the stern seat. The instant he started to paddle, it struck him.

He had lost all sense of direction.

He sighed. He glanced in every direction. No lights. Nothing…nothing but thick endless fog. Even the boat bow was barely visible!

Suddenly, he got to his feet. Face contorted, he raised the paddle above his head. He beat the side of the boat. WHOPP! WHOPP! WHOPP!

The beagle cowered, watching the youth.

Seconds later, they boy dropped to his knees. Breathing rapidly, his wrath shifted to the water. SPLAT, SPLAT, SPLAT!

Finally exhausted, he stopped, elbows resting on the edge of the boat, his head bowed. Then he felt the tongue lapping his right arm, but, still, he did not look up.

"We're really lost this time!" he cried softly.

Moments passed, then he said, "What are we gonna do, Woody?" The dog licked its mouth and whimpered. Bobby sighed. He looked around again, slowly this time.

Not a light nowhere!

He studied the water. No current, just small ripples.

"Guess it don't matter which way we go," he said in defeat.

Once more, he tried to sense or "feel" for the proper direction. No use, he thought. He sat back on the stern seat. Reluctantly, he started paddling, shifting sides every stroke or three.

Thirty minutes later, he had to stop and bail water again. His body gleamed with perspiration. He stood and stepped to the bow.

"Want a drink, Woody?" He picked up the canteen, unscrewed the cap and poured water in the bailing can. He placed the can so his dog could drink, then drank from the canteen. The fresh water was good. He needed that. He felt like drinking it dry. Better not. No telling how long we'll be out here or where we'll wind up!

His mind in a blank reverie as he was about to screw the cap back on the canteen, he thought he saw something. Was…was it a flashing light? Blasted fog! He was about to call Woody, but the word never came out of his mouth. A loud noise vibrated through the fog.

Another ship's whistle!

He felt his blood run cold. He jumped. The canteen fell from his hand. It bounced overboard and disappeared. He scrambled aft to grab the paddle. Again, the ship's whistle vibrated the air: BAAAWWWHHHHOOOOOOOOOOO!

He felt his heart pounding in his chest. He started paddling like crazy. That light, he though. Where was it? He felt the closeness of the ship, heard the bow cutting through the water. He paddled harder. Fear confused his mind. The boat seemed to be standing still! It---Wait, wait! It is a light!

The buoy just seemed to materialize before him. Slow swells began to rock the little craft. It banged against the buoy. Bobby rushed to the bow. He reached out to grab the floating light. The boat and light fought one another as the ship's wake pounded them. Barnacles crunched. Wood scraped metal.

His arm slipped off between the buoy and the boat.

"AAwwww!" he screamed, the barnacles tearing across his arm. He yanked the arm back in the boat. Pain blurred his vision a moment. He tried to yell, scream. Anything. But it garbled in his throat.

Fingers numb and stretched outward like the claws of a seagull, he gaped at the sight. He felt like vomiting, then with his other hand, he untied the slip knot in the plastic bag that contained his clothes. He pulled out a white shirt. No, he thought as he was about to wrap his arm. He eased the bloody limb over the side of the boat. He winced and gritted his teeth as he dipped it several time in the salt water. As he pulled the arm out of the water, his eyes suddenly grew big.

A dorsal fin slid beside the boat. He froze as the shark circled the skiff several times then disappeared. He stood silent for a short spell, the din of the ship's whistle fading in the distance.

"May…may…maybe it…it was a porpoise," he said, shaking. But he knew. It was deep water out here in the ship channel. His arm felt numb. Talking seemed to help.

He forced a laugh."Heck, Dad told me that porpoises are man's friend." He started wrapping his arm. "He told me once about one that rolled a body from the bottom of the harbor, all the way to shore, and"---He stopped to hold the arm of the shirt between his teeth, then continued---"and he said that where you see dolphins, you can bet that no sharks are around. They kill them by ramming their noses in them." He winced as he checked the bandage. Then he looked at the slow moving buoy. His face suddenly brightened.

"Red, Woody! It's red. We're across the channel!" He jumped up and down. Woody barked and barked.

"Dad always said, 'Red, Right, Returning', when he was bringing the Molly Jay back toward Tugg Harbor. Red on the right. Tugg Harbor is ahead!" He jumped up and down again, then kicked water overboard.

Water?

He looked down. It was up to his shins now. How could that be? I just bailed out not too long ago! He looked at the damaged wood. The cut-offs were hanging loose. The waves! The buoy! He dropped to his knees. He tried to pry the split open. Without two hands, it was useless.

Feeling weak now, he sat in the water, legs stretched across the boat, his back resting against the other side.

An idea!

With his feet, using his back, he pushed. The crack slowly opened. His arm throbbed. Straining, eyes welling with tears, he groaned until the jeans were back in place, using his foot to cram them back in place.

He rested. If only his arm would stop aching. Gingerly, he lifted it. Although the wrap was wet, it looked and felt like the bleeding had stopped. He sighed. Oh, if only he had a bed right now. When he felt water coming over his body, he shook his head. He eased upright. Pain stabbed every muscle. He moaned.

"Kee…keep an eye on the light, Woody. I…I gotta ge…get the water out of the boat again. Gosh, he felt awful dizzy. What's wrong?

The dog stood on the stern seat and barked.

"Good boy." Bobby knuckled an eye, then looked for the bailing can.

Ten minutes later, he stumbled back to the seat. He eased down beside the beagle. The animal looked at him, its ears turned back. It whined as if crying.

"We gotta make it!" Bobby said, dreamlike. He picked up the partial oar and tried several positions to paddle. Pain chilled his body. Then he felt the water back up past his ankles!

Oh, God, he thought. So close. Maybe four or five miles. He dropped the paddle and staggered forward. Trancelike, he found the can and started bailing. He kept dropping the container.

"We…we…we just gotta make it!" he said weakly.

Minutes, maybe hours, passed. He couldn't remember. The water wasn't going down. Gosh, he felt so tired.

As he fumbled with the can, the din of a engine trying to start caused the beagle's ears to perk. Woody cocked his head, listening. He looked at his master, but Bobby didn't hear. Woody jumped off his seat and waded through the water to the youth's side and whined.

"Ge…get back!" Bobby mumbled.

The dog nudged his hand. Bobby felt his anger mount.

"Get back on…"

Wait. What's the matter with me? he thought. Woody's trying to tell me something. "What is it, boy, huh?"

The dog looked in the direction of the noise, then back at the boy, wagging its tail.

Bobby looked and listened.

Nothing.

He grimaced. "You're hearing things!" He started bailing water again.

The engine grinding noise started again, a little louder. The youth stopped.

A motor?

Yes…yes, it was. Then a gruff voice spoke:

"Ah tole ya not to use no plastic for that there gas line! Why'd ya do it?"

Tools banged. Whoever they were, they're getting closer, Bobby reasoned. Another voice sounded in the thick fog:

"That's all I could find. Ain't that fer to Galveston. Thought it'd hold til we got there."

Bobby heard the clopping of shoes on wood. They were near, right upon him. He palmed his eyes, trying to clear his vision. Still, the fog won.

"'Cordin' to mah chart, we're right near, let's see…Tugg Harbor. If ya can patch that line, we'll ease up the channel to the harbor. Blasted fog!"

"Say," the other man said, "Ain't that where you got---"

"Yeah, yeah!" the gruff voice cut in. "Four, maybe five years ago. Now quit yakking and get that line fixed."

A wrench banged. It sounded so close, Bobby felt like he could reach out and touch it. On impulse, he started to cup his hands to his mouth and sound his presence. No, no, he thought. What would they think? What would they do? They might take me back to the Island, too! I sure don't want that to happen!

Suddenly, a huge platform appeared. Bobby gasped. He looked closer, what he could see in the thick fog. Netting hung from a boom. It disappeared up into the fog. A shrimper! he reasoned. He sighed in relief. A real, honest to goodness shrimper. Ugly and old looking. From his position he could not see the name over the window of the wheelhouse.

If I could just…just ease up under the stern platform, I'd be safe. Most of all, hidden!

The big shrimper rolled gently. Boards creaked. Ropes squeaked. The deck platform loomed just inches away. Bobby reached out, straining. His hand fell away. He sucked in a deep breath and tried again. Got…got it! But he felt his strength draining. Every muscle tense, he slowly pulled the boat under the protective giant covering. Safe. Hidden. Out of sight!

He felt around for the bow line. Pain stabbed his left arm, but he found the line.

"Okay," the worker said. "Try it now."

The engine started to grind. Bobby fumbled with the line, trying to secure it to a support. It was difficult with only one hand. And his body was now half under water!

"Wait!" said the worker. "She needs choking." Then, "Okay, try er now."

The engine finally started. It raced several times, then settled to a low, humming sound.

"Take 'er easy. Don't want to bust 'er loose again."

"Yeah, yeah," came the reply.

The shrimper started moving. Bobby felt the gradual motion of the boat as the slack was taken up in the line. Water churned and bubbled past the skiff. He felt relieved now. He eased his head down to rest.

It went under water!

He jerked it up. Holy cow! he thought. His whole body was submerged. With his foot, he edged the can to his side. Pain racked his body when he tried to bail water. The only thing he could do was just to lay flat as he could and scoop water the best he could. But at least he was safe.

For a while.

* * * *

An hour later, he was exhausted from the awkward work. It's useless, he thought. His neck ached from holding it above water, and still he hadn't dropped the water level. If anything, it was worse.

Suddenly, the drone of the engine slowed.

"Should be about a hundred yards or so from that thare lighthouse chapel," a voice said loudly.

Lighthouse chapel? Bobby thought happily, almost crying at the thought of his father's name on the memorial brass plaque. Then he felt the water-logged boat surging forward. It was going to ram the shrimper's stern if he didn't stop it. He tried to turn and position his leg out over the bow, but the boat hit the shrimper, cracking its wood even more.

"Something hit us! Check it out, Marty!"

"Gottcha."

Bobby quickly untied the rope from the shrimper. The boat drifted from under the platform. Heart throbbing, Bobby eased up and peered at the big boat as it slowly disappeared into the fog just as he made eye contact with the Marty guy. Bobby quickly ducked his head.

"Turn around!" Marty shouted. "I thought I saw a head in a row boat!"

"Right. Coming about," a voice responded.

Suddenly, the engine died. The pilot tried to start it again, but the engine wouldn't respond. "Fix that stupid gas line again, then we'll go back and check it out, the pilot shouted somewhere in the thick fog.

Bobby stood up in the bow, water flowing over every side, especially in the cracked bow. He picked up his plastic bag of clothes. He checked the knot to ensure it was tight, then leaned over and let the bag drop into the water. He stepped over the starboard side and quickly grabbed the life-saver bag, using it as a floatation device.

"Come on, Woody. The lighthouse ain't far away. Better yet, find it, boy. You can do it!"

Woody jumped overboard from the rear seat and started swimming.

Suddenly, a dorsal fin zipped past in front of Bobby. Then another one! Wide-eyed, he froze, waiting for the pain that was surely to follow. He closed his eyes. Seconds passed. Nothing happened. He popped his eyes open.

Oh, no, there they are again! Coming straight at him, side by side.

"I won't scream," he said, putting himself in front of his pet.

Something strange happened. The fins stopped several feet from his body. Then turned. Side by side again, they raced away from the boy.

"Porpoises, Woody! Porpoises!" he said loud and happy. Bobby looked around.

The dog was not in sight!

He felt his heart sink. Life seemed to drain from his whole body. "Woody. Oh, Woody," he cried.

Suddenly the animal barked. Again and again. Bobby never felt so relieved in all his life than right now. Renewed energy swelled in his naked body. The barking came from the direction the porpoises had gone. Holding the plastic bag, he paddled as fast as he could toward the barking. Minutes later, he felt the soft sandy bottom. He stood up, the water at his thigh. He waded ashore, dropping to his knees on the white dry sand. Woody met him with whining and licking. He laughed, hugging and squeezing his pet. He felt the tongue on his face, in his eyes, on his teeth and partly in his mouth. Despite the pain, he laughed and laughed.

Moments later, he turned toward the harbor. It was getting daylight now, he noticed. And the fog was lifting, enough that he could see out in Tugg Harbor a bit.

"We made it! We made it, Woody!" he said.

Abruptly, he saw the fins again, one to his right, the other to his left. The porpoises swam toward one another. Before they met, the mammals leaped out of the water, then vanished. Bobby smiled and waved his thanks. He stood in thoughtful admiration for several minutes.

"Dad," he said, remembering the brass plaque. He turned and rushed up the bank. He turned and looked up at the white, rotating light of the small lighthouse memorial.

To the right of the entrance, the square plate glistened with the names of missing fisherman. Bobby stopped several feet away. His bronze body gleamed in the faint morning light. Slowly, he walked up to the plaque. He gazed at it a moment, several tears running down his cheeks. He touched the name: Robert Edward Langley.

"Piece of ca…cake, Dad," he said softly. "Piece of cake." He leaned his head against the plaque. He wept quietly.

The sound of the shrimper's engine broke the morning stillness.

Bobby whirled, then rushed to a nearby bush. He squatted, holding his dog. Pushing branches apart, he peered out at the shrimp boat.

"Good grief!" he said as the big shrimp boat started making a slow turn to starboard. "What a scow!" he added. "Sure needs work!" The name came in to plain view above the pilot house.

Bobby's lips broke into a tremulous smile. But he was happy. Yessir, he thought. No doubt about it. It was her alright!

The *Molly Jay*.

The End

Newport, RI 1967. Photo information not known

DIXIE CUP ANNIE

"Gosh, you a real sailor?" the small girl asked, pulling her shabby coat closer to her thin body.

Joe Keith, cigarette dangling from the corner of his mouth, glanced at the child. He smiled crookedly as he paid the cabbie.

"Keep the change," he said.

The driver took the bills and grumbled incoherently. He rolled up his window quickly and gunned the taxi into the New York traffic. Horns blasted. Tires squealed.

Joe grimaced, watching, hating cities. Why his high school chum, Bob, had ever moved here from their hometown of Marshall, Texas was simply beyond his 21 year old understanding.

"You one of them Navy guys?" the girl asked, looking up at Joe Keith with big innocent-looking dark eyes. Small hands in thin cotton gloves toyed with a frayed electrical extension cord that she had been using as a jump rope when the cab stopped at the curb.

"Genuine Grade-A. U. S. Government inspected and passed," Joe Keith replied, looking up the snow-sprinkled steps, tracing with his blue eyes to the building number above the door. He nodded, then sighed, hunching his shoulders. He pulled his pea coat collar closer to his neck. He wondered if Bob had changed much since school, three years ago. And Brenda, his wife, what was she like?

"Mommy said sailors are bad," the girl said.

"That so?"

"Yep."

"What does your daddy say? He ever in the service?"

"Never had one," the child replied like it was no big deal to be fatherless.

Joe bit at his bottom lip, looking at the girl, then threw his cigarette on the littered sidewalk. Concerned eyes on the child, he pulled out his smokes and lit another one, eyes never off the girl. Finally, he exhaled both smoke and foggy breath which were swept away by a light breeze.

Joe grimaced and picked up the sack at his feet. A six-pack of beer. He snugged it under his right arm and went up the steps, jumping them two at a time.

Inside the building, he shut the door. The hall was cold and silent. Mailbox doors lined the left wall like diabolical sentinels. A dark wooden floor that squeaked when walked on seemed just downright spooky to Joe.

Not a good sign, his young mind flashed, but he mustered a smile as he looked up the worn stairs to his right, recalling Bob's phone words.

'Second floor, turn left. Number B-One, Two.'

Joe walked toward the stairs just as a door opened and shut a short distance away. He stopped. Two bundled up old ladies came his way.

"I tell ya, Sarah," one said in a whisper that shot in the cold air like a bullet, "they just grow up and forget ya ever existed. Jail and prison don't even make them grow up. Why, I..."

Joe cleared his throat lightly.

The women's heads jerked his way.

Joe smiled politely, nodding his presence. Although the women avoided eye contact, he knew they observed as they headed toward the street. At the front door, they spoke softly.

"'magine that, Sarah. Sailor in uniform. Never see them like that these days. Almost forgot we had a Navy. Humph! Not like those dingbats upstairs! They should see this young man and example after him!"

"Yes," Sarah said sadly. "My Melvin was buried in his Navy suit at Pearl Harbor. Why it seems just like yesterday...."

"There, there, honey," the other lady said. She patted Sarah lightly on the back. "Chin up. 'member?" She opened the door and led Sarah outside. She looked back and smiled at Joe before she shut the door.

Joe nodded, smiling pleasantly. Remembering his crippled mother, he promised to write to her again tomorrow. And, yes...he'd call her later today. He turned and walked up the creaking stairs.

On the second floor he stopped, fumbling with the three Broadway tickets inside his pea coat pocket. The *Annie* tickets had cost him a bundle back at that bar. Wouldn't Bob and Brenda be delighted to go and see *Annie* with him? Sure, no problem.

Joe dubbed out his cigarette in a dingy-looking ash can to his left by the dirty wall. The sack under his right arm crinkled as he did, and he thought of a joke he'd pull on Bob. He reached into the sack and pulled out a can of beer. He put it in the left pocket of his pea coat. He'd leave the sack in the hall outside Bob's door. Inside, he'd eventually ask Bob if it would be okay to have a beer, and then he'd suddenly produce one. It'd be good for a laugh. Ole Bob was always ready for humor. It was his nature.

"B, One, Two," he said to himself, turning left.

Floor groaning under the thread-bare gray carpet, he walked slowly, looking at door numbers. The din of rock music came from somewhere. It grew louder as he eased down the cold hall.

At door B-1...2, wait. B-One...Two. The two was crooked, like it had fallen off a dozen times and restuck to the door. The one was correct, nice and straight, but the *two* was ready to fall. The rock music boomed on the other side of the door. Joe winced slightly, wondering how the neighbors put up with it. He raised a fist to knock. A big sign stared back at him.

NO SMOKING. NO DRINKING.

Hummm, that wasn't like ole Bob. So much for the beer joke. He set the beer sack on the floor by the door. Cigarette? Well, he could do without one for a short spell. But as he knocked, Joe Keith felt suddenly pensive. Something was amiss, but his young mind could not fathom the cause.

The door cracked open.

Joe saw a chain, then an eye looking at him. Music blasted out from the narrow opening. He smiled weakly, almost wincing at the noise.

The door shut.

Joe squared his hat better, stood straight, and waited as he heard the door chain being released, then a deadbolt sliding open, then what sounded like a heavy bar being taken off the door, then the regular knob lock being keyed. Then the door opened, but only half way. There stood, ah...Bob?

The obese body, clad in bleach-spotted jeans and a dirty, bright yellow T-shirt, wasn't at all like the quarterback on their high school football team. Scraggly beard, too. That wasn't Bob. Oh, no, look at his hair, all curly like bed springs, and puffed out. But Bob was his fellow classmate, his friend. He fought the impulse to hug him and pat his back. Instead, he offered his hand.

"Hey, Bob, good...good to see you, old buddy."

"Joe, you son-of-a-gun. Come..." Bob cleared his throat.

Joe caught the fleeting disapproval of his Navy blue uniform.

"Come...come in," Bob said, glancing over his shoulder as though fearing someone might see him.

Joe took Bob's slightly extended hand and shook it properly. It was as cold and limp as old celery. With his right hand, Joe pointed at his ear, then toward the radio.

Bob nodded and walked over and turned down the music.

"Better?" he asked. He managed a small smile.

Joe grinned, returning the nod. What was with Bob? He was always so happy, ready for humor and a beer. Trying to contain his disappointment, he glanced the place over.

Cold. It was as cold inside Bob's place as it was in the hall. Don't they have warmth? Clothes were draped over the scant and old furniture. At least Bob hadn't changed in this respect...but, still... Although the place had the odor of a boys gym shower, Joe smiled, bringing his eyes back on his friend.

"Nice...nice place here," he said. "Yessir, nice and comfy. Hey," he added with a laugh. "Remember back in school, the day we skipped math and...."

"Hold it!" Bob said, hand up like a cop stopping traffic. "Spare me the Memory Lane crap, huh? Those days are over. Vanished. Gone forever!" From the pocket of his yellow T-shirt, he pulled out a can of snuff. At the door, Joe had thought it to be shoe polish. With three fingers, Bob put a wad into his mouth.

"Sittdown," he mumbled, then shoved clothes, poster boards, and papers to one side on the ratty-looking couch.

"Nah, think I need to stand. Been sitting all day anyway. Where...where's your wife?" Joe stuffed his hands inside his pea coat pockets, his left hand trying to avoid the can of cold beer.

"Oh, Brenda. Yeah. In the kitchen baking rum cake. For our organization, ya know," Bob said. "I'll get her."

"Fine. Fine. I'm anxious to meet the great woman who tamed you, you ole animal." Joe laughed pleasantly.

Unsmiling, Bob walked past him and pushed open the swing-door to the kitchen.

Joe saw a woman jump back, but the door shut before he could get a decent look at her. He sighed heavily, trying to rid himself of disappointment. A beer would sure help now. He fought the urge to pull out the can inside his coat.

"Get rid of that creep!" a female voice said in a tight whisper behind the swing-door.

"Sshhhhh, he'll hear."

"I don't really care," the girl voice hissed. "What'll everyone think of us when they come in and see that, that guy wearing a military uniform in our... their house? What about the hand posters for tonight? They finished yet?"

"Well, ah, almost."

"Look, Thelma, Ronda, and Slim will be home shortly. Now say good-by to Mr. Navy out there soon! We demo at the square at eight!"

"Brenda, honey, I just can't..."

"Ole buddy or not, what he represents is the very thing our organization opposes!"

Joe Keith felt his neck and ears burn in the cold air.

Organization? Rum bread? Snuff? No smoking or drinking? And who was this Thelma and others that lived in this tiny apartment? Joe thought. Maybe, too, Bob wasn't married to Brenda either! And a demonstration at the square? What was... Joe squared his hat. Just as he started to turn to go to the front door, Bob opened the swing-door and came back, a forced smile on his hairy face.

"Hey, Joe, ole buddy," Bob said. He laughed, obviously forced. "Now, sittdown a few minutes, right? Okay? I have to finish a project, ya know, posters for tonight. I won't be

long, then maybe we'll see about going someplace, you know, just you and me. Brenda, ah..." He glanced back at the kitchen door. "Brenda, you, ah, she'll be out later to meet you." He laughed again. Put on. "Ya know how women are, right?" He looked at the cluttered coffee

table in front of the couch. Squatting, he quickly rummaged through the mess, locating two long envelopes. He picked them up and stood. "I knew they was here. Have to be in the mail," he said to himself.

"Look, Bob, I...I have to be going pretty soon. Hot date tonight. Can't be late,"

Joe lied, fumbling with the *Annie* tickets inside his coat pocket. Damn, what a waste of money, he thought. He figured Bob and Brenda would be nice enough to...

"No, no," Bob replied quickly. "Stay a while longer. I'll be finished with those posters in the bedroom in no time. Then we'll go out and hit a few bars

I know." He laughed. Beside the front door, he dropped the envelopes inside some containers taped to the wall. They appeared like cigar boxes.

Cardboard mailboxes? Joe thought. He hadn't noticed them when he came in. Each box even had a big letter on it. Odd.

Bob had dropped the envelopes through the one with a *G* on it. He saw Joe looking.

"*G* means government," Bob said. "We protest to them all!" He looked at the kitchen door as though he'd forgotten something. "Hey, Brenda," he said loudly. "Better get some more food stamps. We're almost out."

"Slim's getting them," came the prompt reply. "We're his family this month. Next month we're Ronda's. Don't forget. Now get those posters done. Demo eight sharp!"

"Right."

"Oh, yeah, Bob-oh. We're out of flour, too. Stop by the pool hall after the demo and get a bag or two," Brenda roared back.

"No prob for Bob," Bob chuckled. He winked at Joe Keith, Mr. Navy.

"Bob," Joe said. "'C'mon now. Food stamps? Just where do you work? Can I help you out?"

Bob laughed without mirth. "Why, Joe," he said with mock sincerity, "my efforts are expended for bettering our individual rights." He tapped the *G* box with a government-fed finger. "My labors will pay off one of these days. Wait and see." He cocked his head at the kitchen door again. "Hey, Bren," he said loudly. "Make two more loafs of your rum bread. And when we get back from the pool hall, make one out of the white sauce, huh?" He picked up a nasty Styrofoam cup and spit a brown stream into it.

"Special rum on the side," Brenda's voice replied.

Rum bread? Joe thought again. Snuff. No smoking. No drinking. Multi-people living in a single family place. Flour at a pool hall? White sauce and food stamps?

"And the *S* on that box?" Joe asked, pointing.

"*State*, man."

"And the *C* on this one," Joe said, tapping the cigar box, "is for *City*, I suppose."

"We fight 'em all, man." Bob spit into the cup again, then said, "Say, man, you're pretty smart, even if you do look strange in that uniform, especially with that little boy white hat."

"We call it a *Dixie Cup* in the Navy. Remember the ice cream we used to get in the little cup back when we were kids? *Dixie Cup*, we called them. Well..."

"How cute!" Bob cut in, lips tight. He looked at Joe seriously. "Ever thought about ditching that garb you're wearing and really doing good for... for yourself? I mean..."

"My ship picked up the astronauts last week," Joe said proudly. "It was on all the TV news stations. Even Walter..."

"Another waste of government funds!" Bob exploded. "Can't you see it?" He yanked out an envelope from the *G* box and held it to Joe's face, shaking it. "It's all in this! Stand up for your rights, man! This letter to the president ought to pop his cork some!" He shoved the letter back into the cardboard mailbox.

"Wait. Wait," Joe pleaded, both hands up at shoulder level. "Bob, buddy. Hey, you might mean well, maybe you do. I'm no judge, understand? But, hey man, this is America. Remember? United States. *United*. We all have to pull together, you know...for the common purpose. That object is our own government. Right or wrong, we have to stand behind Uncle Sam."

The Washington-fed young man laughed contemptuously. "Man," he groaned, "have you got a lot to learn!" He walked to a bedroom door and vanished, prattling on about rights and self preservation.

Joe grimaced, shaking his head sadly. He looked at the room where Bob was out of sight. On the bed were huge-lettered posters, but he made no effort to clear his blurry eyes to read the contents. With a determined stride, he headed for the hall door.

At the makeshift mailboxes, he stopped. He reached into his coat pocket and pulled out the now tepid can of beer. He shook it vigorously as he went to the radio and turned it up, knowing Bob would think he was staying. He stepped back to the boxes.

"Come seven or eleven. Big dick from Boston, and all that!" he said as he shook the can like he was playing dice. Then he snapped the top tab. Beer spewed everywhere like Old Faithful. He soaked each mailbox, then turned the can upside down inside the letter-laden *G* box, suds drowning the paper, foam coming out the top like a frothing horse's mouth.

"Some beer bread for the Navy, Mrs...or Miss Brenda whoever you are!" Joe said, teeth gritted.

In the hallway, he saw that his beer sack had been taken. Well, hazards of a big city, I suppose. He banged the door shut behind him. The number 2 fell off and dropped to the floor, but the 1 remained, strong and firm in its place.

Outside on the snow-sprinkled steps, he stopped, seeing the girl in rags again, jumping rope with the frayed electrical cord. He lit a cigarette.

He exhaled with relief, putting his lighter back in his pea coat pocket. A slight grimace came to his lips as he once again fingered the Broadway *Annie* tickets.

"Hi there, sweetheart," he finally said, then, suddenly, he felt proud. He dashed down the steps three at a time.

The girl stopped jumping. "Oh, hello, Mister Sailor Man."

Joe squatted in front of the child, cigarette dangling from his lips. He pulled out the *Annie* tickets from his pocket.

"Wanna go see a play, sweetie?" he asked.

"What's that?"

"Oh, it's where people are on a big stage and act...you know, they pretend to be somebody they're not." Joe glanced back up at the building.

"Goody. I would like that." The child's face beamed.

"Fine. Give these to your mommy. She'll know what to do. There's three tickets here. Take one of your little friends."

Brown eyes wide, the girl took the tickets. Smiling, she looked at Joe's head.

"Can I have your hat, too?"

"Whooooa, sweetie. That's a tough one."

"Pleeeee-zzz?"

"They would get all over me if I came back to my ship without my hat, Doll. And, hey, the Shore Patrol would probably arrest..."

Sad brown eyes started to water, halting further words.

Joe stared at the child a moment. He bit at his lower lip, glancing about blankly. He sighed heavily. Finally, he spoke.

"Sure, why not." He removed his Dixie Cup and placed it gently on the girl's small head.

The End

MERCHANT NAVY IN THE HEAD

A sailor's life is tough with having to be away from home for long periods of time. They experience loneliness which often turns into frustration. Some men keep silent, others drink, while many front emotions with humor.

Ending a shipyard overhaul with last minute touch-ups and several cosmetic installations, *USNS Glover (T-AGFF 1)* was tied to a pier at the Norfolk Navy Base on this cold December night in 1990.

New sailors, both Navy and civilian mariners, were still reporting aboard to complete the required number of personnel to operate the Military Sealift ship. Although some of the men recognized other crew members, it would be several months before the whole crew would know one another. Being manned by both Navy and civilian mariners, each group was already kidding the other about being the better part of the crew. The Navy guys were better. No, the merchant mariners were better. Back and forth.

It was one week before Christmas on this cold evening just short of midnight.

> It was the night before sobriety,
> When all through the ship,
> Not a dirtball was stirring,
> Except two Glover louses.
> (some sailors never made good poets, either!)

Ollie Walker (merchant marine), his skull bankrupt of brains by alcohol, tried to ease down the last three steep steps of the ladder that led down from topside. Ollie had just staggered back aboard after having tried to drink the local Navy Exchange Bowling Alley dry of Budweiser beer.

Trying to focus his eyes, he weaved and swayed. He stopped, holding the slack chains that served as banisters on the ladder. Twisting his lips, he belched loudly, then stepped down.

BANG! CRASH!

Ollie Walker fell to the next deck. His head bounced at the corners of two joining bulkheads like a basketball being dribbled down court. Legs tangled, eyes crossed, he sat on the deck holding his head and moaned.

Meanwhile, his head equally brain-dead in a toasted and roasted state, Bill Lester (Navy), stood photo-still the best he could. He weaved slightly in front of a urinal in the spanking-new after ship's head. He whimpered, scared to touch his private part that he had just snagged in his trouser zipper.

Outside in the passageway ten feet aft, Ollie Walker (merchant) grumbled incoherently. Using the bulkhead as a support, he pushed up to his feet awkwardly. He swayed, then palmed the bulkhead in a useless effort to steady himself.

"Stupid wall!" he told the bulkhead. He glanced up and down the empty passageway.

BANG!

Frustrated, Ollie Walker hit the bulkhead. He yanked his hand back and grabbed it.

"Shee-ut!" he grumbled, rubbing his hand, obviously relieved that the passageway was void of people.

Back in the head ten feet away, Bill Lester (Navy), crouched over like a Kiwi and slowly backed toward the door that opened inward from the outside passageway. He was undecided as to when he dared to touch his trouser zipper.

"Ooooh," he moaned, careful not to bump against the wobbly toilet stalls to his left. Bright yellow,"CAUTION CONSTRUCTION" tape criss-crossed the cubicals numerous times like a giant spider web. The shipyard workers would finish bolting the stalls in place the next day. The toilet area to his right was useable, including the three new urinals along the bulkhead where Bill (Navy) had encountered his personal problem.

His butt against the head door, Bill whimpered, almost in tears. He touched his zipper gingerly, then yanked it back. Not a muscle moved from his shoulders down.

Outside in the passageway, Ollie Walker (Merchant) turned right, then turned right again. Three steps told him he was going back where he came from. He stopped, rolled his eyes, staggered and did an about-face. At the head door, he stopped and turned the knob. It turned nicely but the door remained shut.

"Stuck again. Don't them yard birds know how to install nothin'?" Ollie grumbled as he pushed on the door. The door didn't budge. He grimaced, then pressed a shoulder on the thin metal door. It remained firmly in place. Ollie made a sour face, then stepped back. He raised a steel-toed boondocker and kicked the door flat-footed. Both the door and the bulkhead vibrated as the door flew open.

"Aaaahhh!" Bill Lester (Navy) yelled as he rocketed across the new terrazzo deck. Half of his chubby body plowed into a torn-open case of stacked toilet and cases of paper towels stacked to the overhead by the sinks. Paper and rolls flew everywhere. Bill broke free, arms failing.

"Outta ma way, you Navy puke!" Ollie roared. He walked up to a urinal.

Bill jumped to his feet. Relief showed on his face at the sight of being unsnagged. He quickly adjusted himself and zipped up his trousers. Then, looking at Ollie, his face went red, chubby cheeks ballooning out with every breath. He slumbered up behind Ollie. "Just who you calling 'puke', you puke merchant marine redneck?"

Ollie turned, zipper half open. "Scrub you, you swabbie jerk!" he yelled.

"Scrub you!" Bill yelled centimeters from Ollie's nose.

"No, scrub you, anus lips!" Ollie screamed.

"Scrub you!"

"Scrub you!"

Bill pushed Ollie. Ollie pushed Bill. Bill pushed Ollie.

Ollie grabbed Bill in a headlock. He pulled him to one of the operational toilet stalls. He yanked the door open, banging Bill's head. Ollie started pounding Bill's head by opening and closing the stall door.

"Aaah!" Bill cried.

After thirty seconds of head banging, they were both woozy and goofy-looking. Is it a wonder? Ollie had been pounding his own head with the door too! They huffed and puffed, staggering about as though lost.

Regaining a bit of ... should it be called sense? Bill seized the moment, giving Ollie a hard shove. Ollie tumbled backwards, feet busting open another case of toilet rolls and paper towel bundles. Unable to regain his balance, Ollie flipped over picture-perfect into a large plastic-lined trash can. Hit feet shot straight up, knees in front of his face.

"You swinie pig merchant!" Bill roared. He rushed to Ollie, leaned forward and tried to pick up the trashcan. He strained and groaned. Suddenly he expelled gas, the explosion probably heard three piers away were the *USNS Henry J. Kaiser (T-AO 187)* was moored. Even the head bulkheads vibrated! The heat alone almost melted the new lava-like Tarzana deck.

Bill managed to lift the can only two feet up, then he dropped it. Mike wedged even deeper into the container. Huffing, Bill pushed the can over on its side.

"I'll get you! I'll get you!" Ollie yelled.

Bill laughed like an insane villain. He rolled the can as hard as he could across the deck. Hitting the bulkhead, the trashcan stopped, jarring Ollie. Bill's laughter suddenly turned into a coughing fit.

Ollie squeezed out of his prison. He jumped to his feet, staggered a bit. He eyed Bill in his coughing spell. Seizing the moment, he clamped Bill in another headlock. He dropped to his knees and grabbed a roll of toilet paper. He started pounding Bill's head over and over while shouting, "Take that! And that! And that!"

Suddenly like streamers in a Macy parade, toilet tissue went everywhere. Mike pounded and pounded. He stopped and grabbed another roll. He pounded and pounded…and pounded. Then he pounded more. Finally, he slowly stopped, exhausted. He let go of Bill's head and sat on the deck trying to catch his breath.

Bill shook his head, eyes crossed. Holding onto the bulkhead, he slowly got to his feet. Weaving, he looked at the toilet stalls spider-webbed with the yellow "CAUTION CONSTRUCTION" tape. Turning to Ollie, Bill swung a beefy leg over the back of Ollie's neck. He straddled Ollie like a goat. Squeezing his legs rigid, Ollie's skull between his calves, he baby-stepped to the loose-walled stalls. Not giving the yellow tape any thought, he yanked a door open. As he short-stepped to the toilet, the tape stretched and broke whirling around Bill's upper body.

Intent on his mission, Bill waddled up to the toilet's rim, Ollie's head over the bowl of water. Laughing, he plunged Ollie's head down in the cold salt water and started flushing the commode repeatedly.

Mike gurgled and bubbled. He raised up now and then, yelling profanity that probably was heard aboard the hospital ship, *USNS Comfort*, cruising in the Red Sea in *Desert Shield*.

"More salt water for you, you merchant pig?" Bill made an effort to ram Ollie's head again. His expression turned to surprise as Ollie struggled and grunted, slowly lifting Bill off his feet, his head above the stalls. Bill grabbed a wobbly wall.

Mike twisted, causing Bill to fall full weight on the loose wall. Yellow construction tape stretched, broke and recoiled in every direction as all three toilet stalls and doors came crashing over, burying the sailors.

It was a silent night for a while.

Suddenly the middle stall door swung open on its side banging a wall that had been piled on it. Ollie's head popped up from the ruins.

"You dim-witted swabbie!" Ollie grumbled as he pulled yellow tape from his face, neck and shoulders. He out of the shambles, careful not to step on rolls of toilet paper. Looking around, he added, "Boy, the First Assistant

Engineer's gonna be ticked off when he sees his brand-new head! I know he's---

Suddenly Bill sprang up from the devastation, oblivious to the tape stretching from his body. He jumped Ollie and pulled him into a headlock. He grabbed a bundle of paper towels and started pounding Ollie's head. The bundle broke open. Brown paper flew everywhere. Bill snatched up another bundle. After only two hits, more paper thickened the air.

Ollie struggled to free himself. Bill groaned and held tighter. Then he paused a moment, trying to catch his breath. Ollie tried to lift Bill, but exhaustion terminated this idea.

Suddenly Bill let loose of Ollie. Both men sank to the deck, heaving and gasping for air.

For a short spell it was Silent Night again.

"Wh...wh...where you...you...from?" Bill demanded.

"Ttt...Texas," Ollie said, panting like a dog.

"Rea...really? Me, too, man!"

"Zat...zat so? Wh...where...'bouts? Dallas, El Paso, Austin, Houston?"

"Lo...Loo...Longview. East Texas, about---"

"Nah! Nah! Man! Me too!" Ollie's face beamed.

"You gotta be kidding!" Bill's face brightened.

Both men got to their feet.

"Yep, su...sure as shootin'," Ollie said.

"Man, that's a...a freaky thing! Man, two guys from the same state, yeah. But two guys from the same town, same state? Mighty unusual. Hey, names Bill, Bill Lester."

"Ollie Walker here."

Both men smiling happily, they shook hands, then pulled themselves together and hugged, slapping backs.

"Say, my uncle owns The Butcher Shop there---"

"Off McCann Road. Yeah! Eaten there hundreds of times," Bill Lester said, laughing engagingly. He opened the head door for Ollie.

In the passageway, they headed forward, side by side, arm over each other's shoulders while talking about other places, roads, and people they knew in Longview, Texas. Unnoticed by either, toilet paper was unrolling as they sauntered along, the leading wad of paper stuck in Ollie's back-pocket; the main roll still in the ship's head. They laughed and chatted on with Bill unconsciously pulling paper towels from his collar and belt line.

USNS Henry J. Kaiser TAO 187
Desert Storm
Red Sea 1991
Turned 50 yrs. old in the Combat Zone!! Jr. Engineer
Bill Sneed

USNS HENRY J. KAISER (T-AO 187)   01 AUG 91 to 05 DEC 91   UNL JR ENGR/W   127
32000/20706   FOREIGN - OPERATION DESERT STORM 19 AUG 91 TO 21 NOV 91
                               AND ENTITLED TO IMMINENT DANGER PAY (COMBAT).
Mr. Sneed was underway for a total of 303 days, computed as described in enclosures
(1) and (2).

                          Sincerely,

                          R. A. GRAY
                          Master
                          USNS HENRY J. KAISER (T-AO 187)

Photo U.S. Navy, Public Domain

FRUIT OF THE POISONOUS TREE

We didn't start what looked like World War III on the Norfolk, Virginia Navy Base.

Honest.

All me and Ernie wanted to do was to go ashore and have a few beers at the base bowling alley snack bar. Calm, and nice and quiet.

Honest.

With *Desert Shield* having turned into *Desert Storm* just three days before, the base and piers were hubs of activity. Jeeps, tanks, and supply trucks scurried about while rifle-toting, combat-ready guards roamed the base and waterfront roads looking for anything suspicious. The air was as tense and strained as a span wire between two ships fueling at sea. It was definitely not a time for public jokes or pranks.

With our Military Sealift Command ship, *USNS Henry J. Kaiser T-AO 187*, docked at the very end of the pier, I knew we had to walk its full length. We would have to dodge and side-step Navy working parties, railcars, the huge crane on its wide tracks, and pallets and pallets of stacked hardware and commissary goods.

Still new to the sealift command and the *Kaiser* my first ship, I wanted to walk slowly and take in everything. It had been ten years since I retired from the Navy. I had only been in Norfolk once, and I couldn't quite recall anything I saw back then during my earlier young days in the military.

I looked at my wristwatch: 0915. A fifteen minute jaunt from the *Kaiser*, the bowling alley opened at 0900. I yawned, covering my mouth. Since not sleeping much before that long midnight-to-eight morning watch, I was a bit tired. But I had promised Ernie I'd go with him.

Dressed in blue-jeans and a dark green T-shirt (with a pocket to hold a pen or two), I positioned my navy-blue ball cap on my head. Above the bill it read: NAVY RETIRED CPO. Being an observer of life, people and places, I grabbed my notebook that I carried constantly, even on watches. I put it in my left rear trouser pocket. You could never tell when a story idea would surface and if I didn't write it down, it would be totally forgotten. But then sometimes I would tote the notebook for days and not jot anything in it.

I went up to the next deck and knocked lightly on Ernie's stateroom door. From within I heard Ernie cuss a streak, then yell, "COME IN, YOU WATER JOCKY NAVY PUKE!"

Not intimidated, by now I knew it was a habit of Ernie's to feign anger and shout the words that ended some of his stories, and even routine conversations. No big deal.

I turned the knob and pushed the door open without stepping in. I laughed. "Man, that's the kindest greeting I've ever received," I said. "Ready?"

"Hold your nads, Wally Jenkins!" Ernie said as he stuffed his wallet in a back pocket of his khaki uniform. While he wore a khaki outfit, he had no merchant third assistant engineer devices on his collars. Sealift was rather relaxed on any type of uniform regulation, it seemed, which I was glad. The civilian merchants mingled well with the Navy guys, which I was also pleased. I once asked Ernie about why he didn't wear collar insignias. He wore no hat either. His reply was that he hated having the Navy guys salute him so he ditched the hat and rank stuff. End of story.

Ernie and I had only stood a week of watches together. We bonded fairly well. At least we had the common ground of having served twenty years in the Navy. And today would be my first venture off the ship since reporting aboard two weeks ago. I wasn't exactly enthused to hit the beach, but Ernie said he needed a break from those dumb midnight watches; that having a few beers would relax us and we'd sleep better when we came back aboard ship early in the afternoon. "What, with those deck-apes jack-hammering the deck up forward making all that teeth-rattling noise on the starboard side!" Then he let out a volley of profanity about the deck force people.

"Ready?" Ernie finally asked, walking out the door.

"That's why I'm up here, you dirt-bag, ex-Navy Boiler Technician."

Ernie merely smirked, almost pulling his door shut. "Wait! I forgot my bag." He re-entered his stateroom quickly and returned holding a corduroy hand-bag squashed under his left arm.

My brows furrowed. "What's the AWOL bag for?"

"That's in case we make it to the base exchange…no, wait, there's a small store up a bit further after the bowling alley. We'll go there after we tank up."

"Gedunk?" I asked, following his lead to the topside quarterdeck.

"No. Beer! But I'll get some candy and other snacks anyway, just to cover the beer. You know, in case it gets searched when we come BACK THIS AFTERNOON!"

"You'd risk your rank just to smuggle a few beers aboard?" I knew that ship's officers had small reefers in their staterooms. Being a junior engineer, I had no refrigerator, but could have one too, if I purchased it myself. Well, maybe later…

"It don't work that way. You have a lot to learn about Sealift. We're civilians. It's easy come, easy go on most sealift ships. Relaxed. Know what I mean?"

"Sure do," I replied, following his heels.

"I'll show you a secret about this bag once we get ashore and away from these ships, Wally Jenkins."

"Goody," I teased. "I can't wait." I laughed, knowing what I would learn would be good coming from Ernie. I really didn't like him calling me by my first and last name, but I wasn't about to anger him. Maybe he did it so he would remember it better. However, I sensed something strange and eccentric about Ernie that I couldn't put my finger on. But, like he said, I had a lot to learn.

Maybe a few beers would bring out this oddness I felt about Ernie.

Oddness? Well, we all had our own particular idiosyncrasies.

Maybe Ernies would be funny. Humm, maybe it would be a horror story, too! I quickly squashed that thought from my mind like stepping on a bug.

We emerged topside to an azure sky and a bright sun. I squinted and knuckled my right eye. I had heard several men say that Norfolk was having some unusually nice weather for this time of year. Well, I wasn't going to complain. I could handle a 75 degree winter. I was used to fair winter seasons in Arizona. Burn me up, I thought, smiling. I looked up, hearing sea gulls squawk like a bunch of nagging kids wanting candy. Several swooped down while others glided in the air smoothly. That's something I wish I could do, I thought with a smile.

At the quarterdeck, Ernie stopped to yack with the third mate on watch. I eased to the lifelines and looked across the huge cement pier. Whoa! I thought, almost raising my hands at the gun barrel pointed directly at me. It was the barrel a five-inch MK. 45 on the stern of the *USS Samuel B. Roberts FFG 58*, a Perry-class tin can tied up across the pier. Outboard of *Roberts* was *USS Doyle FFG 39*.

Looking down the pier, I saw a host of other Oliver Hazard Perry-class tin cans and Spruence-class destroyers; two other Military Sealift Command ships, the *USNS John Lenthall T-AO 189* and another sealift oiler that I couldn't quite make out its name on the stern; both loading supplies. With blue-and-yellow bands painted around their smokestack tops, it was easy to know they were sealift ships. And man, was the pier busy with working parties, vehicles, and pallets and pallets stacked high at various and congested locations. Toward the head of the long pier were…Darn, were those eighteen-wheelers? Fork-lifts scurried about like bugs. Whatever else was up there at the pier head, we would have to walk past. The scene jogged my memory back to when I was en route to Vietnam in 1966 aboard *USS Dyess DD 880*, and we stopped in San Diego for fuel. Only now the ships were much newer. They had different shapes, were more sleek and elegant, and had high tech guns and equipment. I marveled at the present Phalanx multi-barrel anti-craft guns. Awesome!

"…and when I find him I'M GONNA BEAT HIS HEAD IN!" Ernie said, stressing, of course, his last few words in a loud tone.

As he walked past me, I looked back at the third mate and shrugged. He smiled, shaking his head.

Beat whose head in? I thought. Humm, maybe I better not ask. I quickly followed Ernie down the long slopping gangplank.

"Smell anything…like a cleaner or something?" Ernie asked, twitching his nose, the AWOL bag pressed under his left arm pit.

"Well," I droned, "we are walking beside our ship, its tanks brimming with diesel oil, JP-5, aviation gas and thousands of gallons of Navy distillate fuel for ships. Not to mention one *USNS Lenthall* on our bow. Duuhh!"

"No, it ain't that. Its's---"Ernie yanked the bag from under his arm. A portion of the light-colored fabric appeared wet. He smelled the cloth, then yanked it open. Searching a moment inside, he yanked out a small can of cigarette lighter fluid, its pointy plastic nozzle straight up. Ernie yelled a barrage of profanity, then threw the bag to the edge of the pier. Suddenly realizing that this was an error, he darted to the bag and picked it up, glancing about as if to hope no one saw him. In one swift motion he threw the can of lighter fluid out into the harbor.

"What's with the bag, Ernie?" I asked as he rejoined our walk.

"Shhh!" He tucked the AWOL grip back under his left arm. "Tell you later," he whispered tightly.

My brow furrowed, but I remained quiet. What's with the bag getting damp with lighter fluid? I thought. That bag was empty, yes? I wasn't going to ask.

As we passed the open water between *Kaiser* and *Lenthall*, I got a nice view of the submarines way over at the next pier. They looked like long black cigars partly submerged in water. Activity there was also heavy. Shaking my head, I observed a string of orange life-jacketed men chain-ganging (hand-over-hand) boxes and crates of supplies from a truck on the wharf. I felt sorry for them sewer-pipers having to pass everything down a tiny hatch. Must take forever to stock them up, I thought.

I glanced down so I wouldn't get a foot stuck in the recessed railroad tracks that were imbedded in the full length of the pier.

Evenly spaced also were a set of tracks for the huge crane that towered ahead of us. Below the crane was a boxcar, men off-loading on both sides. The boxcar could easily go under the crane. Then I heard what sounded like a huge jet coming in from our rear. I knew a naval air station was close because I had heard them rumble overhead numerous times while in my stateroom. I drew my shoulders up, so intense was the roar. I raised my head all the way back just as *A-6E Strike Aircraft* zoomed past us on its landing path to the air field, its landing gear down, so close I felt I could reach up and touch the wheels. With the other sights and sounds, this made my pride at being an American exceptionally proud and thankful.

"Man," I said to no one in particular. "AWESOME!" I had to yell.

"YOU GOT THAT RIGHT!" Ernie roared over the rumble of jet engines.

"MOM, APPLE PIE, AND AMERICA ALL AROUND US!" I shouted with a smile.

Within a minute, another fighter jet roared in, this one an *F-14 Tomcat*.

"Hum, hum!" I mumbled. Old Saddam Hussein ain't gonna like this coming in his front door!" I said, but Ernie didn't hear me.

Then I thought, Mucho crap-oh! I missed seeing any of the Spruance-class ship names on their sterns as we neared their mid-ship quarterdecks. There were four Spruance-class destroyers juxtaposed, two on each side of the pier.

Sailors in dress blues milled on quarterdecks with shiny brass ammunition shell casings used as supports for the fancy-laced white-roped boundries. Work continued on the mega pier.

We side-stepped workers and pallet after pallet of supplies. Forklifts roared, their exhaust fumes heavy in the air; conveyor belts whined and clicked as boxes were thrown on the belts and carried up to main decks. Orders were shouted by leading petty officers directing the working parties. Horns beeped and whistles sounded. Every move by machine or man had a purpose. The air was so tense it was almost physical.

Something was missing, I thought. Yes...yes...the laughter and banter among the sailors. But we had a war going on, right?

We sauntered past an eighteen-wheeler, another boxcar, the monster crane, on which a bell clanged occasionally when it had to move a bit. Boy, watch your toes! I thought with a smile.

Whoa! I suddenly thought, looking at the huge cement barricades that blocked the head of the pier. They were the same type of barriers that were used on highways. How did the big trucks ever manage to zigzag...Then I spotted a large crane-like forklift parked by the pier front that had to be used to move the barricades to allow railcars and eighteen-wheelers to get to the ships. M-16 toting security men dressed in combat gear inspected them.

And everything else that sought to come on the mega pier.

We crossed the street and started walking across a huge parking lot jam-packed with automobiles, mostly clunkers, only what the sailors could afford. *No bombs at Tom's*, I remembered from a used car ad in Norfolk. I grinned, seeing the Burger King in the distance.

"This bag, Wally Jenkins," Ernie said, pulling it from under his arm, "has---he unzipped the top and stuck his hand inside---"has a double bottom." He exposed a thick piece of cardboard. "Beer goes in, then the so-called bottom fits perfectly in place. I, ah...what's this?" He pulled out some short-stubbed Roman candles, a wad of firecrackers, bottle rockets, sparklers, and some cherry bombs. "Oh, brother!" He cursed a streak loudly, then said, "Forgot about these in the bottom!" Suddenly he looked about cautiously. He quickly stuffed the fireworks back in the bag, then wiped his brow with his free arm.

We both exchanged glances, knowing what the other thought: *To be caught with bomb equated items on base now would surely mean instant jail time. We would probably be charged as spies, too. Maybe even get shot on the spot!*

"Man, remind me to put this junk in the first trash can we come to!" He added, "Make sure there ain't no base police around when I do, too!"

I nodded as he zippered the bag up.

He cursed loudly again. "Damn zipper slipped off its tracks again. I'll just get rid of the whole thing," he said to himself.

With the bomb material out of sight, I breathed a sigh of relief. We quickened our pace. After crossing the busy street and going past Burger King, we slowed down a bit. I briefly noticed that the restaurant was cram-packed. Better them than me, I thought.

Passing a vacant lot, I observed a rust-colored stray cat licking his privates, one leg stretched straight up. Ernie saw it too.

"Boy, that's something I wished I could do," Ernie said, laughing.

"Oh, yeah?" I replied. "You'd probably make the cat mad and he'd clean your bilges with his claws."

"Funny, funny," Ernie said. "Reminds me of when a guy we called Ragbag found a goat. He and the goat got drunk and he took the goat back to his ship."

"Really," I said merely as a statement, not believing him.

"That's right. This is really a Navy no-shitter. Ragbag hid in the shadows on the pier until the third mate went to make his rounds. He snuck the goat ABOARD SHIP, THEN!"

"And just what did he do about the ordinary seaman that stood at the quarterdeck still on watch, knocked him out?"

"Humph! The seaman was his buddy. NO LIE!"

I shook my head in disbelief. "And just where did he put the goat?"

"In after steering. Goat crapped all over the place. Looked like brownish-black marbles all over the deck. Rolly-pollies, ya know? The first assistant engineer went ape when he undogged the door and went in to check after steering prior to getting underway the next day."

"What happened after that?" I asked, the bowling alley in sight.

"Dunno. End of story. Maybe they had GOAT STEAKS FOR NOON MEAL!" Ernie laughed, his head tilted skyward.

"Boy, I've heard of sea stories, but that one takes the anchor chain!"

"Whattsa matter, Wally Jenkins, GET YOUR GOAT?" Ernie slapped my shoulder, laughing like a snorting hog.

As I still shook my head, I looked back and saw the cat running across the field. Go, cat, go! I thought, before Ernie gets any ideas!

Suddenly Ernie said in a tight whisper, "Hey, hey, hey, police!"

"Okay," I said. "Let em look. We ain't done nothing."

Several police vehicles passed slowly by us, four men in the back of a pickup that had benches. Faces of granite, the men wearing helmets, scanned the area; two on the left, two on the right, weapons propped on their hips, muzzles up in the air.

I swallowed hard as they passed us.

Ernie let out a big breath, softly saying, "Damn a bear's ass! That was close. Think I have to clean my skivvies now!"

Two minutes later, we turned right, on the sidewalk that lead to the bowling alley steps.

I opened the door to the crack and bang of bowling balls hitting pins and the din of conversations. I held the door open until Ernie went past.

For the time to be 0945, the place was already getting crowded. We turned right and went to the snack bar. I bought the first round of beer and found a table near the bowlers. Ernie slipped the AWOL bag under the table and put his foot on it.

"Can't ditch it in here. Look at all the people!" he said.

We ship-talked a while about our Navy days, then Ernie sprang for the second beer. More shop talk and looking people over in the building. The third and fourth round of suds found us more relaxed.

"I ever tell you about my daddy's garden?" Ernie asked, wiping the rim of his glass with a finger.

"Do tell," I replied, smiling. Boy, was the beer good. I felt its warm glow in my stomach. I needed that.

"See, we…no…*he*…had one big garden year after year. Made me and my brother hoe it daily. I'm talking *acreage*! We used to get sick of hoeing… hoeing, hoeing. That is, until we discovered the warm July watermelons. We---"

"Yeah, I know. You guys raped them!"

"True, but that ain't the half of it. He could grow the biggest tomatoes too. I mean really big ones!" Ernie made a shape using both hands.

"And you raped them, too, I know." I wiped suds off my upper lip with the back of my right hand.

"But that ain't the half of it. Yes, we had big times with those tomatoes. My daddy asked us about them, who was it that kept getting in the tomato patch. 'Course we said we didn't know nothin'. Well, one day, he caught us and---"

"And he took a stick to both you and your brother!"

"No, not that."

"What, then? He pin a medal on you guys?"

"No! A fate worse than death itself!" He feigned sorrow and guilt as he placed a hand over his heart.

"What, then, pray tell?" I took a big mouthful of beer.

Ernie slapped his hand on the table and roared, "HE MADE US EAT EVERY ONE OF THEM TOMATOES!"

I spewed a thunderstorm of beer all over the place!

* * *

By noon the snack bar was getting really crowded, including every bowling lane, which I estimated to be forty lanes or maybe more. The wooden busting up of pins was amplified, along with the din of conversations. While a few put coins in the juke box, you could hardly hear it unless you were at a table close to the music.

I leaned to Ernie and asked, "Hey, what about this guy you were talking to the third mate about on the quarterdeck before we left the ship? Said you was going to beat his head in."

"Oh, yeah. That'd be Mr. Wollap. Jerry. He borrowed five-hundred dollars from me down in Charleston, South Carolina. We were good buddies, at least I thought. Right now it's been a year and he ain't sent me no money yet. See, we were on the *USS Glover T-AGFF 1*. He lives in a town near my hometown. You know, we thought we were blood brothers and all that crap. I trusted him totally. Even saw him once after that. Again he promised to repay me. Then I got orders to a West Coast ship. Word got back to him. Guess he thought he'd never see me again. Good-bye five-hundred bucks! I wrote him countless times but no reply. Oh, then my orders to the Hollywood coast got cancelled. But I don't think word got to him about that. I'll run into him some time, some place, then I'm gonna take five-hundred off his face and skull!"

"Jerry Wollap," I said. Name don't ring no bell." I had heard that over fifteen sealift ships were home-ported in Norfolk. They were in and out of port constantly. Couple this with all the clubs and snack bars on the world's largest Navy base, not to mention the hundreds of bars outside the main gate, and it was easy to see why it was unlikely to run into someone you knew. But it happens.

"What's he look like, this Jerry Wollap?"

"'Bout your height, but heavyset. Red hair. Has a goatee on a round face. Bulging gray eyes like a damn cat. No, like one of them weenie dogs with pop-out eyes."

"Apt description. If I ever spot him you'll be the first to know." I took a slug of yellow liquid, feeling it burn nicely all the way down. I belched, a hand over my mouth.

"See him once and you'll never forget that kisser!"

"Say," I said, elbows on the table. "You married? Must be. You wear a ring. What brings you back to a lonely sailor's life at sea?"

"We're separated. No divorce. Never. Too much involved. House, land, all that. So she lives in the house. I send some money. No questions asked. I tried living in town. Didn't work. Then my dog died. I said 'That's it! I'm going back to sea!' In short, the price of love is nothing but grief. End of story! Your reason, Wally Jenkins?"

"Well, first I wanted to get involved with *Desert Shield*. Now it's *Desert Storm* and I ain't seen no sand yet! Thankfully we, the *Kaiser*, us, me, you will depart Norfolk next week to go to the Med, transit the canal and go in to *Desert Storm*. I can hardly wait! Second, I got tired of lying, backstabbing civilians. I needed to be back close to my kind of people. Sealift was the closest I could get. But before this, some stupid civilian got greedy and started using my building and maintenance company I owned as a cover for her embezzling money from a bank. Crap went on for over three years before it was discovered, I found out later!

"'Course the FBI cleared me of any wrong doing, but still it was embarrassing, but most of all, insulting, to have to take a polygraph, you know, me a career serviceman. Married and have one son and one daughter, both teenagers. I hate the separation, but that's life. Thank God I have an understanding, loving, and faithful wife."

Ernie nodded knowingly.

We sat in silence, looking at the snack bar getting crowded with the noon rush. Then, looking at the lanes, I saw that almost all of the forty or so lanes had bowlers on them. Combine the hum of balls rolling down the polished wood and the clatter of balls busting up pins by the hundreds, it was no wonder we could hardly make out the music on the jukebox by the south wall.

Being a tinkler of words and stories, I always played the "What if" game. I pulled out the trusty notebook from my back pocket and jotted thoughts. I noted that there were a set of double glass doors that opened to a sidewalk and the vacant lot we had passed earlier. Then I listed some "what if's":

What if there was an explosion on the piers?

What if the bowling alley caught fire?

What if the place was robbed by a band of armed men?

What if some fool came in and started shooting the place up?

Could we make it to the door?

Would we---

I looked up at the last lane near the wall and saw a man walking toward the front. Humm, the floor there was more recessed than the alleys below us. I could only see him from the knees up. It was a maintenance route to the machines in back. There was a rather narrow door back there. They should have made the building bigger, I thought, grinning.

"Say," Ernie said, "whatcha writin', A BOOK?"

I laughed lightly. "Oh, just a habit of mine, takin' notes everywhere I go. No big deal. Ain't hardly used any of the ones I jotted years ago!"

Ernie nodded, then we both took another slug of beer.

I looked at Ernie seriously, leaning forward and slipping my notebook back in my rear pocket.

He must be a very lonely person, I thought. I felt sorry for him. Then again, what sailor isn't lonesome in some way? I sure felt this way.

"Well," Ernie said. "You'll get back home eventually. Me? I don't give a big rat's ass if I ever get back to Ohio or not!"

"Say, you---"I took a slug of beer and set the glass down "---what religion are you? You believe in Christ?"

"None. Well, actually...I believe in all religions. You know, to CYA. Well, that'd be CMA, in my case." He laughed heartedly.

I didn't even smile. I leaned closer to make sure he'd hear me over the noise and music. "Believing in Christ is the only way you'll ever have eternal life, Ernie. That's a fact."

"How so?"

"God's Word, the Bible."

"And what about the other religions, huh? The people!"

"They're wrong."

Ernie grimaced. "What about the Ten Commandments?"

"Believers of the New Testament live under grace, not the law of the Old Testament. The Commandments just show us we're all sinners, that's all. It's impossible to keep even one of them. God knows this. That's why He sent his son in to the world...to save sinners, not the world."

I was relieved that Ernie didn't mind talking about religion, especially the one and only true religion. Most sailors avoided the subject. But I also knew every one of them yearned for something spiritual. They knew the power of the sea, had witnessed it's awesomeness first hand. They knew something great and powerful controlled it.

"Looky here, Wally Jenkins, how can you talk this Jesus stuff while full of beer and one in your hand? Don't you feel guilty?"

"Not at all, buds. I live by the grace of God. While he holds our very breath in his hands, he knows we all live in a pig sty down here on earth. That's why he's so forgiving of us. Me? I'm just a sinner saved by grace."

I tapped Ernie's right hand.

"You know how long it'd take you to study all the thousands of religions of the world?"

"There's that many?"

I nodded. "The rest of your life! And who knows you'd even live that long? Then it'd be too late."

"Hey, speaking of the Ten Commandments, I have this here brother out in California who lives by every word in the Ten Commandments. Don't drink, smoke, curse, nothin'. Prays every day, too,"

"Lives exactly by them?" I asked, eyebrows raised.

"Absolutely. Scouts honor." Ernie raised his right hand, then put it to his chest.

"Well, I'm gonna give you a round trip plane fare to send to him. I want you to get him here...in person."

"Why you wanna do this, Wally Jenkins?"

"I never met an honest to goodness, pure one-hundred percent liar!" I quickly added, "No offense to you, Ernie."

He laughed lightly. "None taken, Wally Jenkins. So what's the deal with having this eternal life? I know you have to repent and be baptized first. My brother says so."

"No, you don't!"

"Huh?"

"Neither of them is necessary to have eternal life. Hey, and don't get rewards and inheritance mixed up, huh? Even a prayer of forgiveness won't get you eternal life. *Believe*, that's the secret word. *Believe*!

"Whatcha have that might be proof?"

"Hum, ah...the thief on the cross beside Jesus. If you recall...ask your brother, he'll tell you...he was a crook, a thief; he wasn't a Christian, that's for sure. And he had never been baptized, nor repented. Jesus asked him if he believed what he had told him and the thief said, 'Yes, my Lord.' And Jesus replied that the thief from that day forward would be in paradise with him."

"What else you got besides that?"

"Well, here's another taste of truth. You can ask your brother about it. The woman at the well whom Jesus met and explained about the living water of life, and asked the woman, hey, man, she was a whore...if she believed him about the living water of life. The harlot said, 'Yes.' At that instant, the woman had eternal life. Jesus even told her about the men in her life; that the one she was staying with now was not her husband. The woman's eyes almost popped out of her head hearing this! Eventually she realized that he *was* the Christ and believed in him. Hey, you've probably heard John 3:16 many times from your brother, huh?"

"How's that, Wally Jenkins?"

"That God so loved the world that he gave his only begotten son. That whoever, now get this word, *believes* in him shall not perish but has, at that moment of believing, has eternal life. It's so simple even a child can understand it. Bible says so, but it took this dumbass---"I pointed at myself "---sailor fifty years to realize this! Amazing, huh?"

Ernie's mouth turned down, but he at least nodded slightly.

"*Believing* in Christ alone for eternal life. Nothing else! Somewhere in the book of Proverbs in the Bible, it states, '*Trust in the Lord with all your heart and lean not on your own understanding.*' What part of that is not understandable? And would you ever accuse John 3:16 or even John 6:47 of being lies?" I poked at my chest, adding, "Not this old sailor. No, sir!"

"Hey, man, I drop ten or twenty dollars in that outside gift box by the base chapel steps once in a while. Gotta earn all the points I can muster!"

"Oops, no good, Ernie. Eternal life cannot be bought or earned. It's a free gift from God."

"I suppose that's in the Bible, too, huh?"

"Ephesians 2:8 and 9, I think. For grace you have been saved. And that not of yourselves. It is a free gift from God. You can't buy it or earn it. Eternal life is not a reward for the good we may do, so we can't take credit for it. Never! Otherwise it would no longer be a free gift. Also in---"

"ERNIE KEGAL, YOU OLD OHIO KNOTHEAD!" a voice roared like a cannon from somewhere in the crowd.

We looked to our left. A rangy man of about thirty dressed in a motorcycle jacket with chains and other garb common to biker people pushed a through group. When he was almost at our table, I saw he had on wrinkly-looking black trousers that looked like leather. He had long black hair tied in a ponytail, and sported a goat-tee on a congenial face with dark penetrating eyes. He appeared about ten years younger than me or Ernie.

Ernie's eye's beamed. He looked briefly at me as he got up, saying, "Randy Mussco from Brooklyn. We served together aboard *USS Jouett CG 29* out of San Diego." He stood just as Randy got to him. They embraced, slapping backs.

I smiled happily. It was always good to run across old friends, especially military people. I envied them both. The camaraderie among service people was unequal to its civilian counterparts. It was closer...like being kin, and it lasted until you took your last breath on this earth.

"Wally Jenkins, meet Randy Mussco," Ernie said, patting Randy on the shoulder. "Randy's a sealift person, too."

I stood and shook a warm friendly hand. "Pleased to meetcha, Randy."

"You still aboard the famous *USNS Comfort*, that floating hospital ship?" Ernie said, quickly adding, "Here, Randy, come alongside." Ernie pulled out a chair, patting its back.

"Nope, they fired me...I think." Randy laughed. "Tried to get friendly with some of the nurses!" He took the chair and sat. "I'm aboard that grocery store, *USNS Saturn T-AFS 10*. We just got back last week from a drug run."

I knew the drug run meant a trip to the Caribbean.

"I tell you, Wally Jenkins," Ernie said proudly, a hand still on Randy.

"This here's one of the best engineers that ever worked for me back when I was in the Navy. He might look like biker trash---"

"Thanks," Randy said, smiling.

"---but I guarantee you, he's one helluva snipe!"

"Hey, you ready for this?" Randy said as he looked around surreptitiously. He slowly pulled out a pint of whiskey from inside his leather jacket.

Oh, brother! I thought.

Randy slipped the bottle to Ernie under the table.

"Never turned it down. You remembered," Ernie said, whatever that meant between them. Looking about furtively, Ernie held the jug at table level, unscrewing the cap. The place was too crowded for anyone to give a rat's bean about the bottle. Truth be known, anyone of them would have taken a slug if they were offered.

Ernie took a long pull. He swallowed and made such an ugly face that even the devil would be frightened of.

Ernie quickly grabbed his beer and swallowed, chasing the burn going down his throat.

I winced. *Boilermakers*!

"'Kay, you're next," Randy said to me.

"Not for me, Randy," I replied, adding, "I learned my lesson years ago about them boilermakers. Beer only, thank you. Guy's gotta know his limitations, I say."

"Ch...chic...chicken!" Ernie managed to groan. He coughed and cleared his throat uselessly, his face red.

Me and Randy laughed.

"Round's on me, guys," I said standing. "Your flavor of beer, Randy?"

"Just like yours," he replied, indicating the empty cans on the table.

"You got it! But, man, look at that line up there. Back as quick as possible." I weaved past tables and people standing.

For some cryptic reason, I had a fleeting vision as I looked over at that below-ground-level narrow path that led back to that skinny door behind which the bowling machines were located. Odd, then the mumbled thought vanished. Hum...

Glancing back, I saw Ernie take another slug of whiskey. I felt my own throat burn! Man, he's gonna get blowed out of his skivvies 'fore long. We really need to be getting back to the ship. Oh, well, one more beer won't hurt. Smelling cooking hamburgers, onions and other grilling treats, I took my place in line and waited. I was on a mission. Beer!

Looking at the double glass doors on the side entrance, I spotted two pay phones on the wall near the jukebox, thinking I should call home to check on matters, but the loud talking, plus the music, plus the bowling pins busting up, it just wasn't conducive to be phone chatting now. Well, after this beer, I'd get Ernie back to the ship, then go back to the head of the pier and use one of the numerous pay phones there. Anyway, Linda often accused me of being hard of hearing, but I informed her, whether she liked it or not, that I had 20/20 hearing. With her being a registered nurse, I enjoyed saying dumb things just to hear her laugh. Oh, gee, I thought, it was horrible being away from Linda and our teenage boy and girl, Austin and Linda Kay. Life was so cruel at times. And I, like the base and the fleet sailors, felt the tension in the air, what with being at war …again, and missing our families and all. And some of us may not get back home at all!

Something had to break the tension and ease the stretched nerves, but… what?

Twelve minutes later, having seen Ernie down three more boilermakers, his face as red as flank speed firebricks in a boiler furnace glowing at 3,000 degrees, I thought, Oh, no, he's definitely consuming the fruit of a poisonous tree! I better watch him; get him back to the ship in one piece. That's what *shipmates* did, you know: *looked out for one another.*

At the counter, I hesitated about getting Ernie another beer. I grimaced and bought three beers anyway. One more and that's all! We had to be getting back to the ship. I was already a bit light-headed myself, like floating in a dream but knowing the world was still real around you. At least I could navigate, and I was glad we were fairly close to the *Kaiser*. It was a walk in the park.

No prob, Bob!

I laughed to myself as I circled all my fingers around the cold cans. I turned and started moving slowly through the crowd towards our table.

Can't let Ernie get out of hand, that's for sure, I thought.

And we can't forget his AWOL bag. And I wondered why he got so concerned with it being soaked with cigarette lighter fluid. It was probably dry by now anyway. Big deal.

I blew a small laugh as I weaved and twisted past tables and sailors. Nowadays you couldn't distinguish a merchant mariner from Navy people. Well, some you could by their hair style and gaudy civilian clothes.

Not like the old days…the Old Navy! I thought gloomily.

"Oops! 'cuse me," I said, bumping into someone. The man scowled at me. I smiled back. "Sorry."

Not very friendly! I thought, almost to our---

Suddenly Ernie stood up, pointing at the snack bar line. "YOU! YOU SOB!" he hollered. He started pushing and shoving through the crowd.

Whoa! I thought, placing the beer on the table. I looked at Randy Mussco my mouth agape.

"I'LL KILL YOU, JERRY WALLOP, YOU SNAKE IN A SHIT CAN!"

I felt my heart go to my toes. Oh, no, the guy who never paid him his $500 dollars!

The men in Ernie's wake started pushing and shoving, too. Several men were caught off guard as they had had their beer glasses to their lips. Elbows pushed the mugs up, cold beer spilling all in their faces.

By then Ernie was upon the red-haired, bulging-eyed Jerry Wallop. He jumped on him like a horse, taking him to the floor. More beer was spilled, again in numerous faces.

A barrage of yelling profanity erupted like a volcano vomiting red-hot lava. Hundreds of fists swung in the air connecting on jaws, heads and eyes.

Suddenly my neck stung as a fist came from somewhere. I fell to the floor. Down on all fours, I shook my head trying to regain my senses. Someone stepped on my right hand. I yanked it up, shaking it to relieve the pain. I looked around, seeing nothing but shoes and knees.

Several of the snack bar ladies screamed.

I got to my feet. I ducked several swings. The whole place was in an uproar! Tables turned over. Beer spilled everywhere.

A real donnybrook! Man alive, John Wayne needed to be here! Even Roy Rogers, Gene Autry and for sure, Randolph Scott and Tom Mix!

I looked for Ernie. Nowhere!

For a fleeting moment, I saw Randy Mussco going to general quarters on a few skulls, his fist hammering away. Smiling, he seemed to be enjoying himself. A few other men were grinning too.

Tension relieved!

Suddenly I felt instant pain. I hit the floor again. I rubbed my jaw. Angry? Yes! But I had to find Ernie and get the hell out of this place before the base police stormed the doors. I started crawling on all fours towards the snack bar.

No good, I thought. Can't see anything. Stupid!

Shoulders hunched, I got to my feet. I dodged a few fists, then grabbed a chair. I climbed on it and looked over the flailing arms and fists.

No Ernie!

I happened to look over on the bowling side where the shoes were issued. To my amazement, three men laughed, holding bowling balls up, poised on the carpet in the direction of the snack bar side. In unison, they took three steps and let the balls fly!

I looked where I thought Ernie had been. Then ten or twelve fighting men toppled over and out of sight in perfect harmony as three balls on the regular all alleys' made perfect strikes, the clatter of pins rumbling the air.

I felt giddy. I laughed. It was like an awesome dream.

Then my chair was knocked out from under me. I hit the floor hard just as the lights went out. Amazing. Just like in the movies! Where was John Wayne at a time like this?

Then the sound of police whistles pierced the air repeatedly. I knew they would start swinging clubs and hauling men out, while other officers would guard and nab attempts of escape at every door. This included the double glass side doors, next to the vacant lot where we had commented about the rust-colored cat licking itself.

I had to find Ernie, and quickly!

Dodging legs and shoes, I made my way toward the snack bar again. I only went a short distance when I cracked heads with someone. We both looked up at the same instant.

"Ernie! Thank God," I said.

"Whooo…whooo…who are…are…you?" Ernie slurred, eyes glassy and terribly blood-shot.

"It's me, Ernie. Wally Jenkins. We gotta get outta here and fast!"

"Where…ah…where are we? I think a dog pissed on me!" Every word was an effort and slurred.

"Never mind that! We gotta get outta---"

Suddenly I thought of the below-the-knee-maintenance walkway to the machines in back by the wall. With the lights out it was pitch black over there. Only the outside light streamed in from the doors. Shadowing any brightness, the hundreds of bodies blocked further seeing down the bowling lanes.

Just what we need. Perfect! I thought.

"Way…waynt. Gotta…get…my…beer!"

"Forget that!" Then I remembered. "Wait here. I'm gonna get your AWOL bag. Stay put!"

I eased back to our table and grabbed the bag. I put the handle between my teeth so I could crawl. "Follow me, Ernie!" I said the best I could. "I have your bag," I mumbled loudly.

"What…bag?"

"Just stay on my heels!"

"Ri…right. Let's get a beer first."

"Shuddup! C'mon!" I motioned quickly with a hand.

Dodging legs and shoes again, we made our way to the maintenance walkway. I kept looking back to ensure Ernie was following. Several times bodies fell over our backs while Ernie kept mumbling he wanted another beer. Then he kept asking, "What bag? What bag? Where's my beer? What bag?" Then he said, "Hey…you…Wal…Wally…Smith. That cat…just scratched my…leg."

151

Feeling my way, I crawled down the steps. I turned and pulled Ernie down the three steps. Together we groveled toward the narrow door in back. I kept groping a hand in front of me when I felt we were near. Finally, I felt wood, then the door knob. I turned it and we crawled in. I shut the door behind us. It was pitch black. I took the bag handle from my teeth.

"Gimme your lighter, Ernie!"

"'Kay."

I found his hand and retrieved the *Zippo*. With the door shut, it was safe to fire it up. I did. The flame danced on the wall.

"Gotta be a door here somewhere," I said.

"Wait…I for…forgot something," Ernie mumbled.

"I got your bag right here. Don't worry," I said.

"Wh…what…bag? For…forgot my beer." Ernie started laughing for no reason.

I just grimaced, looking for that door. We…ah, yes! I thought, seeing our outlet. Ask and you shall receive! I thought, smiling. I pushed the door open. Bright sun spilled in.

I squinted, holding an arm to my forehead.

"Whoa…you…I forgot something."

"I gottcher bag right here."

Ernie started his laughing gig again.

I pulled him outside and shut the door. I had no idea where we were. There were buildings and objects I didn't recognize. I eased back to the bowling building and slowly peered around the corner. Busy way up there, definitely *yes* outside the double glass doors by the vacant lot, but they would not see us. Even if they did, the police would assume that we were workers or something. No problem. I knew the pier was to our right. South. I pulled on Ernie and we started walking. He staggered badly so I took hold of him, my right arm over his shoulders like we were just chums, walking and minding our own business under the January sun.

An *A-6E Intruder*, wheels down, came roaring our way on the much used landing vector to the Naval Air Station to our backs. As before, the whining jet commanded my attention. I looked up. Even with my beer-soaked skull, the sight and sound made my chest swell in pride at being an American. It was the sound and sight of red, white, and blue; and Freedom. So close was it, that I saw the pilot a second or two. I waved my left hand at him, but he probably didn't see me.

After we had walked a block or so, Ernie said, "Egy…Egyptians."

"What, Egyptians? What are you talking about, Ernie?"

"Wha…wha…what you, you said back…there." He thumbed the air over his head repeatedly. "About…ma…may…mace?"

152

My brow furrowed. *Mace?* Man alive, ole Ernie's brain was fried!

We walked past one building, then a smaller one with a narrow space between it and the one we passed.

"Hey, weri'sig...gotta...gotta pee. Hole on, willya?"

I let loose of his shoulders and he stumbled to the structures and disappeared. Two seconds later, he reappeared. "Gimme...ma...bag...huh?" He laughed like a pig snorting. "Got...have...we, uh...well" He laughed, then vanished again.

Waiting, arms folded across my chest, I grimaced shaking my head. Oh, well...

Several minutes passed, then a cat screamed and growled, then screamed again.

"Gotcha, you sumbitch!" Ernie stepped back in sight holding his AWOL bag closed up by the zipper.

I remembered that he had said earlier that the zipper gets snagged or caught occasionally.

"Now just what are you going to do with that?" I asked, indicating the bag.

The cat continued its awful growl and whine while it fought uselessly to escape. Ernie hoisted the bag and pressed it against his chest, his face turning red with the effort. "Go ahead, sc...scream and claw all you want. I gotcha now!" He laughed and laughed.

I reasoned that the fabric was thick enough that the cat's claws couldn't penetrate it. I looked at Ernie. "Just what do you plan to do with that damn thing, huh?"

"Gonna...take...going to take it back to the ship for El...Elmo. He loves ca...cats." Ernie started his laughing gig again.

"Well, I ain't gonna be no part in getting that animal aboard ship!" I said adamantly.

"Not...no...not to, Egyptians!" Ernie said, his mirth continued. "And mace, 'member?"

I turned and started walking again. Ernie soon followed. Egyptians? Mace? What does that mean? He's just goofy now. Too many boilermakers!

A short time later, I looked to my right. Burger King was a block away. Crowded as usual, I reasoned as we crossed the street and entered the same monster parking lot with its many clunkers resting like dogs patiently waiting for their masters. *No Tom's at bombs*, I thought. Hey, did my muddled mind confuse matters about that used car ad in Norfolk. Oh, well...

Oh, no, I thought moments later.

Just how does Ernie think he's gonna get past the guards at the head of the pier? They inspect every container coming on the pier. *No exceptions*!

I hoped that the cat would somehow escape…soon!

The ships' masts sure looked wonderful to me in the not too distance as we crossed the parking lot. Before crossing the street, a wad of sailors and mariners stormed down the street and hurried across the road and got in the long line. They laughed and made jokes about the bowling alley. I figured they must be the fortunate escapees from the melee. With that battalion of sailors crammed in at the bowling joint, some were sure to break free, I thought. Good for them. But now I was worried about how Ernie was going to smuggle that cat in the bag past the rifle-toting guards.

A Navy *A-7 Corsair* strike aircraft, its jet whining loudly, flew low en route to the Naval Air Station. I paused and looked up. Cheering, the sailors, mariners and pier workers showed their appreciation looking up and waving hats or hands.

Crossing the street, I saw we had to get in a long line that bordered the cement barricades.

About hip high, there were two barricades that butted ends, forty feet before we had to produce our Military Sealift Command ID cards for inspection. I held Ernie by the arm as we took our spot in line. The cat must have exhausted its strength. There was no movement of the bag. Good.

Peace at last.

I smiled and waved slightly, even said, "Hi" to the men who had to turn back on the other side of the barricade and walk to the left turn on the opening of the inside barricade, then repeat the process two more times as they zigzagged to the open pier.

"Shhhhh!" Ernie breathed to the passing men as he leaned over and dropped the AWOL bag on the other side of the barricade. The guys nodded and smiled, knowing he was going to pick it up after passing the guards. They themselves loved to trick the guards too. They passed in silence.

"Ernie!" I said in a tight whisper. He only laughed and slapped my back. I grimaced and nodded as I pulled out my ID card. Well, if he had to lean over to retrieve the bag, he would have surely fallen over the barricade, I reasoned. Helping Ernie find his ID, we eased forward.

"Yessir, Sarge, sir," Ernie slurred, standing at weaving attention in front of the Marine guard. He saluted awkwardly.

"Shuddup, Ernie!" I said, then quickly to the guard, "Too many boilermakers. I'm taking him to the ship." I produced my ID. The guard hinted a smile, but then went straight-faced. He nodded approval. I shoved Ernie to the right, towards the second barricade starting our zigzag walk that would lead us to the open pier.

Suddenly Ernie tripped and fell. He moaned some profanity.

I leaned down and picked him up. Engaging in chum mode again, I put my arms across his shoulders and guided him along.

"Almost fourteen hundred hours, Ernie. Time for the rack soon, huh?" I said, hoping his boilermaker flooded brain would forget about the bag when we came to it.

"I want another beer!" he slurred, mouth drooling.

"No, not that. We're on our way back to the ship now. Don't forget...we have that rusty midnight watch again tonight. We gotta get some sleep!" I felt his body going limp. I hoisted him upright again as we came in sight of the bag to Ernie's right. With my left hand, I reached across my chest and took Ernie by the chin. I turned his head my way. "Say, explain to me about this Egyptian and mace stuff again, Ernie." I heard laughter on our heels as other men followed.

Only partly hearing Ernie, I looked at the bag and saw movement. Hum! The cat was re-energized! Well, he had eight more lives left! I thought, seeing part of his face pushing against the partly opened zipper. Well, if he gets out, he'll head straight for the guard entrance...hopefully. I started to smile, then went frozen faced as I saw two of the men behind us thump their lit cigarettes towards the bag. One bounced off the barricade, ambers flying a moment before the butt settled a quarter of an inch away from the lighter-soaked material. The other butt rolled under part of the bottom which was sticking up a bit.

Oh, brother! I thought, letting loose of Ernie's chin. If the bag catches fire, it'll flame up instantly and go to ashes. I didn't even want to think about the firecrackers, Roman candles, bottle rockets, and the cherry bombs under the false bottom! Nosir, they didn't exist!

"'C'mon, Ernie. We have to make tracks! And fast!" I held him tighter as I quickened our pace.

"Huh?" Ernie mumbled.

"'Cuse me, 'cuse me, 'cuse me," I said as we passed people ahead of us.

"Wasss th...russ?" Ernie kept asking.

"Shhhh!" I said in his left ear.

Within seconds we were going down the open pier. I breathed a sigh of relief. But this was short lived!

Suddenly a barrage of profanity came from the guys behind us. Then various men roared:

"WHATTA HELL WAS THAT?"

"A BIG RAT!"

"IT'S A BEAVER!"

"NO, A RABBIT!"

"NO, IT HAD A TAIL!"

"IT'S A SCRUBBIN' CAT!"

At that moment, I felt it run between my legs. Wasn't no way I was going to drop Ernie and run after the animal and claim it was ours. No, sir!! No, the cat had to run its course. Well, it would eventually slow down and rest, and someone would pet it, maybe give it food, and take it home…perhaps, I reasoned.

Boy, was I ever wrong!

The cat ran down the pier.

First attack was on the conveyer belt operator, his hand on the speed control knob. He let out a yell as the cat scratched his back and shoulders. This caused him to push the control to full speed. The workers on the ship laughed at the sight until the cat jumped on the conveyer belt and headed their way at flank speed on top of the hundred-pound sacks of sugar the ship was loading.

Only four men managed to escape the cat's claws. Jumping on three shoulders, the cat boarded the ship in a run on the Spruance-class destroyer, heading aft towards the quarterdeck. Hot on its tail, four of the workers took off after the cat, two with spanner wrenches in their hands.

The men on the pier hollered warnings, a few laughing. The conveyer belt operator had his shirt off looking at the red streaks across his shoulders.

The quarterdeck Petty-Officer-of-the Watch saw the cat coming and assumed a stopping position, hands spread out like his legs and partly squatting. The OOD, a boot Ensign, took a double look at the trouble coming their way. He pushed off from the lifelines where he had stood, elbows on the lines, and tried to beat the animal to his watch stander.

Brooking no slack in his speed, the cat leaped and landed for a split second on the Petty Officer-of-the-Watch's head. The sailor screamed. He threw his hat off his head and felt his wounds. His face turned to instant anger. He drew the .45 pistol from its white scabbard and took awkward aim at the cat dashing to the ship's port side. The OOD was on him in a flash obviously shouting, "NO!" He grabbed the pistol arm and threw it skyward just as flash of fire exploded from the barrel. Then both men ran to the port side, looking forward where the animal had obviously run.

The cat reappeared running back to starboard in the open mid-ships passageway. It proceeded aft again. At the sight of the same spanner-wrench-wielding-workers coming his way again, he turned and ran forward. At the first ladder, the feline dashed up the steps and continued his forward movement.

At the sound of gunfire, the other ship quarterdeck watches ran to the side of their ship, looking desperately to where the sound had erupted.

All work on the pier had stopped. A few ducked behind crates, thinking they were being shot at.

The conveyer belt workers rolled in stitches because they knew what had happened.

High above the workers, the crane operator roared in mirth. Why not? He had a bird's eye view of the action below.

The Spruance-class cat was now at the forward work station where pallets of hundred pound sacks of flour were being unloaded. All the tie-down straps had been cut loose for ease of off-loading the pallet. When the cat saw the workers by the pad, there was no more going forward. In an effort to break his run, he leaped on the shoulder of the boatswain's mate in charge and made clawing jumps from the backs and shoulders of the other men. He finally leaped on the unsecured sacks of sugar.

The crane operator busted a gut, laughing. In mirthful pains, his feet accidentally hoisted the pallet where the cat had drawn himself up hissing at the sailors. Up they went, flour and cat.

For a fleeting moment, I looked back at the people behind us. They had all stopped walking and stood galvanized, looking at the pallet up in the air.

But my mind was not on them. It was what I saw coming up from behind the barricades.

Black smoke!

The AWOL Bag had caught on fire!

I held my breath, knowing what was coming next…and very soon!

Still laughing uncontrollably, the crane operator's foot must have moved elsewhere as the pallet, flour, and cat swung toward the pier. It went past the statue of men looking up. It swung over the railroad boxcars to the 01 level of the Spruance destroyer, identical to the one it had departed from across the pier. At the split-second pause in the momentum before it started to swing back from where it came, the cat seized the iota of time and jumped off. With no workers around, the cat stopped, trying to get a sense of direction.

Again the crane operator's foot must have slipped. The pallet lowered in mid-air, heading toward the open boxcar doors.

Suddenly there was an explosion, then popping noises as the fireworks in the burning AWOL bag ignited.

The pallet of flour bags swung inside the boxcar. The cable grew instantly rigid. The pallet stopped inside the car as flour bags rocketed out the other side. Hundred pound bags burst open, hitting the doors going air borne. Other bags hit the conveyer belt rig while others slammed against the side of the Spruance-class destroyer. A snow storm of flour cascaded down on the pier workers.

At the sound of the fireworks, the cat rocketed aft.

Suddenly the Roman candles ignited. Red, orange, blue, green, and yellow sparks streaked the air above the ships. Then the cherry bombs exploded.

BOOM!

BOOM!

BOOM!

BOOM!

The whole Norfolk Navy Base was in the picture now, including the Naval Air Station.

From the first Spruance-class destroyer, the boot Ensign didn't wait on his Petty Officer-of-the-Watch to perform the task, nor did he inform his CDO (Command Duty Officer). He ran to the ship's 1MC loudspeaker. He grabbed the mouthpiece and held it to his lips, his other hand ready to sound the general quarters alarm. He pressed the mike button. The little red light came on, indicating the system was activated. You could actually hear him breathing over every speaker. He shouted nervously:

"NOW GENERAL QUARTERS! GENERAL QUARTERS! GENERAL QUARTERS! ALL HANDS MAN YOUR BATTLE STATIONS. THIS IS NOT A DRILL! REPEAT, THIS IS NOT A DRILL! ENGINE ROOM. MAKE ALL PREPARATIONS FOR EMERGENCY GETTING UNDERWAY! And he then pressed the all too familiar sound every sailor knows. The general quarters alarm:

DONG! DONG! DONG! DONG! DONG! DONG! DONG! DONG! DONG!

By then red and blue overhead lights of police cars, fire trucks, and other emergency vehicles flashed like a circus at the head of the pier. Uniformed people jumped from units, weapons drawn.

In the harbor, blue lights flashing, several Harbor Police boats arrived, followed by numerous Coast Guard patrol boats. Even a large Coast Guard cutter was standing by, topside gun manned, along with M-16-toting crew members.

Oh, brother! I thought. Oh, brother! Oh, brother! That's all I could think of. I hoisted Ernie back up by the shoulders. I half-ran, half-walked down the pier, half-dragging Ernie.

Every ship docked at the pier followed the first Spruance-class destroyer's decision. Ships' 1MCs' came alive with the general quarters alarm, including preparations for emergency getting underway. Up and forward sailors ran on the starboard side of the ships, while down and aft others ran on the port side of the ships. Soon big gun mounts swiveled, testing their movability; then barrels moved up and down.

Oh, brother! Oh, brother! Oh, brother! I thought, and quickened our pace even more. Sirens wailed from the distance as they headed for the pier, overhead lights flickering or flashing.

Suddenly out of nowhere, four *F-14 Tomcats* swooped down, one right after the other like angry wasps. They zipped low over the pier as though they were looking over the situation below. Instead of landing ahead as usual, they rocketed skyward, their rumbling vibrating the air.

Almost to the *Kaiser,* I heard another all too familiar sound filling the air. One of the outboard docked destroyers sounded three long heavy blasts from its whistle.

WHOOOOOOOP! WHOOOOOOOOP! WHOOOOOOOOOP!

The roar indicated that the ship was free from the pier---BEWARE---and was backing down. Get out of the way!!

Damn! I thought. And NO harbor tug to assist them as required.

Oh, brother! Oh, brother! Oh, brother! Oh, brother! Oh, brother.

Exhausted, but almost to the *Kaiser,* I stopped at the edge of the wharf. I eased Ernie down and leaned him against the two foot bulkhead that bordered the pier edge. He was babbling something I couldn't understand. Bending forward, I put my hands on my knees, breathing deeply as I tried to catch my breath. Looking up, I saw black smoke issuing from *Kaiser's* funnel. I reasoned that the big diesel engines had been started. Line handlers were running to their stations aboard ship.

"I...ua...ah...ah think...ahma gonna puke!" Ernie said, positioning himself on his knees and turning toward the harbor.

"You go right ahead," I said. I stepped behind him and held him by the belt and trousers so he wouldn't go overboard.

Several minutes passed.

I looked toward the head of the pier. What a mess! What a mess! Oh, brother!

"Hey," Ernie said, wiping the spittle from his mouth with a handkerchief. I let loose of his trousers. "Did...ah...did I miss anything?"

I turned and looked at him, hands on my hips. "No, Ernie, not a thing." I paused, then said, "Even your bag's gone. History. Oblivion. Never to be seen again." I knew he was still woozie-headed, very much inebriated, but in a limbo state of mind; if that can be understood even in my own beer-bloated mind.

Ernie's mouth ballooned out several times. He sighed heavily. "I...wass that about Egyptians you said. Mace was something like free? Oh, I do... don't...know. Forget it."

I shook my head. "Dunno, either," I replied. This set me to thinking that whatever it was that I had said earlier to Ernie, he remembered it. No ma...

mace…mace…Humm, what rhymes with mace? Then it hit me. I felt my eyes widen. "Grace, mace!"

I quickly squatted and looked him in the face. "Grace? Grace? Grace? Do you mean free grace, like in the Bible I was telling you about earlier?"

"Ye…ye…yeah. That's what I said all"---he hiccupped"---all…all along. E…E…E…Egyptians!"

"Ephesians? Do you mean Ephesians?"

"Ah…ah…ah do. And that's "---he pointed a shaky finger at me---"what ah…sa…sa…said all along…too."

I leaped up, smiling at the sky, hands spread wide from my hips. "He understands! He understands! Thanks, Lord! Thanks for looking out for us ding-batters down here, especially sailors."

I put my hands at my sides and looked at the drunk merchant marine engineer. *My shipmate.* I want him to understand even better after he sobers up, I thought. *Including me!*

Well, at least the seed had been planted!

Yessir! I smiled happily, then turned and looked at the pier action. My grin vanished!

Oh, brother! Oh, brother!

We didn't start what looked like World War III on the Norfolk Virginia Navy Base.

Honest.

All me and Ernie wanted to do was to go ashore and have a few beers at the base bowling alley snack bar. Calm, and nice and quiet.

Honest.

The End

Author Bill Sneed in Corpus Christi, Texas
With daughter, Alison, who is 37 yrs old now!

Other interesting (?) info about my military career that I am sure millions of service people can relate to. Thanks for your viewing, and I welcome comments:

horsedogbill@gmail.com

And be sure to visit my website for other military-related subjects.

www.writerbillusn.com

If you would like your military info and photos
on my website, please let me know, and
give me your written permission, too .

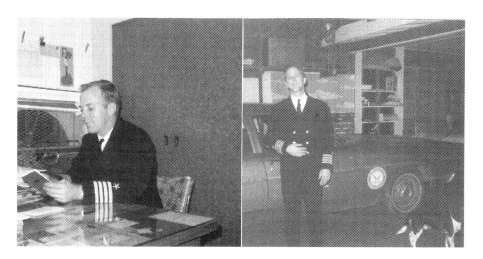

No, I am NOT a Navy Captain. But I wore their uniforms before they did. Here's how:

In July of 1969 when I was a Navy Recruiter in Corpus Christi, Texas, Neil Armstrong and Buss Aldrin walked on the moon. It was a First for mankind. They were promoted to full captains, USN, on their return trip back to earth. I met the Houston Navy Recruiter in Victoria, considered the half-way mark. The Houston Recruiter gave me their dress blue uniforms and I delivered them to NAS Corpus for their four stripes to be put on the uniforms. After they were completed I brought them home where my sweetie wife "Tootie" took photos of me with their coats on. Big deal, huh? Well, I thought it was. I wore their uniforms Before they did. History in the making, right?

I just can't have this book published without mentioning my sea-going Dad, who was serving in Vietnam before I was! His merchant ship was contracted to haul cement for runways. After his death, I wrote a book-sort-of about my merchant marine father. A feature news article was written afterwards. The feature is *after the following news article of 1964* about my Dad's Vietnam exploits:

Willie E. SNeed - 2ND ENG.
1907 - 1986
S. MERCHANT MARINE
1964
Galveston County Newspaper

War in Viet Nam Real for Sneed

164 —

"You don't have to be told there's a war over here." Thus writes W. E. Sneed of League City.

Sneed is not a serviceman. He's not even a young man. But he is serving his country in Viet Nam.

W. E. Sneed

25 NOV 1965
KAoh su ng
with sailors

from Submarine
USS SALMON
SS 573
VIETNAM?

A merchant seaman for the past 30 years, he left the states in July aboard the merchant ship S. S. Warm Springs for a normal foreign run to Calcutta, India. He expected to return by October.

While in Saigon in the early part of October, the ship was contracted for military purposes by the U. S. government.

"At night you can see flares, guns going off and bombing," he writes. "Even in the engine room aboard ship, you can still hear the wartime sounds ashore above the noise of the engines and boilers."

Sneed's son, William, was home recently on leave from the Navy. Of his dad's Viet Nam duty, he spoke of how extremely proud he was. "It even goes beyond the word 'proud'," he said. "To

think that Dad, at his age and a veteran of World War II, is again at the service of his country.

"Yet, there are boys and men in this country roaming the streets rioting, causing trouble and simply being useless to their own nation," he said.

A look of sorrow creased his young brow as he continued, "I wear my uniform with great pride but I feel uneasy about the fact that I am in the Navy and safe in the states while my Dad is in Viet Nam. It should be just the other way around."

William, who has been in the Navy for three years, has made several foreign trips including Cuba and Italy. He recently volunteered for duty in Viet Nam. His home port is Boston, Massachusetts.

Meanwhile, Sneed's wife and William's mother, Lovie, keeps the home fires burning awaiting her two men. Of course, she's had to change homes since her husband left. They had their home up for sale before Sneed left and its recent sale forced the move.

However, her son was home to help with the actual moving and several good friends rallied to her aid.

She echoed her son's words that "everyone should salute and say prayers for all in Viet Nam, military and merchant seamen alike."

Dad - Willie Sneed with
Jeff Moore QMC, Jack Aldridge
MMC, Jerry Alridge MM1 &
Dick Smith HM2

Served aboard over 100
MERChant Ships during A
SEPT. 14. 1939 33 YEAr Sea Service.

William E. Sneed

All in the *Family*

The Marshall News Messenger
Sunday, November 2, 1997

Men dedicate lives to service

ONE MERCHANT SEAMAN
WILLIE E. SNEED
2nd. ENGINEER
1907 - 1986
ONE NAVY SON...

By ANGELA WEATHERS
News Messenger

Being a man of the sea has its ups and downs, but a life of service is the life for three generations of the Sneed family.

"I remember seeing Dad go to sea in the middle '40s, during the invasion of North Africa in World War II, and saying that is when his hair started turning gray," said Bill Sneed, a retired 30-year Navy veteran who followed in the footsteps of his father, Willie Sneed.

"He said he tried not to think about the ships blowing up around, tried not to think about it, but death was always imminent," Sneed said. "In 33 years, he served on 85 ships."

Sneed jokingly said he didn't even know this country had an army until he had served in the Navy for five years. His father's choice in careers had a lot of influence on his decision to become a merchant marine, he said.

During the Vietnam conflict, Sneed served three or four different tours of duty as a steam engineer in the Navy.

"We sat off the coast and lobbed shells, star shells, that brighten things up like daylight," he said. "A few times shells hit the ship, but we backed up the DeNang River and received some enemy fire. We could scoot out if the enemy fire got too bad because the Captain chose to back in, a prudent decision."

After his retirement, Sneed found himself under enemy fire again, serving as third assistant engineer for the Military Sealift Command during Desert Storm.

"We were carrying 5 million gallons of aviation fuel on the Henry J. Kaiser," Sneed said. "We didn't have to worry about being hit, because if we got hit, we wouldn't know it. We'd disintegrate."

Finding himself in a combat zone with hostile fire all around at the age of 50 was a little ironic, Bill thought.

The late Willie Sneed and his son are not the only Sneeds to live through hostile fire. Alan Sneed, Bill's oldest son, returned from Spain and war-torn Bosnia in March of 1996.

Alan is now a steelworker, who joined the Navy 4 1/2 years ago, and is currently stationed with the 20th Navy Construction Regiment in Gulfport, Miss., his father said. During his duty, Alan was promoted to "E-4" a designation given to only 26 steelworkers. He also was selected as "Sailor of the Quarter" during the first part of 1997.

Sneed said his younger son, Aaron, 23, tried to enlist, but couldn't because he is allergic to bee stings.

"It just about killed him," the elder Sneed said. But, Aaron overcame the disappointment to become valedictorian of the Kilgore College Police Academy after graduating from Marshall High School in 1993.

Aaron, a state licensed and commissioned police officer, currently on reserve, is awaiting a civil service test that hopefully will put him on the police force full time, Bill Sneed said.

"It makes me feel great, like a true, blue-blooded American," to have my sons carry on the tradition of service to the public. He said fear (of punishment) and common sense kept both of his sons straight and out

ALAN, BILL AND AARON SNEED are pictured in front of the flag that graced the casket of their grandfather, Willie Eugene Sneed, in 1986. Sneed started the tradition of service as Merchant Marine as a lieutenant during World War II and the Vietnam conflict.

of trouble, creating a perpetuating effect from father to son – the tradition of the American way of life.

"When the kids were real young, Aaron wouldn't even come to me, he didn't know me because the ships I served on would be gone six to eight months at a time," Sneed said. "My wife Charlotte would keep the home fires burning, continually praying and worrying."

Accepting the consequences of his career choice, whether good or bad, meant for Sneed putting his nose to the grinder, he said.

Sneed currently works as a security guard at Texas State Technical College in Marshall. He also is an aspiring author, who has written and published a journal "One Merchant Seaman ... One Navy Son", a book about his father, written after Willie Sneed's death in 1986. He has also received praise from the American Literary

Services and Mary M. Lee, English instructor for TSTC and Panola College, for another novel he wrote .

Editorial director Robert Boyce of the American Literary Services wrote Sneed in September, asking for the rest of his manuscript to "Black Oil Chief, USN." Boyce said Sneed's manuscript has excellent market potential.

Lee said she approached the manuscript hesitantly, but could not wait to finish it, reading all she had during one weekend, horrified at having to wait until Monday to get the rest of the book.

"Bill Sneed's book is a book that I would assign without qualms to my class. I would also give it to my 88-year-old mother knowing she, too, would enjoy it," Lee said. "My husband, an ex-Navyman, has read it and found it to be technically accurate as well as most enjoyable."

'There is only one cure for Seasickness - To sit on the shady side of an old church in the country.' John Lubbock 'or be a Seabee!' Bill Sneed!

William "Alan" Sneed
3rd Generation of Sneed Family in US Navy

As you can see, I am very proud of not only my merchant marine dad, but both of my boys as well. William "Alan" saw action in Bosnia, while my youngest son, Charles "Aaron" saw action on the streets fighting criminals as a police officer. As mentioned also, I am equally proud of our daughter, Charlotte "Alison", who had military experience in Scotland and Florida during her earlier marriage. You can see that they are referred to by their middles names: Alison, Alan, and Aaron.

Now, back to my efforts to get a transfer to a ship that was going to Vietnam back in 1966:

Through some connections and my urgent transfer request, I was transferred from the *USS Compton DD 705*, home-ported in Boston, Mass. It was a reserve trainer ship (voted my favorite ship of my 20 yr Navy career). I reported aboard a Vietnam bound destroyer just short of departing Newport, R.I. This fine ship was the *USS Dyess DD 880*.

I got to Vietnam just as my Dad's ship had returned to the States. You'll note in the photo with the beer drinkers, that my Dad really favored service people. If you ever walked into a bar with him inside, your money was no good. He would buy every round!

And Dad wasn't afraid of the Viet Cong (Charlie) No, sir! . I had a cousin in-country there. Dad's ship was anchored in Siagon Harbor. He went ashore and took a taxi cab way out in the damn boonies looking for his nephew!!! Man, can you beat that? He could have been killed very easily. And, yes, he did locate my cousin. Needless to say, but they had a great visit. Boy, was my cousin ever surprised at the sight of his Uncle Bill in of all places, the hot deadly jungles of Vietnam!! The rather infrequent times that my cousin and I have the chance to visit, he still marvels at the story about my dad visiting him in Vietnam!!

REPORT OF ENLISTED PERFORMANCE EVALUATION
NAVPERS 792 (Rev. 6-59)

| | OF REPORT |
| 17 NOV 64 | To 16 MAY 65 |

| NAME (Last, First, Middle) | SERVICE NO. | RATE ABB. | PRESENT SHIP OR STATION |
| SNEED, William Earl | 511 25 18 | BT2 | USS COMPTON (DD-705) |

INSTRUCTIONS

1. For each trait, evaluate the man on his actual observed performance. If performance was not observed, check the "Not Observed" box.
2. Compare him with others of the same rate.
3. If the major portion of his work has been outside his rate or pay grade

during this reporting period, evaluate him on what he did. Describe what he did in the "Comments" section.
4. Pick the phrase which best fits the man in each trait and check left or right box under it. (Left box is more favorable.)

1. PROFESSIONAL PERFORMANCE: His skill and efficiency in performing assigned duties (except SUPERVISORY)

| NOT OBSERVED | Extremely effective and reliable. Works well on his own. | Highly effective and reliable. Needs only limited supervision. | Effective and reliable. Needs occasional supervision. | Adequate, but needs routine supervision. | Inadequate. Needs constant supervision. |
| ☐ | * | X | | | * | * |

2. MILITARY BEHAVIOR: How well he accepts authority and conforms to standards of military behavior.

| NOT OBSERVED | Always acts in the highest traditions of the Navy. | Willingly follows commands and regulations. | Conforms to Navy standards. | Usually obeys commands and regulations. Occasionally lax. | Dislikes and flouts authority. Unseamanlike. |
| ☐ | * X | | | | * | * |

3. LEADERSHIP AND SUPERVISORY ABILITY: His ability to plan and assign work to others and effectively direct their activities.

| NOT OBSERVED | Gets the most out of his men. | Handles men very effectively. | Gets good results from his men. | Usually gets adequate results. | Poor supervisor. |
| ☐ | * | X | | | * | * |

4. MILITARY APPEARANCE: His military appearance and neatness in person and dress.

| NOT OBSERVED | Impressive. Wears Naval uniform with great pride. | Smart. Neat and correct in appearance. | Conforms to Navy standards of appearance. | Passable. Sometimes careless in appearance. | No credit to the Naval Service. |
| ☐ | * | X | | | * | * |

5. ADAPTABILITY: How well he gets along and works with others.

| NOT OBSERVED | Gets along exceptionally well. Promotes good morale. | Gets along very well with others. Contributes to good morale. | A good shipmate. Helps morale. | Gets along adequately with others. | A misfit. |
| ☐ | * | X | | | * | * |

6. DESCRIPTION OF ASSIGNED TASKS

P.O. In charge of Fwd Fireroom. Stands top watch and coordinates all repair work in his space

7. EVALUATION OF PERFORMANCE

SNEED's performance is extremely effective and reliable. He is a conscientious worker and inspiring to his men. No sailor has greater loyalty for the Navy and is willing to go to the extent that this man will to help his shipmates. His leadership greatly improved the appearance and performance of the forward fireroom.

I was Duty Master @ Arms on this cold night. The drunk sailor was standing on a log-like fender between ships!

*8. THESE ITEMS MUST BE JUSTIFIED BY COMMENTS IN ADDITION TO THOSE IN ITEM 7 ABOVE

When duty calls for a quick decision and immediate action, this man will always be at the scene, ready to help. On the evening of 23 May 1965, SNEED jumped into the 47°F harbor water of Halifax, Nova Scotia, without hesitation, to save a shipmate. SNEED is the kind of a sailor who can be counted on at all times, no matter what the job may be. The Navy can always be proud to have such a man in its ranks.

| X SEMI-ANNUAL | ☐ TRANSFER | ☐ OTHER | 16 MAY 65 | W. J. SNEED, LCDR, USN Executive Officer |

(top of evaluation) Of the many evaluations I had
in the Navy, this is my favorite one.

(bottom of evaluation) Do I remember this night?
You Bet! That water was sure cold!

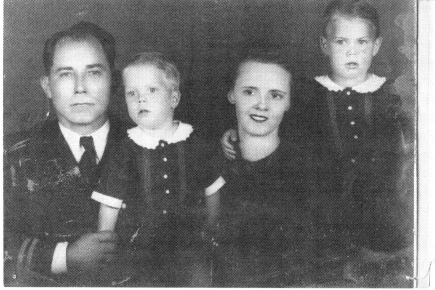

Willie Eugene SNEED
US NAVY & WWII Merchant
Marine Engineer
1907-1986

WilliAM Earl SNEED
"Billy" NAVY CAreer, MArine
EngineeR & Police/Deputy sheriff
DEC 4, 1948 to

Louie Lorona
(Carter) SNEED
AUG 19, 1966

Charles Eugene SNEED
March 12, 1941 \ 18 yrs
March 15, 1959 / OLD
(Sr. High School) Car Accident

1945 photo. Note lieutenant stripes on Dad's sleeve. That's me he's holding.
Of this American-serving family, I am the only one living now. Charles died
in '59, car accident in his sr. year in high school. He was also in the Navy
Reserve. Mom died in 1966, and Dad in 1986.
Photo source/information unknown and untraceable

Author, Bill Sneed. Photo taken shortly after he was commissioned as a 3rd
Assistant Steam Engineer in Florida, 1992.
Photo by his wife, Charlotte "Tootie" Sneed

Marshall, Texas after a Veterans Day meeting. They call
me, what…"Boot Camp?"
Eat your heart out, I'm retired!!

1975 aboard USS Jouett CG 29 on bridge wing
With son, Alan, and daughter, Alison, in San Diego

The Marshall News Messenger
Sunday, January 20, 2008

Courtney Case/News Mess

LIAM 'BILL' SNEED, an author and retired Navy man and ex-merchant marine engineer, sits at his desk where he wrote his recently publish
el, Black Oil Chief USN.

TALE FROM THE SEA

ocal man draws from experiences in Navy to write novel

I debated whether to put this feature news article in this book.
Then I figured it would not fit in any other novel I plan to write.
So, it goes here. I'm not good at scanning stuff as you can see, but
I think it's clear enough so that it can be read. Many thanks!

ROBIN Y. RICHARDSON
News-Messenger

William "Bill" Sneed sailed the seas, cutting across the waves as a chief boiler technician and Merchant Marine engineer.

During his 20 years in the U.S. Navy, he saw combat, was exposed to foreign cultures and developed friendships while discovering a hidden passion for writing that was too strong to ignore.

"It became addictive," he said of writing. "If I didn't write something every day, I felt like I was kind of losing out on life a little bit."

While other sailors used their small wheel books to record daily logs, Sneed would use his to write narratives of his journeys — trips to Greece, Italy, Spain, Turkey and the Red Sea.

"We'd jot notes," he said. "I got to where I jotted notes about countries and people and places I'd visit, and my thoughts about the cruise we were on."

The more he wrote, the more his fascination for writing flourished. He became so intrigued with his newfound interest that he took advantage of his off time, enrolling in writing classes.

"While I was in the Navy, while my ship was in Long Beach, Calif. in the yards...I was probably in my early or mid 30s when I went to some schools.

WILLIAM "BILL" SNEED is pictured with his wife Charlotte.

Courtney Case/ News Messenge

"I took two screen writing classes in Hollywood. I took two college classes — one in short story writing and one in novel writing."

He also studied film and wrote his first screenplay. "That was "so awful, I wanted to shoot myself," he said, snickering.

His luck eventually changed. After retiring from the Navy, he sold a 27-page short story for $327 and won an international short story writing contest with the entry of his 3,000 word short story.

"It won third place and $50 for me," he said.

Now, at age 66, Sneed has published his first novel, "Black Oil Chief USN," which is already receiving rave reviews from critics. One in particular was written in the Jan. 6 edition of the *Galveston Daily News* by Mark Lardas. Lardas compared Sneed's writing to American sailor and writer Richard McKenna.

"The author draws upon his experience as a boiler technician and naval experiences for the plot and incidents that fill the novel," Lardas wrote. "Described from the perspective of the boiler room, the action gets as engaging as anything similar written by Richard McKenna. 'Black Oil Chief USN' is peppered with such vignettes, making the post Vietnam-era Navy come to life."

To read such comments is rewarding to Sneed, especially since he wrote the novel 26 years ago, trashed it only to revive it in 2006.

"I thought, man, to get equated with Richard McKenna alone is a great gratification. Maybe I've done my homework. I'm going to study some more," Sneed said, noting he is also a self-taught author.

Terry Miller, executive director of the Tin Can Sailor Association, wants to offer Sneed's novel to the organization's members.

"I gave it three out of four stars — a worthy read," she wrote Sneed in an e-mail after reading the book. "...it was a really riveting tale and held my interest throughout."

Sneed, who works as a reserve deputy for the Harrison County Sheriff's Office, started writing the novel shortly after retiring from the Navy. Then, he only had three chapters written to present to an agent.

"He liked it. He said, 'I hope this is not all you got,'" Sneed recalled.

Sure enough, it was all Sneed had. He managed, however, to think of a plot, create characters, draw from his own naval experiences and turn it into a "sailor's novel." He ended up trashing it after joining Cypress Valley Bible Church in 2000. "There was so much profanity in it," Sneed explained. "Then, I had a stupid sex scene in it that was sick. When I joined Cypress Valley Bible Church, I got to thinking, 'Well, that goes that novel. I'll have to throw it away. That's exactly what I did. I trashed the whole thing — notes, smooth drafts, rough drafts — everything. I burned it up."

At least, that is what he thought.

Last November, while searching for something in his shop, he ran across three old floppy disks of his book.

"I thought, 'Hmmm. What if the Lord's telling me I can do something with this stupid book after all?'"

He decided to try. Luckily, a man was able to transfer the contents onto a CD, retrieving about 95 percent of the book.

"All the rest of it was gobbledy gook gone," Sneed said. "But, being the author, I knew what was going on, but I had to go back and reconstruct my characters, and put my spiritual theme in there.

"I wanted to underscore and reshape my characters so that they were good people," he explained. "They were in the old one, but there was so much profanity.

"I removed the profanity, sex scene and made the three women Christians."

The three young women characters, who are in their 20s, now sing songs of praises and utter prayers during the hardships of the crew's journey.

"They kind of promoted the sailors on the ship to be Christians," Sneed said.

One character in particular, Chief Boiler Technician Phillip Keith, the main character and an unbeliever, eventually learns about courage, faith and destiny through the action-packed novel.

According to the summary of the book, Keith is just three weeks short of his much-anticipated retirement. He is expecting a smooth trip to the United States from the Philippines. Events take a plummeting turn when he is reassigned to an old World War II destroyer to ensure its safe return to the States.

He has to get accustomed to the modern day Navy where women are assigned to the boiler room. He has the challenge of uncovering a drug smuggling operation on the ship. When a violent storm sends the ship coasting down the dark waters of the Pacific, Keith feels helpless. Not even the ship's mascot, a loyal beagle, can save them, Keith learns.

"I made Phillip kind of a hard core person," Sneed said. "He didn't believe, yet he wanted to believe. Even Kris tells him everybody has a spiritual need. There's a spiritual being living in you that's thirsty for something. It took the whole book for him to realize that."

Sneed said the book is appropriate for all ages.

"It's now a novel where I can give it to a 12-year-old, he can read it and understand it," Sneed said.

In addition to the spiritual message, Sneed hopes to show the life of the military in his book.

"Any branch of the military whether it is the Army, Navy, Air Force, Marines, Coast Guard — it's all about people — getting along and working together," he said. "No one person can be an individual. You all have to work as a team because defense of our military is what it's all about.

"If you don't work as a team, it's not going to function."

The bonds that are built in the military are just as strong — another aspect Sneed reveals in a colorful way through his book.

"You got humor and laughter in it," Sneed said. "I wouldn't trade all the times with the guys and gals for nothing. It was fun.

"I even expressed it was something he (Phillip Keith) was going to miss when he retired — the unity of that close-knit organization — the military."

Sneed, who enjoys traveling with his wife, Charlotte, in their motor home with their two Rottweilers, is making traveling plans to promote his book.

"I'll probably take my dogs with me — one of them anyway. The only bad thing about riding with the Rottweilers is they want to drive once in a while," he said, chuckling.

Contact features editor Robin Y. Richardson at 903-927-5965 or ryrichardson@coxmnm.com

Duty Stations of CPO Bill Sneed

1. USS Howard D. Crow DE 252	Galveston, Texas	Reserve while in high school
2. USS Robert H. McCard DD 822	Charleston, S.C.	Regular Navy
	Reported aboard July 1960 as a Seaman Apprentice (E-2) worked my way up to Petty Officer 2nd Class by Jan 1964 (E-5)	
3. USS Compton DD 705	Newport, R.I. then Boston,	Advanced to Petty Officer First Mass as a reserve trainer Class (E-6) (Because my Dad was in Vietnam, I Requested a transfer to any DD that Was Vietnam bound, then:
4. USS Dyess DD 880	Newport, R.I.	Vietnam bound!
5. USS Charles H. Roan DD 853	Newport, R.I.	Discharged in Jan '68.
6. As a civilian, I sailed aboard two Sunoco ships, one as a "wiper", Then one as an "Oiler". I quit when the ship returned to Beaumont to reenlist back into the Navy	Beaumont, Texas Jan '68 to April '68	Met Charlotte Crowell (RN) Married April 19,1968, then headed Long Beach, Calif to await orders.
7. USS Bennington CVS 20	Long Beach, Calif	3 ½ wks after marriage, I got orders to "bird farm" *Bennington*, already loading ammo in Pearl Harbor, Hawaii!! Gone from May until December!!
8. Recruiting Duty (1968-1972)	Corpus Christi, Texas	Advanced to "Chief", daughter, Alison born (first shore duty in 8 years!)
9. USS Downes FF 1070	Long Beach, Calif.	Sons Alan, then Aaron born
10. USS Jouett CG 29	San Diego, Calif	Another WesPac Cruise, 7 months!
11. USS Barbey FF 1088	San Diego, Calif	Another WesPac Cruise, 7 months!
12. SIMA San Diego (shore duty, last!)	San Diego, Calif	Retired from the Navy July 1980
13. Military Sealift Command	Norfolk, Virginia Sept '90–Sept '92	Sailed as an Oiler, then a Jr. Engineer, then passed C.G. test for 3rd Assist.
USNS Glover T-AGFF 1 USNS Henry J. Kaiser T-AO 187 Redstone T-AGM 20	Norfolk, Virginia Cape Canaveral, Florida Wake, Island/Pearl Harbor, Hawaii	Combat Zone of *Desert Storm,* Jr. Eng. USNS 3rd Assist. Engineer (licensed engineer)

Worked for Sealift for two years. Was only home twice! In Sept 1992, I came home, vowing never to go back to sea again!

In 1992 I worked as a security officer at TSTC (Texas State Technical College). Seeing the future, I attended night school to become a police officer. Passed state test and got my commission in 1999, and later TSTC formed their own police dept. During my off time I worked as a reserve deputy sheriff. After 10 years at the college, I had to retire due to agent orange prostate cancer from Vietnam '66 and '68, plus several other medical problems. I retired completely Dec 31, 2003 at the age of 62. I didn't plan it this way. It just happened. Well, God's in control of everything, right> that's not a question!

My hobbies are gardening, reading and writing. We also have a 2000 Monaco Diplomat 38' motor home which we enjoy traveling in with our Rottweiler's, Annie and Lucy, and the garage sale reject dog, Mattie (in photo below). In April Tootie and I will be married for 41 years!

New Book Prologue

(Title undecided)

Retired Navy CPO, Phillip Keith jerked his head behind his sheriff's patrol vehicle just as a pistol fired from inside a one-story brick building forty yards away. The bullet tore into his left front headlight, glass flying, narrowly missing his head. He was squatted on his heels, back pressed against the fender and tire, his service weapon drawn.

"Phil! Phil!" his black friend said in a loud but tight whisper from his own patrol car parked to the right. "You okay, shipmate?"

Phillip Keith rolled his eyes. "We ain't exactly back in the Navy aboard a tin can, Boomer," he said, but added, "Yes, Chief Boats, I'm okay. Any ideas? These guys are holed up but good in that, ah…brick outhouse!"

"Woodman's' Ox building," retired chief boson's mate Lucas "Boomer" Newman said. "Old geezer lodge of some sort. Was here on a signal seventeen two months ago. Dead ox. Guy musta been two hundred years old!"

"Like you, Boomer?" Phillip Keith grunted a laugh. "Back door?"

"Funny, funny. See Spot go. Go Spot, go. Har-har. Back door's mid section. Might could make it beings it's dark."

"Let's wait a few. See what they do. Calvary should be here soon too."

In the tense atmosphere, the two new-to-civilian-life military men waited.

Both Navy men had retired in San Diego, California. Eleven months ago the chiefs' had been stationed aboard the *USS Doubleday* in Subic Bay, Republic of the Philippines. The night before sailing for the three week voyage back to the State, Phillip had been transferred to a vintage World War II destroyer, *USS Biscay*. Any thought of an easy trip back to San Diego were dissolved when he was confronted with women aboard this combat ship.

Compound this with crew conflicts like he'd never had before, then drugs and murder, well, it wasn't exactly a pleasure cruise. Not to mention being thrown overboard in a storm! Phillip shuddered at the memory. But two matters surfaced like a life preserver popping up from the ocean's depths:

His love for Kris Palmer, and his belief in Jesus Christ alone for eternal life.

But, like the military, here he was in a uniform again with the potential to legally kill.

"Life's a real trip" Boomer had once said.

Boy, he had that right! Phillip thought, his boyish-looking face grim. Still squatting, legs pressing his arms as he held his .40 Smith & Wesson weapon with both hands, muzzle toward the ground, he nodded, glad the boatswain mate was at his side.

Boatswain mate, Phillip Keith thought, remembering another deckhand during his early Navy years. Willie Weed. Why he thought of Willie Weed now he didn't know. He just popped into his mind. Willie Weed had saved his life when a Florida cop was going to bash Phillips' head in with a nightstick during a bar brawl. The cop had the big stick poised to strike when Willie Weed grabbed the cops hand and said, "You ain't hitting my buddy with that log!"

Phillip nodded, thinking again he was glad his black friend was at his side. Only it wasn't Willie Weed this time. It was Boomer.

Phillip and Boomer had met aboard the *USS Compton DD 705* when they had just ten years in the Navy. As first class petty officers, they had been promoted to CPO (pay grade E-7). During the gut-busting humorous chiefs' initiation, Phillip learned that his black friend hailed from Texas, and Boomer had said, "Dugford, Texas. Population fifteen thousand. Ain't grown any since I left. Even when I was a kid there. Fifteen thousand!" Boomer had laughed that squawking tone and walked around, arms pumping while doing his rooster neck-strutting jive. The military crowd hooted, hollered and did cat calls.

It was a delight to not only be from Texas together, but Phillip knew his dad was moving to Dugford when he retired from his merchant marine sea career. Eight years later, he and Boomer served together aboard *USS Doubleday* before Phillip's sudden transfer to the old tin can, *USS Biscay.* The women, the crew, the drugs…the cold sea that night in the dark Pacific. It was all history now. Even the sobriquet the fire room snipe gang started calling him later---

Black Oil Chief, USN---

History. Gone. Vanished.

Except the memories of cute Kris Palmer. Now, almost one year later into

"After Navy Life", the memory of her back in San Diego still dominated his every thought.

"Yo, bro," Boomer said in a tight whisper. "What's the plan? We smoke these dudes out? They deserve it!"

Phillip sighed, then started to look over the patrol car hood. Then changed his mind. "Wait a few more," he said, red-and-blue lights strobbing the pine forest all around. "Sheriff and posse should be here shortly."

"Yeah? They better hurry. Momma's fixin' East Texas steak tonight. Can't miss that!"

"East Texas steak?"

"Watermelon!"

Phillip grunted a laugh. Boomer Newman. Quite a character.

Military friendships were unparalleled and unequal to its civilian counterparts. The camaraderie was more akin to brothership, family. One had to experience it to understand the real value service people put on bonding. And it didn't just exist during an enlistment. It carried over for a lifetime. And here Phillip was again with his shipmate, Lucas "Boomer" Newman. It couldn't get any better than this!

Although only five feet, six inches tall at one hundred and fifty-two pounds, Chief (ex-chief, that is) Lucas Boomer Newman was stout as a marlinspike and as tough as a shot-line monkey fist that had been dipped in varnish twenty times and dried like steel each time. Sable skin hinted a glowing blue hue while small dark eyes mirrored both humor and an intelligent mind. Unlike his southern counterparts, Boomer's voice tone was distinct, clear, and commanded attention. Neither men were like the usual over-weight chief that Hollywood depicted in movies; the ones who had rough-sound voices, pockmarked faces, bulbous noses and big beer bellies.

Phillip Keith, who would turn forty years old in a month, was lean and muscular like a boxer in training. At five feet, nine inches tall, his one hundred and sixty pounds was distributed on his frame like a Greek god. Attributing his health to the hard physical labors of being a shipboard boiler technician, he (and Boomer) jogged and lifted weights three times a week. While they both smoked and drank (beer only), both men kept these vices to a minimum. Some old habits were hard to break, they reasoned. Phillip's ocean-blue eyes were set in a boyish-looking face that he often disliked for not showing his age with a few crow's feet, wrinkles or gray hair on his blondish-brown head. His voice was firm-sounding but gentle.

"Whachew jerks waitin' fo?" a voice roared from the open window of the brick Woodmen's Ox Lodge building. "You law pukes 'fraid to die?" An evil-sounding laugh echoed over the night air and piney woods.

Civilians! Phillip Keith thought, frowning.

During his eight months in law enforcement, he'd witnessed many bad sides of the civilian world. He had come to hate it. Civilians murdered, molested children, starved infants, abused spouses, robbed, raped, and sodomized one another just to name a few sins. And some committed suicide to end it all. True, this happened in the military, but it was generally isolated cases. Humans were humans, no matter where. But the civilian community…

Suddenly a shotgun blast erupted, the sound echoing through the woods. Pellets peppered the passenger side of Phillips patrol car, glass shattering.

"Now what?" Boomer hissed. "I'm getting mighty itchy to do them murders' in. They killed two people back at that convenience store. Father and son, man. That ain't good!"

Phillip waddled back to the rear of his car which was parked slightly angled in front of the bad guys' window some forty yards away. More angled, Boomer's unit was to the rear and right of Phillip's vehicle with open space of ten yards.

The cool night air carried the faint sounds of sirens miles away.

Phillip looked at the building, but the open window was just out of his sight from this rear car position. But Boomer was in view now. Phillip squinted his eyes, frowning at the flashing lights on Boomer's patrol car.

"Boomer. Cut your overheads."

"Right." Head low, Boomer shuffled to his door and opened it. The red-and-blues abruptly stopped.

Repeated shots rang out from the open window. Boomer's windshield exploded.

"Stupid jerks!" Boomer said, teeth gritted. He raised up slightly, weapon above his head. He fired quickly. Flame and smoke filled the air.

"No. Get down, Boomer!" Phillip shouted. He stepped out slightly from behind his car, firing his gun at the now visible building window. He looked at Boomer just as he was hit…once…twice. Boomer was slammed back by his partly opened door.

"NO! NO!" Phillip yelled. No concern for his safety, he ran to his buddy. On his knees, he looked at the blood pumping from Boomer's midsection, hip, shoulder? It was everywhere. Boomer's forest-green shirt was soaked!

"Lord, no. Lord no!" Phillip screamed to the sky, adding, "Boomer! Boomer!"

Laughter echoed over the woods from the building.

Phillip's head jerked at the brick structure. Then he pulled Boomer back to the safety of a huge pine tree trunk. He glared back at the building, lips tremulous. Moments passed.

"Okay, buds," he finally said to his shipmate. "This is for you and me!"

He dashed back to Boomer's car. He reached in and started the engine.

He ran back to the rear of his own car. The ground exploded with dirt and pine straw, bullets narrowly missing his heels. He opened the door and started the engine. He hit the toggle switch for the red-and-blues to flash on. Next he turned on the overhead "side" lights. He flicked on the "takedown lights". The building and lawn front lit up like a football field. He skirted back to the car's rear. He dashed across the open space, his face firm while quickly firing the ten rounds from his magazine. At Boomer's door, he ejected the clip and inserted another ten-rounder. He slid behind the steering wheel. He glanced at his car, knowing that the takedown lights would only blind the killers for a minute or so, and that they couldn't see anything behind the brightness, regardless. He gunned Boomer's engine several times. Face resolute, he floor-boarded the gas pedal. Wheels spun and smoked on the asphalt. Then the patrol car shot toward the open window, gaining great speed with every inch.

Elbows straight, knuckles white on the steering wheel, Phillip clamped his teeth. The car busted into the building. Bricks tumbled in through the busted out windshield. Hundreds cascaded the roof top. Two-by-fours cracked. Insulation tore out. Sheetrock exploded in an avalanche. Debris flew. Dust fogged the room. Then radiator steam spewed from the hood front.

Suddenly a human form folded across the hood front, a shotgun flying from a hand. Phillip pushed the gas harder. The vehicle plunged across the room. The front push-bar nailed the other man making a useless effort to escape. He was pinned against the rear wall. The car stopped. Phillip jumped out, weapon in hand.

Outside, tires screeched on the parking lot. Sirens wailed. Three sets of red-and-blues flashed the pines like a giant forest fire. Men jumped from the vehicles.

Phillip fired at the first form across the hood. He emptied the gun. By rote, he reloaded another ten-rounds. Shooting from the hip, he emptied the gun on the pinned man. Then, face sweaty and dirty, he stood there transfixed.

Suddenly a tall uniformed man appeared from behind.

Breathing heavily, perspiration dripping from his chin, spittle from a corner of his mouth, Phillip dropped the gun. He never felt the hand on his shoulder, nor the Texas drawl of the sheriff.

"Think we got us a real problem here now, Deputy Keith!"

*   *   *   *

Fifteen-hundred miles west on the San Diego, California Naval Base, Daryl Lacy adjusted the binoculars pressed to his gray eyes. Yes, there she was, pretty as ever!

Kris Palmer.

"Like it or not," Daryl Lacy mumbled, "You're still mine!"

Kris Palmer would always be his. He would make sure she understood it better…this time.

Daryl Lacy and Kris Palmer. It would soon be Mr. and Mrs. Daryl Lacy. That had a nice ring to it. He loved it.

Lowering the binoculars, Daryl peered over the dash of the clunker-navy guy-car he had hot-wired at that big parking lot further down the base harbor road. He'd made a wrong turn in looking for her ship, *USS Biscay.*

Why not steal a car? the inner voice asked. *You could cruise the base and learn the piers in case the ship moved. Why, with that sailor's I.D. you took off the bar counter downtown last night, you could even scout the Navy Exchange, purchase things, but, hey, you better find some chump uptown to alter the photo, huh? If you're gonna play Mr. Navy, you need to look like a sailor. Get your hair cut and trim that beard. This might be 1981, relaxed Navy rules and all that, but you sure don't want to get caught. You've gone too far to have that happen. Now, get a car and start looking!"*

Driving on the harbor front road, he had found the *USS Biscay* docked at another pier a mile away. Base is bigger than I thought, he reasoned. So he parked on the lot and blended with the rest of the cheap vehicles that young sailors drove. He'd just leave the car here. Navy people would never look for a stolen car on the base it was taken from.

Dummies!

The car would be here tomorrow when he returned to watch Kris Palmer. He was going to watch her every move…where she went, who she was with, what they did…even what she ate…everything! Why it would---

Suddenly a ship behind the USS Biscay blew its whistle high on the forward smoke stack, indicating it was underway, free of the pier and under its own power.

Daryl Lacy frowned at the noisy interruption. He scratched his beard, then brushed his long black hair out of his eyes. Yes, he had to get a haircut and his beard trimmed. They might get suspicious at the main gate again and stop me next time. Boy, that would end everything. His stomach knotted at what almost happened this morning.

At the naval base main entrance, he had stood aloof, watching what others did as they walked past the gate guards. The guards were nothing but civilians in uniforms wearing guns. The military, most in civilian clothes, merely showed their I.D. at the guard standing across the street at the guardhouse in the middle of the roadway. Boy, the military was sure relaxed now, he remembered thinking as he sauntered toward the entry. With the early morning traffic, this made it even more a piece of cake. But as he flashed the stolen I.D., the guard gave him a stare, then almost halted the rush hour traffic, but obviously changed his mind and motioned him through.

Whoa, close call!

Yes, he would have to find a barber somehow. Why hadn't he thought of this? Oh, too many beers last night in downtown San Diego, with that ignorant-looking skinhead dressed in that bright orange dress or skirt or whatever, trying to bum money from him and calling himself a priest. Some people...

Later, after the fortunate chance to steal that military I.D. from the careless sailor getting stoned with his billfold, car keys, a wad of crumbled money and the I.D. on the bar, he should have been out trying to find a barber shop. Then this morning, the mere thought of locating Kris Palmer after over four years fogged his memory.

Kris, he thought. Daryl pressed the binoculars back to his eyes. He felt his heart throb at the sight of her again.

Four years, my dear. Four years and I found you. You thought you were so sneaky disappearing on me, huh? Well, I done more research after reading that letter, sweetheart. It gave me direction. Solid. Concrete. I know your ship, too. *USS Biscay*. And it was your best friend back in Ohio that let you down. Only Linda Walker didn't know I dug through the trash when I saw her reading a letter. A lucky shot in the dark, but it paid off. Linda Walker never recognized me with my long hair, beard, and sunglasses, especially since I had been gone to Alaska for two years. I last saw Linda was a year after high school graduation, then I spotted her with your letter three years later. Ha-ha. Here I am back in your life, only you don't know it yet. And the inner voice spoke again:

"And it will be until death do us part this time, Kris Palmer. There's no turning back!"

*   *   *   *

The .38 Saturday Night Special looked real. Fact is, it was. But the cylinder was loose on the frame and the firing pin was broken off, so it rendered the weapon useless. But seventeen year old Johnny Cupp didn't care. He was just going to use it to scare the clerk into giving him the money.

And tonight was the night.

(under construction. Top Secret. You know what I'd have to do if I told you!ha)

*   *   *   *

Another part/section of the prologue will read:

In the mothball fleet of the US Navy Base in San Diego, hidden in a back bay bone yard, a seagull glided down smoothly from the salt-laden air. Toes spread wide, it landed on the tip of one of mount 51's gun barrels of the *USS Waldron DD 699*. Curious, the bird looked left and saw other kin resting on various topside structures of *USS Compton DD 705*, *USS Robert H. McCard DD 822*, *USS Vogelgesang DD 862*, *USS Orleck DD 886*, and *USS Charles H. Roan DD 853*.

As though satisfied, the gull strutted its neck several times, let out a squawk, then looked to its right at *USS Tabberer DE 418*, *USS Samuel B. Roberts DE 413*, and *USS McClelland DE 750*.

(I will relate to other Navy ships in the "red-lead" fleet all like they were standing by to be called into the service of their country again, but they were lonely, depressed and rusting badly. I will end this part by)

"On these terms, the ships' waited." Or something to this effect.

There is another part to the prologue, all, of course designed fire up the reader's interest in wanting to read more...the usual 'What happens next theory.'

Jeremy Richardson Dec 2008, Great Lakes, Illinois
Jeremy is a special friend of our church family, and a member
of Cypress Valley Bible Church in Marshall, Texas

Jeremy is to be recognized for his decision to join the worlds' greatest Navy. Jeremy was having a really hard time since he got married. His wife is pregnant and he was working two jobs to make ends meet. "Congrads" Jeremy on your wise choice in life. You have a bright future ahead now. Stick to your schools, do your best, follow orders and you can't go wrong. And thanks for your "belief" in Christ alone for everlasting life. We're all very proud of you back here in Marshall, Texas. You should see your mother and sister's faces beam at the mention of your name. Would your mom happen to have a picture of you in her purse? About 500!! That's how I got this one!

God bless you and keep you safe, sailor.

In conclusion of this book, a special "Thanks" to my *mucho amigos*, Albert and Nono. Thanks for the wonderful memories and your decades of friendship.

Billy Sneed

Across the fields of yesteryear,
He sometimes comes to me.
A little lad just back from play;
The kid I used to be.

Author unknown